When the Small Creatures Wake

Brigid Griffin

Published by Write on the Tyne

To N, of course.

Chapter 1
January 1982

Midge Kenny woke early; she was always the first up and about. She looked over at Wendy's bed. Only the top of her head was visible, a tangled bird's nest of auburn. It must have been after 3 am when her older sister had come in, pissed. Trying to be quiet in the dark, sitting down suddenly on the end of Midge's bed like a clumsy puppet with its strings cut, crushing her foot and waking up Jasper. Just the tip of her lit fag glowing in the dark as she wrenched off her tights and dangly earrings, before stubbing the fag out in a saucer on the bedside table and falling into bed, the rest of her clothes intact.

Midge enjoyed the peace and warmth for a few minutes, pulling the scratchy nylon quilt close to her neck. She sighed, dreading having to put her feet out of the warm bed. She felt irritated and tired already, her eyes gritty with lack of sleep. Midge idly watched the streetlight filtering through the thin curtains and listened to feet running past the window — wondering if it was someone late for work or someone running away from something. Jasper was curled up against her feet, purring. A tight, warm ball of tiger-stripes. She loved the weight of him under her toes. Every night she lay poker straight in the narrow bed, her arms crossed across her chest like a small medieval crusader in his tomb, feet resting on a stone lion.

Eventually, she got up and roughly pulled a jumper over her nightie with a groan, wincing as her ears got caught in the neck hole. Jasper didn't move as she shoved her bare feet in some gym pumps and padded out onto the freezing landing. The pumps were too tight. She had grown again and now she had to wear them with the backs flattened down. She could see her breath in the air and she hugged herself, rubbing her upper arms. It wasn't as cold as it had been earlier in the month, when it had snowed for three days straight, but there was a bone chill of coldness in the house.

Jean's door was half open, the bedside lamp had been left on. Midge could see her mum's bulk, humped under the eiderdown, one white pudding-like arm exposed. A man's tattooed hand was loosely gripping the soft flesh of her shoulder. She couldn't see anything else of him. Sometimes she saw nothing of the men, sometimes she just heard them. Midge looked away. She always felt slightly sick and embarrassed about Jean's visitors.

What was it with Mum and these blokes? They were always idiots or creeps. They were often gone before the house was up, scurrying out in the dark. Hoping nobody knew they'd been there, disappearing up the street with their guilt. Some of them would hang around afterwards, sitting at the table in the kitchen, playing at uncles, jolly and red faced with the drink. Grabbing at Jean as she made them breakfast or a brew and making a lewd comment about their nighttime activities.

Midge sometimes wondered with dread if this was all going to happen to her in time. Or if it was just a conscious choice on the part of her mum. Did Jean actually like any of these blokes? Or was it just something to pass the time? She never got used to the awkward embarrassment when she came downstairs and saw another unfamiliar, shifty face. None of them ever stuck around, not the ones who seemed nice, anyway. They'd vanish, never to be seen again. Gone into the Bermuda Triangle of one-night boyfriends.

One time, Midge had seen a bloke going through her mum's bag. He'd got up early and didn't know there was anyone else in the house. She had slipped downstairs and seen a weasel in a Harrington jacket with a wet moustache who looked about sixteen, emptying Jean's bag onto the kitchen table and picking up coins from the rubble. Midge quietly watched him with resignation as he slyly folded a tenner into his jeans pocket before he clocked her and gave a violent start. Midge opened her mouth to say something, a small freckled hand held out as if to ask for the money back, but the words were stuck in her throat and she felt tears coming. He mumbled something about looking for a lighter and then legged it, banging the front door so hard the glass rattled.

Some of them tried it on with Wendy, coming downstairs after a night with Jean and seeing her daughter's white and fox coloured body stretched out on the settee. They didn't get far, though; Wendy didn't take any nonsense from men — she'd seen how her mum had been messed around by them for years and wasn't going to go down that road.

Midge adored Wendy, happy to be safe in the shadow of her confidence, cockiness, and glamour. None of that with Mum, mind. Jean carried on looking, searching for answers through men who never understood the question. Midge jerked back her head and gagged, softly closing the bedroom door on the stale waft of beer, Elnett, sex, and cheap aftershave. She continued walking across the landing; the floral carpet, threadbare in parts beneath her feet and clattered downstairs. There was no point in keeping quiet, Jean and Wendy wouldn't surface before dinnertime and slept like stunned mullets.

Christ, it was a shithole downstairs and stunk of fags and chip fat. Absolute devastation. Midge always thought the house looked like it had been burgled when Mum had a party after the pub. She stood on one bony leg like a small stork, tiredness making her feel ratty. Jean's bag hung off the banister, with most of the contents on the floor underneath it: purse, comb, makeup, fags, lighter, receipts, tampons, bus tickets, chuddy, and screwed up tissues. Half a packet of Polos and a Fisherman's Friend stuck to the carpet.

Always the fucking same, she thought. *I'm the kid here, but I'm looking after everyone else because you can't be arsed to behave like adults.* She scooped up the crap from Jean's bag and stuffed it back into the opening, angrily wiping the sticky fluff from her fingers. One shoe was lying on its side by the front door, a warped oval of white plastic, with the metal rod of the heel poking through and the insole hanging out like a yellow hungover tongue. A man's leather jacket hung on the hoover, a tie coiling out of a pocket towards the floor.

Midge went into the kitchen to put the kettle on, pulling a gagging face at the smell. There was all the evidence of a post-pub feeding frenzy. The chip pan had been on, a black cauldron barnacled with decades of burnt on lard and a semi-melted plastic handle. Under the grill rested a brittle, carbonised black square of toast.

A polystyrene tub of green-gold curry sauce was on the table, a fag sticking in the middle like a tiny fencepost. *One day, Mum will bloody burn this place down,* thought Midge, coldly rubbing her mouth with the back of her hand and quickly wrapping up the loaf that had been left out, a knife sticking out of its back. Marg was smeared all over the bench and the floor and had been walked through the kitchen and into the hallway. *Jesus Christ, what a tip.* Midge put the lid back on the crusty neck of a tomato sauce bottle and made a pot of tea. Pouring the boiling water into the teapot, the steam billowing into the freezing air in a hot cloud.

It was worse in the front room. She flicked the light on, the heavy-lined orange curtains only showing the shadows of the party fallout. Jean's best mate, Lynne, was asleep on the settee, covered in a fake leather coat — an inch of black roots visible above a bleached dead frizz of fried, home-permed hair. A foot with its laddered toe hung off one end of the couch. She was snoring like a pig; her face squashed against the cushions, a wet patch under her open mouth staining the velour black.

Midge turned away with gritted teeth. Lynne was one mess that was going to have to sort herself out. She had to clean this place up so she could sit down with her book and pretend they all lived in a normal household. She started putting records back in their sleeves, working efficiently and rapidly from years of practice. Stacking them back next to the player, fighting an urge to put her foot through Shakin' Stevens, who had kept her awake last night howling about a bloody green door.

She moved over to clear the coffee table and hovered over it for a moment, fingers splayed to pick up the greasy forest of glasses. The sticky, manky table top was crammed with ashtrays, cans of lager, and a bottle of vodka with the lid off. A fag end floated in a wineglass half full of something the colour of piss.

After dumping all the glasses, bottles, and cans in the kitchen, Midge crouched down to make the fire. She tipped the ash pan into an open newspaper, watching the warm soot and slack cover Linda Lusardi's tits. She made a wigwam of sticks and screwed up paper in the hearth, placed a few shards of coal from the bucket on top and lit the paper with Jean's *Welcome to Rhyl* lighter, mechanically thinking the tea must be brewed.

Midge held a double sheet of newspaper over the opening, waiting for the flame to draw, watching, mesmerised as a photo of the Manchester City squad disappeared as the middle of the paper inhaled and burned away with a little roar. She gave a satisfied grunt, rubbed the ash off her hands, and looked for her book. Midge was going to spend a contented Sunday morning reading in the chair in front of the fire. She found *Watership Down* underneath the telly, covered by a massive grey bra which she threw onto a chair.

After pouring a mug of tea, she came back into the front room, and opened the curtains, peering at the still dark Sunday morning street through the fag-yellowed nets and condensation streaming down the pane. Most of the other curtains in the street were closed. Midge knew everyone on the road, in all these red brick boxes. She had been born in this house, and nothing ever seemed to change.

Mrs Dwyer from number 43 was walking down to early Mass, handbag over her arm like Mrs Thatcher. Mantilla and gloves on, ready for whatever Our Lord was going to throw at her. *Who the bloody hell does she think she is?* Midge thought, huffing to herself. She always looks pissed off; it must be what God does to you. Coming the other way, shiny in the streetlight, was Baz, the Kenny's dog. Baz was a randy little sharp-faced brown mongrel. He came and went as he pleased, roaming the streets with his curly tail, shagging and scrapping his way around the estate. Midge giggled softly as he cocked his leg on the wall opposite and carried on his way, nose up. He'd been out most of the night, leaving when the music got too loud to sleep.

'What time is it, love?' Midge jumped at the croaking sound from the settee.

Lynne was struggling upright, squinting at the overhead light. Looking like a hybrid of Myra Hindley's mugshot and Frankenstein's monster; kohl and mascara blurred in black rings above her hangover-white face.

'Christ, my head. Pass me bag, chuck. I need to get some paracetamol down me.' Lynne had her head in her hands, nicotine-stained fingers digging into her scalp.

Midge rolled her eyes. 'It's eight. Here, have this brew. There're two sugars in it.' She handed over her mug.

'Ah, thanks, love.' Lynne clutched the Charles and Di mug with both hands. Everyone at school had been given a Royal Wedding mug last year. Midge was surprised it had survived the brutal washing up regime at the Kenny's.

Lynne lit a Silk Cut with trembling hands and inhaled deeply, resting the fag on the foothills of a mountain of dimps, piled in a Harp ashtray while she swilled down the painkillers.

She groaned softly. 'Jesus, I was pissed last night, not even made it home. Terrible. Did we wake you up, love?' She threw her head back in a cracked smoker's bray of laughter and Midge could see right past her silver filled teeth to her red-raw throat.

'Nah, not really,' Midge lied, and wondered who the hell could have slept through the shrieking, cackling, dancing, thumping music, and shouting. She could never understand why people always had to shout when they were drunk.

'They had a good band on up at the Club, Human League songs.' She nodded to Midge, who smiled weakly. 'Your mum was on form. She was up on the stage and we got kicked out, so we went to the Pole Star and there was a lock-in. Trevor had put butties on and we had a right laugh. It was packed.' Lynne was cackling now, restored by tea, fags, and headache tablets.

'Who's he?' Midge jerked her head towards the stairs. Lynne shrugged and drew deeply on her fag.

'Was our Wendy there?'

'No love, she went to the Spinners and then the Carders. I saw her in the chippy. I'd best get up and go. I've got work today and I need to get sorted. If I go in looking pissed again, I'll be getting the arse. Tell your mum I'll call up tonight with the catalogue.'

Lynne struggled up off the settee, necked the brew in one, and started searching for her shoes. Her hair was completely flattened on one side, a creased pattern from the couch cushion denting her cheek. Midge found one shoe under the record player and the other was in Baz's bed, lightly chewed at the toe.

'See you, love.' She squeezed Midge's arm and sailed out with her shoes under her arm, closing the door softly.

'Ta-ra, Lynne,' Midge muttered. She felt the arctic blast of air whoosh in as Lynne closed the front door and she got up. Midge made herself another brew before curling up in Jean's armchair, wrapped in Wendy's fake-fur coat, the fire crackling into life. She opened her book and lost herself immediately.

Chapter 2
January 1982

Bobby Armstrong walked home from school slowly to delay being in the house with Ray for as long as possible. She went into town and bought some tights, had a browse in the record shop, and decided it was too cold to stay out any longer. It was already dark when she reached the estate. The orange glow of the streetlights was turning the wet paving stones to glossy cough lozenges. A fine drizzle was falling. Bobby pulled the collar of her donkey jacket up around her ears and tucked in the thick, inky-black mass of her hair. Her flat, thin shoes slapped on the pavement as she marked out the paces home. She could feel the moisture seeping into her tights. The ice was melting to slush now, the dirty snow patched with black and still piled up at the sides of the road. Lights were going on in houses, curtains being drawn. She could hear the murmur of voices and tellies behind closed doors. She pushed her hands further into her pockets and hunched her shoulders.

Ten minutes was used up having a quiet smoke in the bus shelter near the Carders, and then she realised it was getting too cold to hang around. She flicked the lit fag end into the gutter and watched the glow die instantly.

Time to go home. She waved at Midge Kenny, who was wet through, running the opposite way with something wrapped in a carrier bag, her parka flapping in the breeze. She looked like a little blackbird swooping along through the gloom.

It was probably the Littlewoods catalogue, thought Bobby. It was always being shuttled between the women of the Kenny and Armstrong households. She walked to the railway bridge and marvelled at the icicles still hanging from its entrance like giant teeth; they fringed the black maw, stretching inside the cavity. Lining the roof like the inside of a shark's mouth. Dripping freezing cold droplets on her head as she hurried through, feet echoing and breath pluming.

Ray rarely said when he would be back because he liked to keep Stella on her toes. If he told her when he was coming home, he thought she might have time to arrange for some fancy man to come around for a quick shag and leave sharp, before he got back. Or she might be able to spend an extra ten minutes skiving, watching the telly or reading a magazine instead of getting his tea ready or cleaning the house. The things she should be doing; looking after him and what he wanted.

Ribbon Street ran straight through the Gritstone estate from north to south. Bobby Armstrong lived at the north end, in the cluster of smaller, older, and poorer houses. She used to have Wendy Kenny to walk home with, but Wendy had left school last summer. She was working in one of the few mills in town still operating, shaking her lovely auburn head at Bobby's insistence at staying on into the sixth form.

'You wanna get out and get to work, yer daft beggar. Money in your pocket, get away from school.' She often lectured Bobby while they sat on Wendy's bed, painting their nails, smoking, and listening to records.

Bobby did sometimes wonder if it would be better to leave school now, but her mum was counting on her staying on and getting a place at university, the same as her twin brother Davey. Stella was obsessed about them getting qualifications, bettering themselves. She didn't really know what she wanted, except that it was time to get out of the house.

She left the red brick terraced houses of the town centre behind and walked onto the estate. Turning in at number 8, Bobby pushed the gate open with her foot. It was slightly lopsided, dropped on its hinges and scraped across the concrete. The house was like all the others on this part of the estate; a semi-detached cube with the bottom half rendered in grey pebble-dash and the top half red brick, surrounded by an overgrown lawn, and a straggly privet hedge.

The hall light was on, and in the twilight, a large square of light reflected on the cracked weedy flagstones in front of the doorstep. To the left of the house was a narrow driveway with crumbling tarmac. Wedged in this slender gap was a decaying 1950s Jaguar. The car was pewter grey with burgundy leather seats, glossy walnut dashboard, and a gear stick topped with a ball of the same shining wood. There was a vivid green seam of moss growing between the windowsills and the glass along the rubber seals at the top of the door panels.

Ray had come in all cocky one day, years ago, twirling a car key on a leather fob around his finger. He had been given the car as part payment for a debt and it needed a bit of work to get it back on the road. He would do it up and sell it for a profit. It had been reversed up the side of the house and hadn't moved since, slowly rotting into the ground.

Davey and Bobby had used it off and on as a refuge. If things really kicked off in the house between Mum and Ray, sometimes they would come and sit in the car. It was freezing in the winter, but at least it was dry, and once you were wrapped up in a coat or a sleeping bag with a hot water bottle, it was cosy. It had evolved from being a place to play in when they were little kids to their rusty sanctuary as they grew into adolescents.

When they had been really young, Davey had fantasised about getting the car fixed up and just driving off one day with Bobby and Mum. Driving as far as they could, putting miles and hours between them and Ray. As they got older, they realised that even if they had a taxi running outside the house and Stella's bags packed and sitting on the doorstep, she would never leave him.

The car stayed as it was, as immovable as Ray and Stella, and just as rusted together. Bobby had found Jean Kenny's mate, Lynne, in there more than once, too pissed to get home from the Spinners. Crashed out on the back seat, wrapped up in a coat, and looking like a kidnap victim. Even the cat slept in there sometimes. Tiger had got shut in once. Bobby had spotted his furious face at the window, his soundless miaow making a small cloud of breath on the glass.

One day, Davey was fishing about in the front passenger seat, trying to shift it forward when he could feel something stopping it from moving. It was a piece of metal wedged sideways between the seat and the floor. He fiddled for ages in the tight space, and when he freed it, he saw it was two tubes and a thick piece of wood joined together. Davey held it out in front of him, crossways. They both looked at it, gobs hanging open in shock, knowing what it was from the telly but amazed they would ever see a gun in real life.

'I could have blown me head off. It's a shotgun, isn't it? A sawn-off shotgun?' gasped Davey in excitement, thrilled with his find.

'I think so. Shall we tell Ray?'

Davey shook his head. 'No, fuck that. Let's get rid. We could get into trouble.'

They wrapped it up in newspaper and put it in a bin bag. Davey had watched enough episodes of *The Sweeney* to know he had to wipe off their fingerprints with a tea towel. When it got dark, he took it to the tip, and threw it over the chain-link fence so it mingled with the broken bikes, tellies, and fridges.

Bobby pushed the front door open and stepped into the warm fug of the hall. She could smell fags and hot oil. Stella was in the kitchen, standing over the chip pan and a frying pan of sausages. An open can of beans was next to one elbow, a smouldering fag in a saucer by the other.

'Hiya, Mum,' muttered Bobby, wearily. She let her bag slide off her shoulder to the floor.

'Hello love, you're late,' said Stella, pushing a thick black curl behind her ear.

Stella had once been beautiful. Dark eyed and olive skinned. Rich, blue-black hair piled up on her head. She was still lovely, but her body had thickened over the years and her face looked tired. Too much worry, work, and fags.

'I had to call into work to pick something up,' lied Bobby, noticing the three dinner plates on the countertop.

'He in?' She jerked her head towards the closed door of the front room.

Stella nodded, expressionless. She knew the kids hated Ray, and with good reason, but she didn't like them openly slagging him off. She tipped the beans into a pan and began tidying up, almost tripping over Tiger, who was weaving in and out of her legs, snaking his tail around her calves and mewing.

Bobby picked him up from the greasy chequered lino and hugged his beautiful tabby face to hers, letting him bump her cheek with his head. He was purring like an engine, his whole body rumbling. Bobby sat down with him at the small, wobbly kitchen table, rocking him like a baby. Stella drained the chips in the basket, dumped them on the plate in a steaming golden pile, and added the sausages and the beans. She turned to fill the kettle and then held the plate out to Bobby.

'Take his tea in, will you? While I brew up.'

Bobby sighed, set a protesting Tiger down on the floor, and wordlessly picked up the plate, knife, and fork. She stepped into the cool hallway, shut the kitchen door behind her, hawked and spat neatly into the centre of the beans, before opening the front room door and walking in.

Ray Short was sitting in front of the telly. The room was boiling; the fire going and the air full of cigarette smoke. It was an old-fashioned council house front room, with an open fire and a brown tiled surround. Full of cheap, crappy furniture and everything was fag-yellow. The news was on at a deafening volume. Mrs Thatcher was speaking, her lady-Dalek voice a metallic drone. Ray didn't acknowledge Bobby as she held out the plate of steaming food. He took it off her with his nicotine-stained fingers, put it on the arm of the greasy Dralon chair, bent over it, and started shovelling. Bobby curled her lip at his oafish manner and scowled, just out of his line of vision.

The room bore the stamp of Ray's love of pub paraphernalia. A beer barrel used as a coffee table with a whisky bottle lamp sat on top and a beer towel on the arm of his chair. There was one settee in grey fake leather and two armchairs; one Stella's and the other Ray's. Above Ray's head was a huge spider plant in a macrame plant holder suspended from the ceiling. Bobby always marvelled at its survival. It never got watered and lived directly above Ray's fag-hand, which was rarely idle. Next to the window was a small, dark wooden dresser with Stella's few china ornaments, and a couple of photos of the kids when they were young. There had been lots of other knick-knacks, but over the years, most of them had been smashed.

Ray Short was in his sixties, still immensely strong, just over six feet tall, and thickset. He was wearing his blue boiler suit, one leg crossed over the knee of the opposite leg, heavy work boot dangling. The dour face was large and mottled, with a drinker's complexion, topped with grizzled grey hair. Ray drove wagons for a living and earned good money, most of which he pissed up the wall. Stella came in carrying two more plates, one for her and one for Bobby.

'Where's our Davey?' asked Bobby, sitting down and taking her plate.

'He's away at Chris's house until late.' Stella's voice was neutral.

Davey spent as much time out of the house as he could, too. Although if it was really kicking off, Davey would hang around to keep an eye on his mum.

Ray made a huffing sound of contempt and gestured at the telly with his knife. The teatime news was still on and the picture showed a crowd of men in balaclavas shooting guns over a freshly dug grave at an IRA funeral. A priest, vestments flapping in the wind, stood to one side, mouth moving soundlessly. The news reader's voice was posh, serious, disapproving. Ray grunted, gouged a lump of snot from one nostril with a forefinger, and wiped it on a boiler suited knee. Bobby grimaced and put her fork down.

'Bunch of fucking dirty murdering papes. If I was back in Ireland, I'd have the lot of 'em,' he spat.

The picture changed to a green armoured Land Rover, driving through a windswept terraced street, gaudy republican murals painted on the gable ends of houses. Children with furious faces throwing stones. Head-scarved women standing in doorways, arms crossed. Bobby rolled her eyes, well out of his line of vision. Ray always made a point of slagging off Catholics. It wound Stella up as she and the kids were Catholics — the Armstrongs had been so for generations, ever since they came here to dig the canals as navvies. Both Bobby and Davey went to St Francis's school. They didn't go to

Mass anymore; they had both done their First Confession and Holy Communion, and Stella liked a lot of the old traditions.

Back in Ireland, my arse, Bobby thought. *You're full of shite. You've never been to Belfast. I bet you've never set foot out of England, you'd shit yourself.* She shoved a forkful of beans into her mouth and tried to filter out Ray's bullshit.

She could see Stella stiffening out of the corner of her eye as she mechanically chewed her chips. Ray muttered to himself and carried on eating. He was okay when he was sober, just grumbling and miserable. The trouble started when he'd had a drink.

Bobby finished her tea and collected everyone's plates. She would have her brew, watch the local news when it came on, and then go up to her room. She always had the excuse of homework to get out of Ray's way and could read and listen to her music in peace. It didn't sound as if it would kick off too much tonight. If it kept quiet, she would come down when the sobbing sound of the cornet on the *Coronation Street* theme tune filtered up through the ceiling.

Bobby's room was at the back of the house. It was tiny, but her own. Davey's was a mirror image next door, but much tidier. Papered in woodchip and music posters, it smelt damp and always looked dreary in the daylight. However, on a winter night with the curtains closed, lamp on and the radiator ticking next to her, it felt cosy. Her bed occupied one wall, then there was a small space opposite for her wardrobe and a chest of drawers with a record player on top.

The room was so narrow when she lay down in bed, she could put the flat of her hand on the wardrobe door. Her desk was wedged under the window, piled high with textbooks and plastic folders. Every surface of the room was covered in clothes, makeup, records, and half-drunk mugs of cold tea. She smiled to herself in satisfaction. Stella was always going mental at the state of this room. It was a tip, but was one of the few areas of the house Ray seemed to exert no control.

She sat on the bed, rubbing the space between her eyes, and contemplated finishing her homework. Bobby had an English essay due in at the beginning of next week, but that could wait. She was due to take her A-levels next summer and hopefully, maybe, go to university. But she didn't want to think about that right now — the possibility of failure was too frightening. Bobby longed for university; a way out. But didn't want to tempt fate. If she stayed here, she'd end up like Wendy, or her mum.

She kicked her shoes off and massaged her feet, wondering what it would be like to pack up her clothes, books, and records and go and live somewhere else. Somewhere new and exciting where nobody knew anything about her, and she could start all over again. The thought was weird, frightening, and exhilarating at the same time.

Pushing the future out of her head, she made a brief attempt at tidying up; stacking her school textbooks on one side of her desk, putting makeup back in its bag, picking up clothes off the floor, and hanging them up. She contemplated going round to see Wendy, but the sound of the rain turning to sleet on the window made her mind up. She slid an Elvis Costello record out of its sleeve, placed it carefully it on the turntable with the volume low. Tilting her glossy black head on its side, she picked up a bottle of nail polish, lit a fag, sat on the bed and waited to see if the silence would hold.

Chapter 3
January 1982

Ray couldn't stand any of Davey's friends. They were a threat, with their youth, enthusiasm, and noisy joy for life. He particularly hated Chris Clough, who was bold, camp, clever, and most worryingly for everyone, completely unafraid of Ray.

Chris was one of the few friends that came to the house and seemed oblivious to Ray's simmering rage. Ray accepted him there because he had a nice little sideline moving heavy pieces of furniture and doing house clearances for Jonty Clough, Chris's father. Ray delivered furniture for him in his spare time and was paid in cash. He couldn't bully Chris, or the jobs might dry up. It always gave Davey a bit of a buzz, knowing how much Chris wound Ray up. And it was part of the reason Chris could really push Ray's buttons; baiting him subtly.

Davey and Chris went to Chess Club at the school on a Thursday night, and then usually wandered the streets afterwards, smoking and chatting. Sometimes, they'd pop in the Baited Bear for a pint; a sanctuary for the quieter, more discerning underage drinker. Then they might go to Chris's and listen to records, smoke Jonty's posh cigarettes and sample some of the bewildering selection of obscure liqueurs stacked on the sideboard.

Chris's dad had an antiques shop. It was full of junk and curios, heavy Victorian furniture that nobody wanted, creepy dolls with porcelain faces and horror-film glass eyes, dusty stuffed animals, and boxes of old coins. Books lined the walls and made towers on the floor, climbing in terraces along the top of old sideboards and dressing tables. Tarnished silver trophies filled the shelf above the till and a polar bear skin rug with an eye missing stretched out in front of a coal fire that blazed all year round. It had the peculiar dust and old leather smell of all second-hand furniture shops.

Davey loved it; the old books, the ever-changing weird stock that came and went. There was no hurry, no raised voices, just calmness and good humour. As soon as he opened the door, he felt safe and at home. A sensation he never fully experienced in Ribbon Street.

Jonty Clough was born an antiques dealer. He was rotund, with a jolly, handsome, florid face that was always smiling. With collar length, untidy, greying hair, he wore a cravat, a woollen tank top with holes in it, and an air of casual geniality. He was happiest pottering around the shop, readjusting the pose of a mannequin in a moulting fur coat or polishing an occasional table with a pair of vintage satin French knickers. Jonty could usually be found at the back of the shop, sitting behind an enormous leather-topped desk with his feet up.

Molly Clough had left years ago when Chris was a little boy. Gone in a cloud of perfume, a fur-collared camel coat, and a halo of blonde curls. Chris had a dim memory of her getting into a low, long-nosed orange sports car with a tall, thin man wearing a moustache and a tweed jacket. He held a recollection of her soft voice, leaving clouds of angel's breath on a frosty December morning.

'Now don't be a silly boy, Chris. Mummy is going away for a little while, but you look after Daddy for me like a good boy.'

A little while actually turned into a long time. The next time he saw her, years, decades later, she was in a white coffin, wearing a sea-green dress looking like a sleeping mermaid in a velvet lined shell. When Molly left, Chris didn't remember crying or feeling sad or confused. Molly had never really been there anyway, and he liked being with his dad — who never made him go to bed, or do his homework, or tell him he wasn't allowed to watch something too adult on the telly. Jonty never told Chris what to read, what to wear, or what to think.

What Davey really liked about going to Chris's flat was the calm. There was no shouting, no tension that clung to the cigarette smoke in the air. You could do or say whatever you liked, and nobody would ridicule an opinion or comment. Could talk about politics, music, anything at all and be respected. You could sit and openly read a book without being told you were wasting your time, being a queer, or getting ideas above your station.

And that's why in many ways, to Davey, it felt like home.

Davey met Chris in the first year of secondary school. The Chess Club gathered on a Thursday evening in the library, and Davey was a new member. He had no clue about how to play but liked the names and the feel of the pieces, and the quiet of school out of hours. It was a further excuse not to go home and be under the same roof as Ray. It wasn't until everyone left at 3.30 pm that Davey realised what a noisy and brutal place school was during the day. The corridors were in half darkness, just the ticking of cooling radiators and squeak of his shoes on the lino following him from the main doors.

St Francis's had been built as a new comprehensive in the 1950s. Now, it was all peeling metal framed windows, wired glass, graffiti, and yellow enamel painted walls. In the entrance lobby was a large photograph of the Pope and a dusty glass case with football and athletics trophies. Next to this stood a life-size statue of Our Lady in her faded blue and white plaster robes, looking down on proceedings with a neutral 'seen it all before' expression.

Davey tucked the borrowed chess board and the small sliding box of pieces under his arm and made his way down the central corridor towards the only classroom with a light on. The heating had been turned off and he could already see his breath in the air. He walked into the club meeting room, which was the sixth form common room during the day and smelled of teenagers and disinfectant. Posters were peeling off the wall, and someone had drawn a cock and balls on the advert for the school production of *Macbeth*.

Mr McCauley, the maths teacher who ran the club, was drooping by the doorway, reading the paper and wondering how long he could stick it out before he could nip out for a fag. There were about half a dozen tables occupied, and Davey sat down with resignation at the only table with a single occupant. Bloody Mark King. Nobody wanted to play him. He was such a cocky twat. For the first couple of chess meetings, Davey had been paired up with Mark, a third-year know-it-all with a moonscape of acne on his neck.

Mark taught Davey nothing, but repeatedly beat him in a few moves, smacking the pieces down and barking 'Checkmate,' in a bored robotic monotone, whilst Davey was still floundering and wondering which piece could move where. He could feel his palms getting sweaty and was starting to think chess wasn't for the likes of him, it was for the posh kids. Davey was about to pack it all in and piss off home in the third week, when Chris Clough wandered over. He was burly and handsome with a narrow tie in a microscopically tight knot halfway down his chest, crumpled shirt, and twinkly brown eyes below thick brown hair which stood upright in a stiff quiff.

'Hey, Kingy, do you want to swap places, give Phil Moss a good kicking? He's taking the piss out of me. I'll take your place here if you like?'

He spoke with artificial brightness, as if he was talking to a small child.

Mark stood up, chair scraping back abruptly, and disappeared in seconds, hungry to bully someone else. Chris sat down opposite Davey, moving all the chess pieces back into their starting positions, humming the tune to *Ride of the Valkyries,* under his breath. Davey knew Chris vaguely. They had never been in the same form, but shared some classes together. Raising his eyebrows, Chris flicked a glance at Mark, seated at the next table, rubbing his hands together, ready to browbeat somebody else. Davey could feel himself wanting to laugh.

'Christ, he's such a pain in the arse,' he muttered under his breath, twirling a knight around to face Davey. 'Right, let's start at the beginning. I'm Chris.' He held out a scabby, grubby, and roughened hand over the table and shook Davey's vigorously. 'Would you like me to teach you the basics? I'm a bit crap at it, but happy to show you?' He offered with a broad smile.

Davey nodded wordlessly.

'Did you know the rook is supposed to look like a chariot? The Persians called it a Rukh, so my dad says, that's where it got its name. If you want, when we finish tonight, come to ours for your tea. Dad knows loads more about the names of the pieces and he's a really good teacher, much better than me. If you want to, that is.' He smiled and Davey shrugged, not sure how to answer.

He looked down at the board and suddenly back up at Chris. 'Yeah, thanks, that would be good.'

Chris blithered on, moving pieces carefully and slowly. Explaining what each represented, how it could move, what it could do, telling stories about its history and origins. Mr McCauley wandered between the desks, periodically telling Mark to stop raising his voice. There was a fifteen-minute break halfway through the session, but Chris was in full flow and Davey was captivated. They didn't even go out for a fag.

After the club had finished for the night, they wandered back to Chris's flat above the shop on Mulberry Terrace. It was a steeply cobbled street in the oldest part of town. The area was crowded with disused mills and warehouses — and the river ran its sluggish way behind the buildings, the smell of dampness and decay heavy in the air. Chris led the way, chattering and laughing, gesturing with his cigarette, an orange point of light in the gloom. Davey said little. He couldn't get a word in edgeways and he was quite happy listening to his new friend. Chris took a last drag and threw the fag end into the gutter. It bounced briefly in a shower of sparks.

The Cloughs lived above the shop in a tall three-storey building that had once been a small weaving shed. It was accessed by a narrow doorway and even narrower staircase covered in the oldest, filthiest lino Davey had ever seen. Chris kept up the non-stop flow of chatter the whole time they climbed the steps. The entrance at the top of the stairs opened into a dim landing and Chris flung open a door.

'Hiya, Dad, only me. This is Davey, he's staying for tea.' Chris dragged an apprehensive Davey into the room.

Jonty was lying on the floor, hair wild, arm in the back of a disembowelled telly. He was wearing what looked to Davey like fancy dress, then he realised it was a Chinese patterned pyjama top and a pair of purple corduroy trousers that had probably been fashionable in the 1960s.

'I'm just trying to get this bloody thing to work. The snooker's on in a minute,' he grumbled, getting up. 'Hello, hello!' he bellowed, beaming at Davey and striding over to shake his hand, crushing it in his giant paw.

Jonty welcomed Davey like an old friend, ushering him into an enormous, dilapidated velvet wing-backed chair. A ginger cat the size of a small lion immediately settled on his lap and started kneading, claws plucking at his nylon trousers. Jonty nodded approvingly.

'You're greatly honoured. Bacchus is a very discerning moggy.'

It was the most amazing room Davey had ever seen — like something out of a film — and he was instantly enchanted. It was enormous, taking up almost the whole of the second floor. Large windows looked out onto Mulberry Terrace; they were covered with heavy, rich-looking orange velvet curtains that were slowly becoming detached from their rings. Under one window was a piano, sheet music decorating it, and another cat who was stretched out asleep on the keys.

Davey felt a mixture of excitement and confusion. It was all so weird and unfamiliar, but Chris and his dad seemed completely at ease having someone like him here. It didn't seem to matter to them that he didn't talk or look like them, or came off the estate. He wiped his sweaty palms on the arms of the chair.

He's asked you here as a mate. Just relax, you're allowed to be here. You're good enough as you are.

Davey stroked the cat, who had stopped shredding his trousers and had gone noisily to sleep on his lap. He stretched out his legs and studied the rest of the room. On the opposite wall to the windows was an enormous fireplace. A roaring, crackling fire was raging, and fast asleep in front of this, lying on a zebra skin rug, was a brindle greyhound, tightly curled like a Danish pastry.

'This is the most beautiful room I have ever seen,' marvelled Davey eventually, normally too shy to speak. He couldn't help himself. Everywhere he looked, there was something odd, unusual, or exotic. A kaleidoscope of artifacts casually displayed not for effect, but because they were loved and admired.

'I'm glad you like it, Davey. Please make yourself at home.' Jonty smiled, probing the innards of the telly again and swearing gently under his breath.

When Jonty found out Davey was Alice's grandson, instead of the usual silent disapproval of most strangers, there was a cry of pleasure and recognition. He clapped his hands together. 'Miss Armstrong, a most charming and erudite lady. I remember selling her a telescope. It's an honour. Of course, I see the resemblance to Stella now, you have the same colouring. You put me in mind of Caravaggio's *John the Baptist.*'

Davey smiled, not knowing what or who Caravaggio was, and made an embarrassed sound in his throat, thinking what Ray would say if he could hear this conversation. He glanced at Chris, who started giggling.

'Don't worry, you'll get used to Dad. Beans on toast and a brew okay?'

Davey nodded and hugged the little lion closer to him, who purred in contentment. Davey felt his own contentment; like he had come home. Five years later, it was even more of a home than ever. Davey spent as much time as he could away from the estate unless Ray was really pissed and trouble was brewing. Then he felt like he should be there to check on Stella. And to try to keep a lid on Bobby, who was getting more and more lippy with Ray, challenging him sometimes and winding him up. It was as if she wanted to provoke him into doing something that might break the endless cycle of bickering, drinking, fighting, and hassle between Mum and Ray.

Chapter 4
February 1982

Alice lived where the town ran out into a stutter of condemned-looking stone cottages as the road rose. It turned into a lane as it climbed the Pennines in a ribbon of patchy tarmac, splitting the grey green hills, the heather, and boulder strewn moorland. The people, mills, and houses dropped away as the sheep and curlews took over. Up here, it was clean sky and racing clouds, isolated barns and lone, bent-over trees, sculpted by the wind.

Flint Cottage was set on its own, away from the road up a small track. It faced towards the moors, as if turning its back on the town, crouching amongst the crags. The stone front was painted white, with a peeling blue door set in the middle, like a child's drawing of a house; crooked and plain. Alice's parents, James and Rose, had lived in this house before her.

James came back from the war in 1918, a quiet, gentle man, walking the hills with his sheep and the ghosts of his friends left behind on the Western Front. Changed forever by the smells, sounds, and sights of war, the casualty clearing station and the endless filth, noise, and misery. The simplicity and poverty of the hill shepherd's life seemed like heaven on earth. Recalling the relentless cycle of the farming calendar had kept his sanity through the long years in France and Belgium.

He passed his knowledge on to Alice, his only child. She drank it in, absorbed by the peace of the lonely hills. When James finally retired, the opportunity came to buy the cottage, and he used every penny saved from a lifetime of work to purchase the place. It would have killed them all to live in town, and it meant Alice could carry on with the sheep when her parents were gone.

The front door of Flint Cottage opened directly into a single room with a stone-flagged floor. Inside was very little furniture: a long oak bench, fissured with age, an armchair, and an ancient settee covered in a striped wool blanket. There was no open fire, but an old-fashioned range with a huge, heavy door. In winter, Alice kept the door open, and a fire raged within. A small warming oven which was often used to revive frozen newborn orphan lambs in springtime — tiny woolly bundles wrapped in a towel.

The rough, bumpy wall held few shelves, and these were crammed with random objects Alice had collected over the years. Animal skulls, bird's feathers, fossils, interesting rocks, or branches all had their space. A large telescope stood on its tripod by a window, which looked out onto the moorland behind the cottage. Above this was Alice's collection of books on astronomy, wildlife, plants, and geography.

Alice loved it here and wouldn't live in town if you paid her; a pit of idiots and gossips. The hills were in her blood and her bones. In her youth, she had been to school in town and worked at the mills. She hated every second of the noise, the choking air, the heat, the small-minded gossip, and the people.

Alice was in her sixties, and one of the fittest people Bobby knew. A small woman, with a slight, birdlike frame, she was still strong and agile. She spent all day walking the fells, tending her few animals and her vegetable plot. She owned three scrubby acres of land, bounded by dry-stone walls, which Alice mended and maintained. She had shown her grandchildren how she fixed the walls after the sheep had damaged them by scrambling over, or when time and storms had battered them.

'See the tall, thin, upright stones?' she said as Bobby and Davey looked on. 'They're called soldiers. You find a narrow piece of stone and pop it in the gap. And the narrow through stones, they're called mice, and you must do just the same. Once a piece of stone is in your hand, you don't put it down. You must find a place for it.'

Davey and Bobby stood close while she spoke quietly in her low hill shepherd's dialect. She held a piece of stone out so they could examine it, grey and lichened on her weathered palm. Then delicately but firmly slotted it into a gap in the wall. It fitted perfectly, as if it had been made for just that place. They nodded, captivated, and

Alice watched carefully while they selected their own stones and positioned them in the holes she indicated. She loved teaching them these tasks.

Stella hated the outdoors and as a child; had no interest in any of the jobs Alice took so much pleasure in. The kids were different altogether. They loved all of it; wall mending, feeding the animals, collecting eggs, helping in the vegetable garden. Alice smiled to herself when she watched them at lambing time, rubbing life into a newborn animal lying steaming and bloody on the ground. Or cleaning out the barn, forking sodden straw and shit into the wheelbarrow for the muck heap. Stella had always hated the gore and smell of life at Flint Cottage, but Bobby and Davey drank it all in, asking questions and getting their hands dirty.

Today, Alice was wearing a pair of men's trousers, tied up with baling twine, and a thermal vest with a jumper over the top, which was more holes than wool. Covering this was an anorak, an old one of Davey's from years ago. Alice had a strong jaw, snow white hair marbled with a black streak, braided and knotted at the nape of her neck. Her eyes were large and dark, usually wary from a life spent mostly alone, but they always seemed to soften when she saw her grandchildren. Her face, roughened, ruddy, and brown. Its features still beautiful in their own way with their web of wrinkles, high cheekbones, and slanting almond-shaped eyes.

Alice was a solitary woman. She enjoyed walking alone, roaming the hills above town at all hours and had done this since girlhood. It had earned her the reputation of being the local oddball, possibly a witch. She rescued injured animals and birds, put them back together with care, patience, and a knowledge of herbal medicine that had been commonplace in the hills when her parents were alive. In those days, the vet or the doctor meant a bill few could afford, and there were plenty of free remedies in the plants and trees of the Pennines.

Sometimes, Alice took her bike and went farther afield on her travels, her coat flapping behind like a sail as she swooped up and down the lonely Pennine lanes. She would have a sandwich shoved in one pocket, and an apple in the other, often getting home after dark. In winter, she would sometimes lie down on the sheep-cropped frosty grass, oblivious to the cold, and watch the night sky. Her hands thrust deep in her pockets, she would scan the inky darkness for her favourite stars: Andromeda, Pegasus, Cassiopeia. The dusty patch of the Pleiades and the reassuring swagger of Orion the Hunter, striding across the winter sky.

James had taught his daughter the shapes and habits of the planets and constellations, and the strange stories of how they found their places in the sky. That was another reason she couldn't live in town; the streetlights made it so much harder to see the stars, and that was something she wasn't prepared to tolerate. Alice collected things on her travels. Once a badger's skull, found bleached and resting amongst the gorse. Other times, seed heads, pheasant feathers, bones, pinecones. Once she found a medieval stone cannonball, smooth and fitting perfectly into her hand like a cricket ball, its surface slightly pecked by its long-dead maker.

A favourite place to visit was the small Neolithic stone circle north-east of the town, sitting above the cottage, reached only from a steep scramble up a crag. Here the stones lay mainly buried and fallen over — some with ancient cup and ring marks, swirls and depressions nibbled from the surface. She liked to run her fingers around the whorls, pushing them into the past.

One day, after a storm and torrential rain following a summer grass fire, Alice had found a small bundle, slightly exposed under one of the half-fallen larger stones. She scraped away the loose peat and scree to find an ancient leather bag tied with a leather thong. When she untied it, there, lying on a soft tawny hare's pelt, was the skeleton of a baby. It had a thin cord holding an amber bead threaded around the bones of its left wrist. Alice had wrapped the bones back up and scraped a deeper grave, laying it back down and covering it with soil and rocks, its secret kept safe.

At right angles to Flint Cottage was a small, low-set grey stone outbuilding hidden in a rocky fold of the hills. It had an oak door at one end, silvery with age, and narrow arrow slits in the walls for ventilation. Ancient and crooked, it had withstood the Pennine rain and wind for centuries. The roof was covered in thick slate slabs coated in a patchwork of sulphur and steel blue lichen. Viewed from the cottage, it almost looked like it was part of the hillside itself, growing out of the rock.

Alice went to the barn every evening to prepare it for the animals, who were kept indoors overnight. It was her favourite time of day. A small bare dusty light bulb hung low from the rough cobwebbed beams, spreading a soft light. The barn was one long building with wooden hurdles, so it could be divided into pens of different sizes. At one end was a small space with half a dozen hens fussing and squabbling, getting themselves ready for bed on a low perch. Next to this was a larger pen, empty, but reserved for the ewes when they came in to lamb if the weather was bad. It was covered with a thick layer of straw. At the very end was the largest space still, reserved for Jupiter, the pony.

Jupiter had been bought for a few pounds at the town livestock mart many years ago. Alice had originally gone to buy some lambs, but the quality wasn't good. She sat close to the front of the ring, amongst the flat-capped and overalled men, all dressed in wellies, sludge coloured tweed, and gaberdine. They glanced at her and a few nodded. She was 'Odd Alice' to them. Not really seen as a woman, but respected for her knowledge of animals and herbal medicine. Many a local farmer had knocked at her door for a remedy when they couldn't afford a vet, and more often than not, the bottles and jars of liniment, poultices, or drenches worked, whatever was in them.

She was dressed like a man as usual, her slight figure clad in a boiler suit and an old overcoat belted with a man's tie. The thick black and silver braided rope of her hair fastened with an ancient scrap of ribbon. She sat quietly; coarse, reddened hands folded into her lap like two roughened dry leaves. Animals came and went from the sales ring, but nothing caught her eye — everything was too expensive or too poor looking.

Alice had decided to go home when the mixed lots of odds and sods started coming through. It was getting to the end of the day's business and all the good stuff had gone. Suddenly, a filthy brown pony was chivvied into the ring by a fleshy faced thug waving a stick. The young pony charged round the ring in a blind panic, half wild from rough handling. Its thick winter coat was plastered in dried mud. Eyes rolling in terror, small ears flattened to a plain head with a broad, dirty face. The crowd was thinning out and there wasn't much interest.

The auctioneer was ramping up his monotone chat, trying to get a bit of attention, saying it could be a useful riding pony and it was well bred. A small ripple of laughter ran round the ring at this. A lad from the riding school walked away. The pony was too young, too wild looking, and too much work for him.

Soon, the only people bidding was the meat man hoping to pick up something nobody wanted at a knockdown price, and a lean looking dark-haired man who looked to Alice like a traveller. The reserve price was too high, and the traveller bowed out and it was the meat man's bid. The pony was still being chased round the ring while the auctioneer was winding down his chant. It stopped in front of Alice, coat dark with sweat, legs trembling, and eyes full of confusion and fear.

She raised her hand mechanically, and the meat man shook his head. The pony was too thin, anyway. The hammer came down, and the pony was hers. She sighed, shrugged, and got to her feet. By the time Alice had been to pay £8 at the auctioneer's office, it was dusk. The pony was tied to the back of a cattle wagon and the thug was impatient to go home.

'Does he have a name?' Alice asked, putting her hand up to stroke the pony's neck. It flinched and trembled as she ran her hand over the matted, greasy fur.

He shrugged and said something she couldn't hear, untied the rope, and handed it to Alice. The wagon roared off and Alice and the pony were left in the mart car park, with the last few cars and trailers rattling off into the early evening sunshine. It took two hours to walk the pony home. It had never been led anywhere and its feet were a mess; overgrown, and painful. His mane and tail were matted with lice, shit, and straw. His belly, bloated with worms.

By the time they got to the road above town, the stars were out. The Milky Way, a silver, quivering net above them as they walked. The only sounds were the pony's soft breathing and the padding sound of his unshod hooves. Alice talked to him about the planets and stars as they walked, and his ears moved backwards and forwards, listening to her low voice. She suddenly felt quietly triumphant that she had rescued this pony from the meat man, and only a little foolish that she hadn't bought any lambs. She scanned the sky again and smiled at the brightest planet that had suddenly appeared, hanging low in the western sky.

'There's Jupiter just coming up over there. That will be a grand name for you.'

A barn owl drifted past silently, flying low over the fields, hunting. It turned briefly and looked at them, its beautiful white, heart-shaped face like a ghost. The pony was exhausted and Alice stopped for a few minutes at the plague stone, which marked the beginning of the open moorland. He dropped his head to drink from the rough shallow trough at its base, lifting his head slowly, water dripping from the shaggy fur on his chin — too tired to flinch when Alice stroked his shoulder.

'Not too much further now, and we will be home.'

It took Alice six weeks to be able to touch the pony's head without him rearing up and rushing to the back of the barn, snorting, and quivering in terror. It was slow progress, gaining his confidence. Gradually, she was able to groom him — washing his tail and combing burrs from his mane so it fell in a silky black curtain down his neck, brushing his coat to a burnished dark conker colour. His feet took longer, months of visits from the farrier to trim them back to normality.

Jupiter spent day and night out on the fell in the summer, but in winter, he came indoors at night and was always waiting at the gate on an evening. When Alice opened it, he would trot stiffly into the barn, whickering at her as he came towards her, automatically making for his stall. She would fasten the gate and spend a few minutes talking nonsense to him. She never tired of this; the artificial light on his soft, mossy coat. The sound of him pulling contentedly at his haynet, his muzzle white with age now. Sturdy, woolly legs knee deep in thick straw.

Tonight, when she got back into the cottage, she had company. She was on her knees beside the range, breaking up sticks with her strong brown hands when Bobby knocked on the front door and slipped in, frozen from the walk up the hill out of town. She shut the door behind her and stepped into the warmth, turning her torch off. The cold closed out behind her.

'Hello love,' smiled Alice. 'I'm brewing up in a minute. Do you want one?'

Bobby nodded and eased herself into the armchair, pulling off her gloves and coat and enjoying the warm silence.

'How's your mum?' murmured Alice in her low, harsh voice, snapping away at the pile of twigs.

'She's alright, I suppose,' sighed Bobby, rubbing her forehead absentmindedly, and holding her hands out to the warmth of the range.

A large black and white cat wandered in from the tiny kitchen and settled itself on Bobby's knee, butting her head.

'Ganymede really likes you. He's a funny cat. He hasn't moved all day until he saw you come in, not like Perseus, he never sits still.' Alice chuckled a little, adding more twigs to the growing stack of the kindling.

Perseus, an even bigger black cat, was sharpening his claws on the back of the ancient couch, ears back, and a look of intense concentration on his face. Alice smiled and turned back to Bobby.

'And that useless bag of shit? He's still there at home, I take it?' Alice had no time for Ray. She knew a bad 'un when she saw one and had let Stella know as soon as she clapped eyes on the smarmy charmer. She knew all his stories were lies, especially his war stories.

'Aye, more's the pity,' Bobby murmured, shrugging. She held her hands, palms up, fingers splayed, tilting her head on its side in a gesture of resignation.

Alice could never understand why Stella stayed with a man who did nothing but bully and control her. She had offered her daughter the opportunity to come back home countless times, but she never did. Alice could see it was because of Stella's pride and bloody-mindedness that she couldn't go home. Stella had grown up without a man in the house and had suffered at school for it.

She'd been called a 'bastard' and a 'black bitch', a 'darkie's kid', 'a half-caste'. She craved a man's protection, was validated by his presence. Stella would rather live with Ray, and all his violence, than in freedom and peace, alone. And she blamed Alice for it.

'You don't need a man to look after you. No woman does. You have your brain and you can be just as useful,' Alice would snap when she saw Stella with a black eye or a bruised face. It filled her with sorrow and rage to see her daughter like this. But she knew it didn't matter what she did or said, Stella was determined to see Ray the way she wanted him to be.

'He's a good man, really.' Her voice would start rising as quickly as her temper. 'He puts food on the table. He's a hard worker. He's been a father to the kids, after him, that was supposed to be a father went off!'

She knew it wasn't really true. Everything the kids had ever eaten, worn, or played with had been bought by her. But if she admitted that to herself, then she would have to admit defeat, and the waste of all the years pretending Ray was someone he wasn't.

'Those kids and you, for that matter, would be better off without him, and you bloody know it,' Alice would snap.

Stella would get properly riled then and start shouting. 'And what would you know? You weren't brought up without a father, were you?'

Alice would go very silent and still, glowering at Stella with a steady, hot gaze. She felt some guilt at Stella being brought up without a man in the house, because of the way she had turned out, but Alice wasn't prepared to live with a man for the sake of having one around. Stella needed to kick him out and grow up. She liked her independence and Stella had wanted for little when she was growing up. Everyone in town was poor then. Stella was no different from any of the other kids. If anything, a bit better fed, and healthier living away from the mills.

Alice poured Bobby a strong hot cup of tea and they sat in companionable silence, with only the sound of the ticking clock, purring cats, and the wind rattling the old windows to disturb the peace.

I would love to live here, Bobby thought, not for the first time. She and Davey had fantasised about living here when they were young kids, when Ray had first showed his real personality. And Alice would have them here, in a heartbeat. But they wouldn't leave Stella, not yet, anyway. However, that time wasn't far off — that time was coming.

Chapter 5
February 1982

It was dark outside and only 4 pm. Stella hated the winter. She loathed the draughts in the house and the lack of light. She detested the dreary long evenings sat in front of the telly, one side of her body hot from the fire, her legs turning a mottled corned beef colour. The other side, cold from the ill-fitting windows and doors that never got fixed or replaced. Most of all, she hated sitting and listening to Ray; his droning on and complaining at everything that came on the telly. If it was the news, he was moaning about Northern Ireland and the Troubles,

'Bastard Catholics, fucking Micks. All the fucking same.' Or race riots. 'Uppity black fuckers, they should be grateful, or fuck off back to where they came from.'

When Davey reminded Ray that most of the people rioting were third generation Britons, he was met with a volley of abuse. Thatcher, job losses, dole queues. It was all there for Ray to pass comment on. If it wasn't the news, he complained about *Top of the Pops*, or Stella and the kid's favourite, *Coronation Street*. Or any and every drama or documentary unless it was *Dad's Army* or cowboy or war films.

Stella was upstairs, sitting on the end of their bed with its silky pink nylon quilted counterpane and its ballerina skirt trim. It was cold and she could see her breath. She stared ahead into the mirror of the white plastic dressing table. The table had a glass top, and arranged on this were three small ceramic containers. They held cheap earrings and rings with coloured glass stones, along with some white plastic rosary beads given to her on her First Holy Communion by a teacher at school.

Stella stared at her reflection objectively, without pity. The tired face, sliding slowly into middle age with its softly sagging jawline. Her dark olive skin now showing open pores and deep grooves from nose to chin, like a ventriloquist's doll. Her eyes, slightly hooded now, but immense black pools fringed with dark, thick lashes. She was still pretty, she decided — could still turn a few heads when she was done up and in her good clothes.

She looked at the backs of her hands. On her right hand, she wore a silver Claddagh ring from Alice. It had been her grandma's and it had been passed down from her great grandma, who had been married with it, in a tiny stone church, somewhere in Kildare. On her left-hand ring finger, she wore a silver ring with a large glass stone. Ray had found this on the floor of a pub toilet, but presented to Stella as a white gold engagement ring with a two-carat diamond.

Her hands were slim, but becoming mottled. The tips of her fingers roughened from work, and the back of the hands woven with raised blue veins. It seemed like two minutes ago that Ray had slid the ring on her finger. *Where did the time go?* The kids had been toddlers then. Now they were adults and here she was, still sitting, waiting for her life to begin.

Her hair was still long and mainly jet black, with a few streaks of grey here and there. She brushed it rhythmically, recalling how much of a fuss she made of it when she was young. Chuckling to herself, it instantly felt like a lonely, hollow sound in the empty room.

When she first met Ray, she used to back comb and spray the life out of it — pinning it up in a beehive and only washing it once every couple of weeks. Sleeping like a geisha so it wouldn't get flattened. All her mates did the same, and nits were rife in the mills in town. Later in the 60s, she ironed it flat, bent over the ironing board, covered with brown paper. It would only stay straight for a while though, before springing up into fat, silky curls.

Ray had been a proper catch back then; tall, good looking, attentive, protective. A mysterious war hero. Although nowadays, she doubted most of the stories. She wasn't daft. She heard people at work and in the pubs calling him a bullshitter and a Walter Mitty. Stella didn't think too much about it though, sometimes it didn't do any good to delve into the past. She pulled a few strands of hair from the brush and placed it back on the dressing table, lost in thought.

It had been good to have a man around, especially as she was on her own when the kids were little. Life as a single parent was a struggle, and she didn't like leaving them at Alice's all the time when she was at work. Other women helped; neighbours, and girls from work, but they let her know they were doing her a favour. She just wanted a proper family; a man to make everything right.

Alice hadn't liked Ray from the start. She saw straight through him from the first time she met him, challenging Stella straight away.

'What d'you need another man for? Look how the last one left you fixed. He's nowt but trouble.'

Alice had been single since before Stella was born. Stella couldn't remember a time when it had been anything other than her, Alice, and Grandma and Grandad Armstrong. She had never heard a man's raised voice until she got with Ray, and after that, she heard nothing else.

Stella massaged the back of her neck, and then under her eyes, disliking the fact the skin stayed pleated where she had rubbed it. But he was here and he was looking after them all. She didn't have to be on her own like her mum had been, living hand to mouth and bringing her kids up in the hills like little savages.

Stella looked beyond her reflection to the padded headboard behind her. Ray's side of the bed had a dark, greasy stain from his head on the pale imitation velvet. Above the bed was a faded wallpaper pattern of pink roses, repeatedly intertwining a pale green trellis. Stella remembered the day she and Ray had papered the room.

He had been an arsehole that day, snapping when she let the paper curl back before it was properly pasted and kicking off when the pattern didn't match up perfectly. They hadn't been together long and he'd just moved in with her. It was the first time he had hit her. She had shouted back at him when he dropped the pasting brush on the carpet and he slapped her so hard across the face she had a sore, red cheek for days. Without even realising it, she tapped her fingertips on her cheekbone, expecting to feel tender, raw skin.

The idea of leaving had come into her head many times, half-formed, usually after a battering, when she felt really low. She kept the intention hugged to her consciousness where nobody could see it. A treasure, a hope, a precious thing to bring out in secret when things got really shit. Something to feed, nurture, polish, and luxuriate in. She always ended up dismissing the ideas as impractical; two kids, no money, a failed relationship, on her own again.

Sometimes she thought about going back to Alice, back home up the hill. But she told herself, there wasn't enough room there. Stella was too proud, always losing her nerve and making excuses. Telling herself she was too old to leave, to start again. She rubbed her upper arms, shivering. It wouldn't do her any good feeling sorry for herself. He would be back soon, and she needed to pull herself together. Ray wasn't that bad. She could be an annoying bitch and should cut down on the booze. He had told her so enough times. Maybe he was right, maybe it was all her fault. That's why he wouldn't marry her.

Stella stretched, pulling her cardie closer round her shoulders. It was freezing in the room now, but she didn't want to move. That would mean going downstairs and finishing hoovering the front room. She wondered briefly what it would be like to just have herself to look after, to have nobody else to worry about.

Once, after a really shitty Christmas, she had gone so far as to cobble together a small deposit for a tiny, damp flat on Jacquard Street — but had bottled it at the last minute. She wondered where all the years, chances, and opportunities had gone. Her and Ray, stitched together somehow like a badly mended shoe.

Ray had eroded her self-confidence, her *Stellaness* so much that she almost didn't know who the woman was looking back at her. A half version of herself, with the energy and life removed. Her essence dulled and diluted. She pulled her rings off, having to screw the Claddagh around to force it over her knuckle. It left a dent and a band of white flesh. She rubbed some moisturiser into her hands, smoothing the cream into the creases of her fingers. They were workers' hands, she reflected, not idle lady's hands.

Stella worked part time at Earnshaws. Ray liked the house to be nice and tidy, and he wanted to keep his eye on her. He had made her reduce her hours because there were too many men there and left alone to her own devices, she'd get up to all sorts. She didn't mind going part time, mill work could be boring. She had a mundane role in the accounts office now, adding up the weight of bales of fabric before they went off to the dyers.

Most of the women there didn't get a chance to do the more interesting jobs. One thing she did love was the factory banter and the social life. The mills in town had football teams and outings, nights out and other events. Most people sat down together at brew time and dinner time in the canteen. When the Barnaby holiday came around, there was the fortnight mill closure and the exodus to Blackpool on the train or coach.

She smiled when she thought of her and Jean Kenny running riot on the front at Blackpool when they were younger. Eating candyfloss, out dancing every night until their feet were like puddings. They used to share a boarding house room to save money, sleeping in the same bed and flirting with countless young lads from other mills all over the north. Then, before they knew it, back on the train home to reality; skint, hungover, and happy.

The sound of the key in the door broke her trance, and her stomach plummeted in its familiar lurch of fear. Stella jumped up and left the room to run downstairs, already ready to gabble and sound defensive. She nearly tripped on the ruckled up carpet on the way out of the bedroom. She looked over the landing and Ray was standing below, under the light. He had a bald patch starting on the crown of his head. Stella smiled with grim satisfaction and started walking slowly downstairs.

It was mince and mash for tea. Ray threw his keys on the little table by the phone, walked past Stella without comment to the kitchen and the fridge, then sat down in front of the telly. She heard the soft snap and hiss as he opened a can of lager, and she went into the kitchen to sort out the tea. The kids weren't in; they spent more and more time out of the house now. She couldn't blame them, but it made her feel irritated and sad recalling how noisy and chaotic the house was at this time when they were younger.

The mince was already cooked, a grey congealing mass in the frying pan — it just needed heating up. The potatoes were overcooked and almost liquid in the pan. They looked like wallpaper paste. Stella threw them in the bin and put the kettle on, ripping open a packed of Smash. He'd never notice, not if she chucked some gravy on top. She looked for the Bisto, listening to some quiz programme blaring out from the front room. Within five minutes, Ray's tea was ready, and Stella took it in, waiting to gauge the mood.

She had her tea sitting in her armchair, looking at the telly. 'What's been going on today, then?' Stella said in a deliberately cheerful voice. The adverts were on; a woman was dancing up and down a lounge, singing, and sprinkling a giant can of talcum powder on a carpet. She looked demented.

'Nowt much. Had a run over to Leeds, and then Bolton on the way back. Rained all the way. I'll have to tell them that the wagon needs a new tyre. If I get pulled over by the coppers, I'll be in bother.' He said all this with his mouth full of food, and a thin rivulet of gravy trickled down his chin.

She turned away, inwardly gagging. Finishing her tea, she got up to draw the curtains against the winter blackness and banked up the fire with more coal. She put the big square fireguard around it, and brought a washing basket in from the kitchen before draping socks, knickers, shirts, and trousers over the top of the guard — the legs of the trousers hanging down as they steamed gently. By the time Ray was finishing his fifth can, they would be ready to turn over to dry on the other side and by the time they went to bed, the washing would be crispy and dry.

It was tinned mandarin segments for pudding. Stella tipped some into two little metal ice cream dishes Bobby had nicked from work and gouged a couple of holes in the can of evaporated milk. She liked the way the milk separated into tiny cream-coloured balls when she tipped it on the fruit. She took them in on a tray, and curled up in the chair again, opening a can of lager and a fresh packet of Silk Cut. Stretching out her feet, she picked up *The Bitch*. Stella loved a Jackie Collins novel, she and Jean devoured them with a passion, indulging their fantasies of a life of wealth and glamour, designer clothes, yachts, racehorses, black satin sheets, penthouses in New York and handsome young lovers — all of which were in short supply in Gritstone.

By the time the late news had come on, Stella had drunk a few cans, and Ray more than a few. He was on the whisky now. A newsreader with enormous glasses and a serious face was delivering a feature about unemployment. The number of people out of work had reached three million, he intoned. The manufacturing industries are in terminal decline, an economist has said. Coal, steel, shipbuilding, textiles, and car production were all struggling.

'We're lucky we are still in work, but you can tell we're on borrowed time,' remarked Stella. 'Nowhere near as many orders as a few years ago, and no more overtime or bonuses. Jean says at least two mills are going to close this year in town. When she was talking to one of the lads who service the overlockers, he said Manchester is in a right state.' The drink had given her voice a slight nasal lag.

Ray grunted and took another gulp of whisky. People would always need wagons. Things always needed shifting from one place to another. He really didn't care, as long as he had what he wanted. Stella was getting worked up. Ray seemed unmoved by the hardship being inflicted on manufacturing towns and cities, particularly in the North. He didn't care that people were struggling and communities were being slowly destroyed. She fixed her eyes on him, but he wasn't really listening to her, just looking at the screen.

'I worry about our Bobby and Davey. What kind of world are they going to come out into after school? There won't be any jobs, they won't be able to get on.' She shook her head and reached for her fags again. They had slid down the gap between the cushion and the chair and she scrabbled for them, irritated. Ray was silent.

'Don't you care?' Stella was always agitated when he didn't respond and went into one of his surly shrug moods. She lit a cigarette and smacked the lighter down on the chair arm, temper rising. Inhaling deeply, Stella stared at the ceiling before letting the smoke out in a long, furious, trembling jet.

He looked at her coldly and belched, insolent and expressionless. Then he leant towards her and sneered in a sing-song voice, 'No, I don't care. If they wanted proper jobs, they'd be out there now, looking, instead of staying at school filling their heads with shite and thinking they're better than everyone else.' He sat back in his chair, smiling, satisfied that he had infuriated her.

Stella was furious. 'They're doing their A-levels to better their chances.' Then she couldn't help herself. 'They don't want to be *just* wagon drivers or mill girls,' she spat. Jackie Collins had slid to the floor, and Stella was bolt upright in her chair now, eyes hard.

Ray took a deep, measured, slow breath and turned his flushed, Spam-coloured face towards her. 'This *wagon driver* has kept that pair of snotty bastards for years, you stupid, ungrateful cow!' He pointed at her with his brown, bent fag-finger and waggled it threateningly.

There was a bit of spit forming at each corner of his bluish lips. He rested his fag on the foothills of the overflowing ashtray, piled up with dimps like a stinking fruit bowl. Stella felt a sudden, familiar stab of fear, and licked her dry lips. She knew she had gone too far this time.

The front door clicked softly. Neither of them heard it above the telly and the slanging. Bobby slid into the room, a blast of cold air following her. The room was full of fag smoke and the fug of damp washing. She had heard the raised voices when she unlocked the door and knew what was brewing. Bobby sat on the settee in between their chairs and said nothing. She met Ray's eye, feeling the loathing for her coming off him in waves.

Come on then, you twat, she thought, maintaining a neutral expression. *You're the big man, aren't you? Are you going to come at us both?* He was much less likely to hit Stella if she was sitting between them. After thirty seconds, she picked up Jean Kenny's catalogue and started flicking through it mechanically, not even looking at the pages as she turned them.

Chapter 6
February 1982

Bobby worked at the Minerva Café on Saturdays and every Thursday evening after school. She had been doing this since she was fourteen. It was hard on your feet running around all day on a Saturday, but she was having driving lessons and wanted to save up for her own car, so every penny counted.

George and Maria Angelides were the owners. A dour Greek couple who had inexplicably ended up in Gritstone in the 1960s. The café was on the edge of the indoor market and occupied a corner of the main street. It was always busy; mums with babies, workmen, shoppers, and market traders. After school, it was packed with school kids. There wasn't anywhere for older kids to go until the youth club opened at 6.30 pm, and if you didn't want to go home straight from school, it was the only place to go to get a coffee, smoke, and hang around with your friends. There were other cafés in town, but this one played music and you didn't get kicked out after ten minutes if you didn't keep ordering more food or drink.

Today was a Thursday shift, straight from school. Bobby nipped into the ladies to get ready. Tired, already late for work, and not looking forward to the next few hours. She pulled off her school clothes quickly and stuffed them in a ball in a carrier bag, dragging on her uniform of worn, flat pumps, thick black tights with a ladder just starting on her ankle. She wriggled into the crumpled, tight skirt worn well above the knee that Maria always muttered about and shoved her arms into the once-white shirt, before tying the strings of the black apron twice around her waist.

Her thick mass of hair was back-combed and pinned high on her head with a stack of grips which shed themselves into people's food throughout the shift. Bobby peered into the dusty mirror, dissatisfied with her shiny face and the dark blue shadows under her eyes. She wiped the surface with her sleeve. It was going rusty at the edges and gave off a slightly blurred reflection. She put on a coat of shimmery lipstick and another layer of kohl under her long, black pupilless eyes, and smoothed a raven-coloured curl back from her forehead.

George hammered on the door, making her jump. 'You gonna be in there all day? Customers are out here waiting!' he roared.

Bobby pulled a face in the mirror and sighed loudly. 'Coming, George,' she yelled. 'Here we fucking go again,' she muttered to herself and unlocked the door.

The good thing about this job was the speed at which the shift went. It was flat-out busy — making tea and coffee, running out food, clearing tables, and taking orders. Occasionally, someone would order something exotic from the menu, like a fruit salad, and Bobby would be sent on an emergency mission to the fruit shop to locate a banana.

Bobby knew a lot of the customers from off the estate, or kids from school. There were regulars who came in for a chat, and the odd perv who would make comments or try to touch her up when she put down plates of food. She learnt to keep her distance with these men, leaving the plate of food on the edge of the table or asking Neville Croft, the Saturday boy, to take out the food. Neville was a cheery boy, fourteen stone at the age of sixteen with a squint and horrific body odour.

The café had been built as part of the market in the early 1960s, and its décor remained unchanged. A speckled lino floor which looked filthy, regardless of how often it was mopped. Twelve tables seating four people each and a corner booth upholstered in red leatherette with small slashes in its seat oozing dirty yellow foam like pus. The metal tables were topped with blue Formica pocked with fag burns. Each held a plastic menu propped up between a paper napkin holder, salt and pepper pots, tin ashtray, a brown sauce bottle and also ketchup in plastic tomato-shaped containers, with a red scab of dried sauce on the spout.

One wall comprised windows looking directly onto Market Street, and another was covered in a large mirror and a picture of the Acropolis which was tinged yellow with two decades of cigarette smoke and grease. The far end of the café was taken up with a long counter, the till, and the coffee machine, and beyond this the tiny, cramped kitchen, perpetually steamy with the fryer and the dishwasher going continually.

Thursday evenings had been quieter recently. It was Gritstone's late night shopping day, but in February, most people didn't want to hang around the market. The days were short and cold, everyone was still skint after Christmas.

Midge Kenny appeared after school. She bought a pot of tea and sat in the corner booth immersed in her library copy of *White Fang* while she waited for her sister. She was curled up inside her parka, knees drawn up underneath her, small face almost hidden in the coat hood. Bobby thought she looked like a tiny, shrunken Eskimo, book propped open with one hand, the other around her teacup.

At 5.15 pm, Wendy strutted in through the door straight from work like a copper-coloured queen. Her tabard covered in a raincoat, collar up, beautiful hair shimmering under the lights. Bobby snatched five minutes to sit down with them until George rang his bell on the service hatch to make her move. Midge and Wendy left and the evening dragged. Sleet pecked the windows and the cars outside made a steady whooshing sound as they splashed past. Bobby stared out into the dark, past her reflection as she automatically emptied ashtrays and collected dirty plates — willing the time to pass more quickly.

A group of grammar school boys came in when Bobby was trying to get tables wiped down and the floor swept in the back of the café. She usually put *Reserved* signs on the back tables so she could get a head start on cleaning up when George turned the closed sign around at 7.30 pm. There were four boys and they made straight for the back of the café and sat down at a table, its surface still wet from Bobby's cloth. They flicked the *Reserved* sign on to a neighbouring table, it skidded on the wet surface and clacked against the sugar dispenser. Oblivious to anyone else, they chattered loudly and lit fags.

Bobby walked over, hackles already rising, and said evenly, 'This table is reserved. Please could you move to the front of the café?'

One of the boys, fair-haired with a pink complexion, just shrugged, and two others smiled. They were probably her age, or maybe older. They had sixth form badges on their expensive looking wool blazers. Bobby thought about her and Davey and their ill-fitting nylon blazers with shiny elbows, and was filled with fury.

Why did the grammar school lads always look different? Bobby could never put her finger on it. It wasn't just appearance, there was something else. Arrogance, posture, the confidence that anything they asked for they would get, and anyone who looked and sounded like Bobby would do it for them.

'No, we can't,' a flat, posh voice came from one with red hair with red rimmed blue eyes. He didn't even look at her. He was reading the cracked plastic menu with exaggerated nonchalance. 'Four white coffees. Does anyone want anything else?' he drawled.

'Chips. I'll have some chips,' rapped one.
Bobby took out her notebook and scribbled down the order with her much-bitten biro, raging inside. She turned to go back to the counter and one of them said something. Bobby couldn't catch it, but another boy hissed, 'Don't.'

She longed to go back to the table and throw a boiling pot of tea at those posh twats, but it wasn't worth losing her job over. Bobby returned with their drinks and food, keeping her eyes on the table, feeling the back of her neck burning.

They were watching her with amusement, and the rude one said, 'Thank you' in a loud and exaggerated manner when she turned to go back to the counter.

She was suddenly aware of her shiny sweaty face, laddered tights, the bobbly pilled fabric of her skirt, the greyness of the white blouse, and the food stains on her apron. It hadn't crossed her mind before they came in. She had felt good enough. Now she felt grubby and rough. Bobby carried on cleaning and stacking up clean cups on top of the coffee machine.

Eventually, the *Open* sign on the door was flipped over to *Closed,* which was the signal to help Maria empty the bins and sweep and mop the kitchen floor. The older woman's ankles were so swollen the skin lapped over the top of her shoes and her thick little body moved slowly and stiffly as she worked. Her grey head was bent over the top of an overfilled bin bag, fumbling the plastic into a knot with her crooked, puffy fingers. Bobby reached over and picked it up to carry out to the skip in the freezing, icy yard. They worked in companionable silence, each completely lost in thought.

She could hear George cashing up, muttering over the till roll as he recounted, trying to find out why he was two pence short. After filling up the stainless-steel serviette dispensers, she washed the ashtrays, tipped clean cutlery into trays, and threw the dirty tea towels into laundry bags.

The posh lads were finished now. Bobby reckoned they had spun out the coffee and the chips for as long as possible to wind her up. She ignored them when they came up to the till, leaving them to George. As they left, the red-eyed one let the door slam so hard, the glass rattled, and she could hear a bray of laughter in the wet darkness beyond the fogged-up windows.

Bobby went over to the table to clean up, stacking the cups and saucers, and ashtray onto a tray. Under a saucer was a folded-up scrap of paper. She was about to throw it in her bin bag with the fag ends and the dirty serviettes when she saw it had writing on it. It was scribbled in a slanting, exaggerated hand.

Bobby, I'm sorry about my friends, I'd really like to talk to you. There was a phone number. Which of them had written that? And how did he know her name? For a second, her stomach fluttered with excitement. They had all behaved like a bunch of arseholes, so she was surprised and flattered. Unless it was a trick. Get her to ring up and then take the piss out of her. She could see them now, all crowded around a phone receiver, listening while she politely asked to speak to the lad who had left her the note.

Her face felt hot. Pushing the paper into her pocket with embarrassment, she started wiping the table down in a flurry to distract herself. Then she took the scrap of paper out again, shook her head as if to rattle some sense into it, crunched the note into a ball and shoved it into the bin bag. Fuck it, she was sick of people like that — people who thought they were better because they had money, or a uniform to hide behind. Then almost instantly, she forgot about it. George was waving a small brown envelope with her wages in it. It was home time.

The following Saturday, there was a large white envelope waiting for her at the café. George wasn't impressed. He handed it over to her and muttered something, but Bobby ignored him. She looked at the writing on the envelope. It was unfamiliar. Scribbled on the back, it said: *Do not open until tomorrow.*

Fuck that. She took it into the toilet at her break time and ripped open the envelope. It was a hideous Valentine's card, with a cardboard back and a padded satin front — covered in a large picture of a kitten with enormous pale blue eyes, sitting in a basket of ribbons. There was some daft verse which she didn't read and then a message which said, *'Ring me, M xxx'*

It was the dick from the grammar school. Bobby had forgotten it was Valentine's Day tomorrow. She was half revolted by the hideous card, and half flattered — she'd never been sent a Valentine's card before. Digging her nails into the padded front, Bobby tore the kitten in two, then crammed the card into the sanitary towel bin, muttering under her breath. She was still convinced he was taking the piss.

Bobby put it out of her mind after that and had completely forgotten about the grammar school cretins until two Thursdays later. As she left work at the end of her shift, one of them was waiting outside. Maria and George had just locked up and wandered off, and Bobby was fumbling for her fags, rummaging in the bottom of her bag in the dark. She was aware of a figure leaning against the shop front opposite the market and thought he looked familiar. Ignoring him, she carried on walking home through town, him falling in to step beside her.

'Hello,' he said. The voice was wary, quiet.

Bobby clocked him from the corner of her eye, turning to glance at him without expression. It was one of the quieter, smirking boys from the group. Tall, with wavy light hair and eyes which looked colourless in the streetlight. Bobby realised who he was then and made the connection with the note and the naff card. She made a grunting sound of begrudging acknowledgement and carried on walking, eyes straight ahead.

'I left my phone number on the table after I came in a couple of weeks ago with my mates,' he explained, pushing his hair back with his hand, smiling slightly and inclining his head. 'They were being rude.' His voice was flat, local, but with a careful edge to it, as if he was trying to sound more polite, more polished.

'I know,' Bobby said abruptly, staring straight ahead and taking a drag on her fag, hitching the strap on her bag further up her shoulder.

He stared at her profile in surprise. He wasn't used to being ignored, especially by a girl. Especially by a girl *like this. She was very pretty*, he thought, *but common. That's what his mum would say, anyway.*

'I just wanted to apologise for my friends. For the way they behaved,' he continued, speaking quickly now, hands splayed out, palms upwards in appeasement. 'I'm Matt, by the way.' He held his hand out, changing tack.

She just glanced at it and increased her speed, staring grimly ahead. He quickly let it drop to his side.

Bobby suddenly stopped and stared at him. Her eyes narrowed and she smoothed her hair back away from her brow, flicking her fag end into the gutter.

'Then why didn't you say something at the time? Or didn't you have the balls?' she snapped, and carried on walking, faster this time, wanting to get rid of this arrogant prick.

He just walked faster, and used a wheedling voice this time. 'I'm sorry, yes, I should have done. I don't know what I was thinking.'

Bobby carried on. She was nearly halfway home now. It was drizzling. She was tired and hungry, and just wanted to sit down in front of the telly with her tea and a brew.

'It's okay,' she said wearily. 'It doesn't matter.'

He followed like a shadow as she crossed the road onto the estate, wondering if she should just go into the phone box near the chippy and pretend she had to make a call. Not far to Ribbon Street now, she could get rid of this idiot. He was quite nice looking in a way, she conceded, but completely irritating and so persistent.

'Good, that's great. I wondered if you wanted to come out with me one night? Maybe for a drink, or to the pictures?' He spoke quickly, trying to wrap up the deal, eyebrows raised in invitation.

Bobby turned around and stared at him incredulously. Home at last. Thank Christ.

'No thanks,' she spat and turned in at her gate. She slammed it so hard it rattled back against the latch, the rotten wood wobbling.

Matt stood gawping in surprise as she marched up the path and let herself into one of the shittiest houses on the estate. *Fucking stuck-up little slag,* he thought with outrage, and carried on home through the drizzle, which was turning to rain now. *What a bloody nerve, turning him down. He could have any girl on this estate.*

Matthew Thomas wasn't easily deflected from his purpose. Every Thursday and every Saturday, he waited for her outside the Minerva and walked home with her, trying his best to charm her. The first time he had seen her in the café, he had been attracted to her. The dark eyes, skin and hair, that deadpan sexy expression. He also thought she was a piece of trash, but he didn't like rejection one bit, had rarely experienced it, and decided it was his mission to have her.

The only potential fly in the ointment was that psycho stepfather of hers. Matt had never met him, but when he asked around about the Armstrongs, it was quickly made apparent that Ray Short was a fucking maniac who didn't care who he battered.

After a solid four weeks of badgering and stalking, just to shut him up, Bobby agreed to go out for a drink with him. She had started to find his persistence amusing. He was a complete dick, but she supposed there were worse looking lads in town, and she could feel herself weaken under the flattery. She could go for this drink and if it all turned into a nightmare, she could just tell him to piss off firmly, and that would be the end of it. But first, she had to discuss the matter with Wendy, whose encyclopaedic knowledge of the ways of men would provide all the advice required.

Chapter 7
March 1982

Wendy and Midge's room was cosy and fuggy with smoke. Wendy had the little portable electric heater going full blast with both bars on. Jean would go mental if she found out, but she wouldn't — she was out on the piss. Midge was downstairs watching telly and Wendy was stretched out on one bed, Bobby on the other, drinking cider and listening to The Specials. Wendy was painting her toenails alternately black and white, with a newspaper spread out under her feet to catch the polish, humming along to the music.

Bobby was flicking through a copy of *Smash Hits* and chain smoking, wondering what she was going to wear on her date with Matt. She heaved herself up into a sitting position on Midge's bed and shoved the pillow between her back and the wall. The room was in total chaos. It looked like a crime scene — every surface covered in Wendy's clothes, makeup, records, empty crisp, or fag packets. In contrast, like a small, calm oasis, Midge's bed was tidy. Faded candy-striped sheets tucked in tightly, covered with a bobbly orange nylon quilt cover. At the side of the bed was a tower of books and an alarm clock with a dinosaur's face.

'He sounds like a total dick,' was Wendy's verdict when Bobby related the saga.

'I mean, is he fit?' She demanded, staring at Bobby intently through thickly mascaraed lashes, wanting to know in forensic detail everything about his appearance, clothes, what he had said and when.

Bobby shrugged. 'He looks okay, I suppose.'

Wendy rolled her eyes theatrically at this apathy. 'I don't know why you're wasting your time on him.'

'I know, but I thought I might give it a go.' Bobby looked at her friend for approval or dissent. 'He seems to like me. He's been chasing me for weeks now. Perhaps he might be okay when I get to know him?' reasoned Bobby. She gave an exasperated sigh. 'And anyway, I'm bored. It's just school and listening to The Arsehole at home at the minute.'

Wendy said nothing, slowly shaking her head, face blank and mouth hanging open. 'Well, you wanna get out of that school and get a job, while there's some left,' she warned, waving the miniature brush at Bobby before screwing the cap firmly back onto the polish.

She had a point, Bobby conceded. All that seemed to be talked about at the minute, either on the news or at home, was unemployment and the dying out of the traditional manufacturing and mining industries. A Job Centre had appeared in the middle of town, replacing the old Labour Exchange. It was all carpet-covered dividing screens and grey plastic modern looking desks. There were a lot of closures at the smaller mills in town, and people were now travelling to other places for work. That was almost unheard of a few years ago. Until recently, a person could live and work their whole lives in town without ever having to leave if they so wished.

Wendy ran her hand through her glossy red bob, her fox-coloured eyes dancing. 'Here, look what I just bought with my wages.'

Pushing the point, she dragged out a Dorothy Perkins shop carrier bag from under the bed and pulled out a black and white checked dress in one hand and a pair of white stilettoes in the other, grinning. Wendy blew all her money on clothes and records. There were always plenty of men around who bought her drinks. Jean was forever grumbling that she never paid enough board and squandered her money on luxuries. Wendy didn't give a shit. She reasoned she was here for a good time, not a long time.

'Lovely,' agreed Bobby, leaning across the gap between the beds to stroke the dress and pick up the shoes to examine.

But she couldn't do it. She wanted to stay on at school, despite the powerful temptation to leave, to have nice clothes, and to buy records whenever she wanted. She wondered briefly what she would have bought if she had that much money to spend on a new dress and shoes, before firmly pushing the thought out of her head.

Wendy was locked into it now, like the others at work. Living for the weekend and for Earnshaws mill closure at the Barnaby holiday. Ruled by the demands of the catalogue and Christmas clubs, a slave to the clocking machine. Eventually, Wendy would get married to a lad who worked at Earnshaws, she would have babies and she would be another mill girl, getting pissed in the Carders or Spinners on a weekend. Bobby didn't want that, but she didn't want to go away to university and leave her mum alone in the house with The Arsehole either. She handed back the shoes and watched Wendy fold up the dress, trying not to feel envious.

Wendy was rifling through the narrow wardrobe she shared with Midge. There were about three items belonging to Midge, and one of those was an ancient First Holy Communion dress. The rest was taken up, crammed with Wendy's clothes and shoes. She dragged out a red jumper from a bin bag and threw it on the bed along with a pair of red high heeled fake leather boots.

'These will look good on you. You'll have to shove some newspaper in the toes of the boots, mind, those are a six. The jumper will look great if you wear it with your black jeans or I can lend you a skirt.' Wendy dragged another bag out from under Midge's bed and rooted through it. 'Here, I love this one.' She fished out a scrap of stretchy sequined nylon roughly the size of a hairband and held it out.

'It's okay,' said Bobby, quailing at the skirt. 'That's a bit short for me.'

Wendy shrugged and shoved it back in under the bed. She selected a pair of imitation gold hooped earrings from her extensive jewellery collection housed in a Quality Street tin and handed them to Bobby.

'Make sure he buys all the drinks,' advised Wendy sagely. 'And do something with your bloody hair. You look like a gonk.' She looked serious for a moment and they both collapsed back on the beds with laughter.

Matt arranged to meet Bobby at the corner of Market Street after she had finished work on Saturday evening. She had slipped into the market staff toilets and changed into the outfit Wendy had lent her, stuffing her waitress uniform into a carrier bag and shoving it into the cleaner's cupboard. Bobby brushed her hair smooth and coiled it on top of her head, pinning it into place and spraying it solid, all the while thinking, *I hope this is going to go okay and I don't look a mess.*

She redid her makeup with a slightly trembling hand. It was quite tricky in the dim light from the filthy bulb and there was no decent mirror, only the small compact she had in her bag. She tied a soft dog's tooth scarf borrowed from Stella around her neck, fastened her donkey jacket, popped in the earrings and hobbled through the empty market in the unfamiliar, too-big boots. She took a deep, shaky breath to steady her nerves and pulled the coat straight, pushing her shoulders back and striding purposefully to the street exit just as the security guard followed her to lock up the gates.

Matt wasn't there, and it was starting to rain. She stepped back into the doorway of the café which offered a bit of shelter, wishing she'd remembered her brolly. She wrapped her arms around herself to keep warm and tried not to look at her watch. However, 7 pm came and went and the rain came down harder. It was soaking the red boots now. She could feel the newspaper in the toes turning to soggy papier mâché.

Bobby closed her eyes, fighting the urge to cry. What an idiot. *Why had she bothered to agree to this? Of course he wasn't going to turn up.* She trembled with cold and fury. She could feel mascara slowly making its way down her cheeks. Bobby was just about to storm off home at twenty past when he appeared around the opposite corner to the market, smiling. Almost strolling, his stride calm and confident. She exhaled slowly, feeling a mixture of anger and relief, forcing herself to appear unconcerned.

'I'm really so sorry, something happened, and I got delayed.'

He opened a massive golf umbrella and put his arm around her. Bobby could smell something, a familiar smell, sweet, feminine and floral. She couldn't place it.

'You look lovely. Let's go somewhere warm and have a drink.' He glanced at her and then jerked his head towards the corner of Market Street.

'Okay, yeah.' Her voice sounded small and she allowed herself to be steered towards the end of the street.

Bobby thought they would go to the Baited Bear. That was the usual place for underage drinkers like her, but no, he had a car. A very smart white Mini parked around the corner. He ushered her into it quickly, opening the door and holding the umbrella over her as she stepped in. She had never been in such a clean car before. The air freshener smell was overpowering, though. She ran her hand along the glossy dashboard in a soft, stroking motion and turned to him as he folded himself into the driver's seat, jamming the wet umbrella into the footwell behind her.

'Is this your car? It's very nice.' She flipped down the sun visor and made surreptitious attempts to repair her rain-damaged makeup in the mirror with a tissue and spit.

He shrugged, settling down now he had got away with being late. That stupid cow he was seeing from school had made a fuss when he said he had to go out for dinner with his mum and dad and couldn't see her tonight. He had to listen to a tearful rant and make all sorts of promises before he left and drove like a maniac across town to pick up Bobby. Lying came to Matt as easily as breathing. If it meant he could get what he wanted, he felt no guilt or regret.

'Let's go somewhere nice and quiet so we can talk. It's the least I can do as I kept you waiting in the rain. I'm so sorry.'

Bobby felt herself thaw slightly and settled back into the seat, stretching out her legs in the sodden boots. They drove out of town towards Manchester. The tiny windscreen wipers flipping loudly back and forth, audible over the music on the radio, which kept crackling out of signal. The streetlights gave way to darkness and the narrow beam of the headlights picked out the wet tunnel of hedges as they travelled through increasingly narrow country lanes. Occasionally, a rabbit darted out of the undergrowth in front of them. A fox appeared for an instant, staring at Bobby with eyes like green-yellow triangles before loping gracefully through the bars of a gate.

Eventually, they arrived outside a small country pub in a village she had never heard of. Bobby thought it was oddly romantic and so completely different from town. The headlights lit up cottages built from stone with neat hedges and a small village green with a perfect child's drawing of a duck pond. It was nothing like the wild bleakness of the moorland around Grandma Alice's home. The windows of The White Hart were welcoming pools of light in the darkness.

It was pitch black and Matt took her arm as she stumbled out of the car in the borrowed high-heeled boots. She muttered a thanks and wondered for a second if Ray would do the same to her mum, suspecting not. *He would probably leave her lying in a puddle and step over her to be first to the bar,* she thought. There was no factory stink out here, just the wet green and mud smell of the country.

Matt relaxed. He thought The White Hart was just out of the way enough that the other girls he was seeing wouldn't be here and spoil things. Bobby had never been anywhere like this. He could tell by the excitement in her eyes, and knew that she was impressed. He felt no guilt whatsoever. He hadn't made anyone any promises, and what they didn't know wouldn't hurt them. Opening the ancient door with the low, thick stone lintel that led into the bar, the light and warmth rushed out. Matt smiled at Bobby and inclined his head for her to go ahead of him.

Bobby scanned the room. The ceiling was low and beamed. The bar crowded and full of jolly chatter. There was no jukebox or fruit machine. The walls of the pub were bare stone, decorated with faded hunting prints, horse brasses, and ancient wall lights. There were a few small circular tables dotted around on the worn flagged floor and a large open fireplace. *This,* thought Bobby, *is definitely not a pub where anyone need worry about getting glassed.*

Matt pointed to a table close to the fire. Bobby hurried over to sit on a small floral padded stool, feeling self-conscious and bedraggled in her damp clothes. She stretched her clammy hands out to the spitting flames, shoving her handbag under the table with her foot.

Matt went to the small stone-fronted bar and ordered a pint of bitter for himself, and half a lager and lime for Bobby. He didn't even ask her what she wanted, but she said nothing, content for the moment to absorb her surroundings while he spoke to the landlord. A small grizzled salt and pepper coloured terrier walked over and settled itself in front of the fire with a grumble.

Bobby warmed up. She shrugged off the donkey jacket and put it over the back of a chair, where it gently steamed in front of the open fire. Her toes pressed into the mush of the wet newspaper. Cautiously, she started to relax. However, the evening turned out, it was better than sitting in her room doing homework or refereeing the slanging between Mum and Ray.

Matt observed her critically as he carried the drinks back from the bar. He thought she looked ridiculous in her cheap clothes, plastic earrings, and fake leather boots. But she had a beautiful face even though her makeup had been inexpertly applied and her hair was like a bird's nest. These faults he was prepared to overlook if at some stage he could get a shag out of her. He wondered what her dark-cream skin looked like under that tight red jumper and jeans. He just had to be patient and spend a few quid. That's all it would take with a girl like this.

Throwing, a couple of bags of crisps on the dimpled, beaten-copper circular table, he placed the drinks on tatty, stained beer mats. He sat down opposite, taking up most of the table with his forearms, leaning forward to take a mouthful of beer.

Bobby picked up her glass, had a sip of her drink and muttered, 'Cheers. Thank you,' in a small voice. She took out her cigarettes for something to do. Usually reasonably confident, she suddenly felt shy here, out of her comfort zone of the estate or the café. She offered the packet to Matt, who shook his head with a small pursed-mouth expression of dislike.

'No thanks, I don't.' He said with a slight edge to his voice.

'Yeah, horrible habit, I know,' Bobby said in apology.

She shoved the packet back in her handbag. She was suddenly surprised at herself and put it down to nerves. Sitting back, she listened as he talked. School, politics, cars, pubs, university, his friends — he had something to say about everything. Bobby smiled and nodded. It was a relief not to talk about her family and she was dreading him asking. It slowly dawned on her she need not worry on that score. He wasn't remotely interested; he was happy to talk about himself and voice his many opinions. In the Armstrong household, this was agreed to be the behaviour of a gobshite, but for the moment, Bobby let him get on with it.

'Where do you live?' She eventually got a moment to get a word in.

There was an uncharacteristic pause of hesitation before he looked away towards the bar, then back across to Bobby before saying blandly, 'The corner of Elder Avenue and Dixon Drive.'

'Oh, so you're on the estate as well, then.' She smiled.

'Not really,' he frowned before correcting her. 'Near to it, I would say.'

Bobby observed him while he was talking. Very pale blue eyes and colourless lashes, wavy fair hair brushed back off his forehead like all the posh kids wore it, a slightly weak chin, and good skin. His teeth were even and white, and Bobby suspected he had been to an orthodontist. Not a plain face, but not a handsome one either. She couldn't work out if she fancied him or not. She was wondering why he had asked her out, as she hadn't been able to speak more than a couple of sentences so far. *Maybe he's shy, and that's his way of covering it up,* she reasoned.

Matt drank slowly. Bobby assumed it was because he was driving. She, however, was drinking a bit too quickly. *Probably the nerves* she thought. She could feel her face getting hotter and sweat was trickling down her spine into the small of her back. More drinks arrived. The heat from the fire was becoming unbearable. Even the little dog had admitted defeat, getting up and wandering off, panting. He drained his pint and got up. Bobby fished out her purse and held out some money, but he waved it away.

'My treat. You don't have to pay for anything.'

When he went up to the bar to buy another round, she nipped to the ladies. She ricocheted off the doorway as she entered the toilets and walked to the mirror. Looking at her reflection, she took a few deep breaths. Her dark complexion was flushed. Her hair, now it was drying out, was a frizzy mess — twice the size it had been when she left work. She tamed it down with a wet comb and reapplied more lipstick. She felt dizzy, but thought the date was going well. Bobby had little experience with how couples interacted with each other, other than her mum and Ray. They would have been at each other's throats by now.

When she returned to the table, there was another half a lager and lime waiting for her.

'Thanks, but I think that had better be my last.' She giggled as she sat down a bit too heavily on the wobbly little stool.

Matt smiled slowly, and through the haze of fag smoke and booze, Bobby thought he might look okay after all. The conversation had dried up slightly. He had evidently run out of opinions for the moment. He reached over and moved a coil of hair away from her cheek. It bounced upwards like a spring.

'You look lovely. That hair is amazing. Does it take a long time to curl it like that?'

Bobby gave a shout of laughter that made a couple of people turn round. She put her hand over her mouth to stifle it. 'God, no, this is just how it is. It's uncontrollable. I don't really do anything to it.'

Matt grinned and shrugged, 'Well, I like it, anyway'.

Bobby smiled back and dropped her eyes, sipping her drink and feeling her face getting even hotter. It was a clumsy compliment as she knew exactly what a state her hair looked like, but she was flattered and amused.

The pub was filling up now, a different crowd than the pubs in Gritstone. There were no overalls in here. It was mostly older people in nice clothes, a few younger girls in shirts with pie-crust collars and pearls, and men wearing tweed and red faces. Bobby glanced at Matt as he took a swig of beer. He wore jeans and a shirt with a jumper that was definitely lambswool, not acrylic. He had polished brown shoes and an expensive-looking leather jacket hung on the back of his chair. Bobby reflected that there was nobody in here that looked like her or her family and friends.

Nobody that was wearing borrowed cheap clothes and a tartan lined donkey jacket. And definitely nobody with skin as dark as hers. *Fuck it, you've just as much right to be here as those posh types. Stop worrying about it.* She sat up straighter and smoothed her hair down, staring coldly at a couple of lads standing at the bar behind Matt, who were obviously talking about her and sniggering. She put her chin up and held their gaze until they looked away.

The last orders bell rang, and Matt ordered her another drink even though she had said no. She glanced at him anxiously, taking the wet glass and adding it to the others on the little table.

He laughed. 'You'll be okay, it's Saturday night after all. Don't worry, relax.' He patted her arm as though she were a nervous old lady.

She was annoyed because she felt really pissed, but said nothing. He was paying, after all. It seemed rude to complain. She took a deep breath and fidgeted in her seat. The waistband of her jeans was digging in, and her feet were hurting in the stupid wet boots that still hadn't dried out. The room was boiling, packed, and cigarette smoke was stinging her eyes. She forced the drink down, trying to focus on speaking normally.

Bobby went to the toilet again, walking slowly and deliberately. Locking herself in a cubicle to have a wee, she pressed her burning face into her hands. She was going to feel dreadful tomorrow and knew she should have been more assertive and said no to the extra drinks. After peeing for what felt like twenty minutes, she clumsily wrenched up her pants and jeans and staggered out. There were two posh looking twenty-something girls by the sinks and they stared at her, then looked at each other and started giggling.

Fuck this, thought Bobby. *I need to go home.* She didn't bother to squeeze past them to wash her hands. Why bother? They thought she looked like a scrubber, anyway. He was waiting outside the loo with her coat, and held it out for her as though it was a mink as she clumsily guided her arms into the sleeves. Nobody had done that before. She felt like a child. It was an unfamiliar feeling and she couldn't work out if it was altogether pleasant. She gave up on trying to fasten her coat up correctly, unable to match up the buttons with the holes.

Matt led the way out of the bar, and Bobby stumbled after him. The air outside was beautiful; full of the clean, damp, earthy smells of early spring. She took a deep breath, dragging it down into her lungs as Matt took her upper arm to steady her. The heels of the boots sank into the gravel with every step as they walked across the car park. She looked up into the clear, sparkling veil of the night sky and was about to point out the constellation of Leo, but decided Matt probably wasn't interested. *He'll likely just tell me how many light years away it is, instead of listening to the story of Hercules,* she thought irritably, hitching the strap of her handbag back onto her shoulder.

He opened the car door with a flourish, and she sank into the passenger seat. The fake gold hoops were hurting her ears now, and she longed to be home, having a fag and a brew. She idly wondered if Matt should be driving at all, after the amount he'd drank.

The Mini headlights picked their way through the country lanes like twin searchlights. Matt was still prattling on. Bobby could hardly hear him over the radio. It was like the sound of the interference coming from the telly when the aerial was wonky, she decided, giggling into the collar of her coat, burrowing down into her seat.

She carried on trying to spot more constellations, stars, and planets through the window, looking for the orangey glow of Arcturus, one of Grandma Alice's favourite stars. She must have nodded off, because within what seemed like a few minutes, he was pulling up outside her house.

'Here you are, safely home.' His smile seemed kind enough. He must have recognised that he had been talking non-stop, 'I hope you enjoyed yourself. I'm not so bad after all, you know.' His voice sounded quiet and slightly hesitant.

Bobby smiled back. 'Yes, thank you for the drinks. I had a good night, Ta.'

Matt nodded slowly and raised his eyebrows.

'So, you'll do it again? Meet me again?' He tilted his head and tapped his fingers on the steering wheel.

Bobby agreed before she could think of anything else. She thanked him again, fumbled the door open, got out of the car and zig-zagged up the path. She focused on the square of light in her front door, hoping Ray and Mum were in a good mood.

Chapter 8
April 1982

Bobby had walked past Matt's mum and dad's house dozens of times over the years. It was the last house on the final street before the estate ended and Elder Avenue began, with its elegant, curved sweep of Edwardian villas and long, perfectly manicured lawns. A thirty-second stroll separated the two, but for Marg Thomas, Elder Avenue represented everything she wanted but had always been denied. This short walk crossed from one world to a very different other. A world of washing machines, no electric meters, Axminster carpets, fitted wardrobes, fridge freezers, and proper central heating.

Whenever someone asked her address, Marg always said, 'The corner of Elder Avenue,' because technically, that was correct, and also because she was a raging snob.

The second she moved into 1, Dixon Drive, as a newlywed, Marg wanted to move on to better things. Keith Thomas was having none of it. He'd been born in that house; his mum and dad had moved into it when it was built. Phillip Thomas, practically still in his demob suit, hoping to swap the sweaty horrors of the Far East for the peace of a brand-new council house, spitting distance from a pub and his allotment. The house had a sizeable garden, a driveway, and was a ten minutes' walk to the Carders. Keith didn't give a shit about living on a road of private houses and loved living on the estate. He had grown up here, his mates lived here, and he knew practically everybody, good or bad. It was home.

Marg had different ideas, and the minute they could buy on the council house Right to Buy scheme, the house began its transformation. They bought it for a song because Keith's family had held the tenancy for so long. It was obvious when somebody had bought their council house. Porches went up, conservatories, cladding, different windows appeared. People wanted to show others that they owned their own home.

Bobby had met Matt after school and he'd suggested they go to his house for a brew. She was interested in meeting his family, as she hadn't met any of his relatives or friends yet. This was their third date after The White Hart. They had been for a brew and cake in a tearoom in Buxton — which Bobby thought was weird because that was what old people did. And they'd been for a walk in the hills, which Bobby did all the time and enjoyed.

However, Matt definitely looked put out when Bobby corrected his directions and knew the names of all the crags and tors. She had to explain that she had practically been brought up in the hills around town, but he was still a bit huffy. Matt was even more pissed off when she strode up each hill with ease. He struggled along behind, despite her dragging on a cigarette the whole time, never drawing breath as she pointed out local landmarks, plants, and wildlife.

She really would have liked to go to some places people their age would normally go; like the pool hall or the pictures. A date at the Baited Bear, or even the Gem, which had a disco once a month, and sometimes live music. Matt always had an excuse. Usually, that town was full of dickheads or that he wanted to get to know her with no interference. Bobby let it go. She was enjoying having someone to go out with. He was generous with his money; always refusing to allow her to pay for anything and although she was unsure of him, it was sort of nice to have a boyfriend, if that's what he was. They hadn't really had any discussion about that yet.

He led the way up the crunchy multicoloured gravel driveway with its white curlicued iron gates hanging on pillars topped with plaster lions. *It's like fucking Graceland,* she thought as she looked around the overcrowded front garden. A bright plastic gnome in red wellies fished hopefully on the edge of a wishing well encrusted with shells. A blind tin flamingo perched in the middle of a small, perfectly mowed stripy lawn; one leg bent at an unnatural angle. Different coloured crazy paving slabs wound a path to a white fountain where a semi-naked plaster nymph frolicked in a shower.

Matt fiddled with his house key whilst Bobby took in the carriage lamps on either side of the front door. It wasn't the standard painted wooden door with the usual big square pane of wire reinforced bobbly council glass. This was a white plastic door with an ornate stained-glass panel of roses running down the centre and a gold door handle. He pushed the door open without speaking and Bobby followed him in, hesitating slightly as she stepped into the hall. She had a feeling she was trespassing.

'Shall I take my shoes off?' Her voice sounded stiff and unfamiliar in her own ears as she looked around the spotless hallway with its smell of furniture polish, gleaming white paintwork, and a telephone table made out of some ornate curly metal. The phone was one of those daft pretend Edwardian sets that was really awkward to use. This looked like a shoes-off house. At Bobby's, you kept them on to keep them clean, and for a quick exit if Ray was kicking off.

'Yeah, best to do that,' Matt responded blandly, pushing his hair back from his forehead and looking back over the top of Bobby's head to see if anyone was passing.

'Where's your mum and dad? Are they at work?' queried Bobby.

'Benidorm,' he said crisply, with a quick sniff.

Of course they were. Bobby instantly knew that she wouldn't have been invited here if they had been at home. Her family were the sort of people Marg Thomas avoided. She smoothed her hair back from her face and put her school bag on the floor. *Yeah, she wouldn't want me lowering the tone.*

Marg wanted better for 'Our Matthew'. He wouldn't be living on the estate after he finished sixth form. He would go to university, then get a good job and marry a nice girl from a family who perhaps lived on Victoria Avenue. They would move into a nice home nearby, possibly with a monkey puzzle tree in the garden. Near enough for Marg to show off and walk through the estate wheeling a beautifully dressed baby in a huge Silver Cross pram.

He would not be marrying a pinched-looking girl off the estate, pushing a screaming, filthy-faced toddler in a knackered second-hand buggy. Shopping bags hooked over the handles, hurrying home through the rain whilst squinting through a cloud of fag smoke, with a home perm and wearing a shagged-out anorak.

Bobby slid off her shoes, noticing the peeling, worn insoles and scuffed toes as she kicked them out of the way under the coat stand. Crossing her arms over her chest, she suddenly felt like she was here for an interview or a test. Matt indicated the front room with a flick of his head and walked through the doorway, sitting down on the cream fake leather sofa. Bobby hesitated, then did the same — perching at the opposite end, frightened to touch anything in case her family might rub off on something. She noticed the settee had a protective plastic covering, which was slippery and clammy. She looked at her toe poking through a ladder in her tights and quickly curled the end over with her other foot, wishing she had ignored him and kept her shoes on.

The front room, or *lounge*, as Matt called it, was full of stuff. Every surface was occupied with china ornaments: ladies in crinoline skirts, a little boy holding a puppy, a demonic-looking clown, and a shepherd. Over the electric fire was an enormous mirror with a thick gold plastic surround made to look like carved wood. She sat up straight, wiping her sweaty palms on the grey knees of her school skirt.

'Well, this is very nice,' she lied, for something to say.

The light was partly obscured by the most flounced and frilly blindingly white nets Bobby had ever seen, bordered by heavy peach-coloured satin curtains. In the middle of the room was a large, heavy looking coffee table on fancy, bowed metallic-gold legs. The table surface was made from a veined green stone. Bobby leant forward and stroked it with a nail-bitten forefinger. It was cold to the touch. Next to some perfectly stacked copies of *Women's Own* was a giant cigarette lighter and an ashtray all made from the same stone.

'It's called onyx,' he drawled laconically.

Bobby noticed that when he said this, he gave a slight sniff afterwards and his head moved back.

'Oh. *Onicks*. It looks heavy.'

He shrugged and nodded. 'Do you want a brew?' Matt was now standing in front of her as though wanting to hurry her up. He had his hands in his pockets and was looking at her with a slightly impatient expression, waggling his head, eyebrows raised.

'Yes, okay then. Thank you.' Her voice still felt awkward in her ears; stiff and formal. To avoid his gaze, she looked down and unnecessarily adjusted her tights.

Matt disappeared for a few minutes and Bobby could take in more of the room. She sat back further on the squeaky, uncomfortable settee.

A small peach coloured miniature poodle wandered in, blending in with the décor. It had discharge coming from its eyes, which had stained the fur under its eyelashes black. It wandered over to Bobby and jumped on her knee, grinning up with a mouthful of rotten teeth and rancid breath. Its scrabbling nails made another ladder in her tights. Matt wandered back in and handed her a small fragile looking flowery cup and saucer. The cup was so thin she could see light coming through it.

'That's Angel.'

'Oh, she's nice,' Bobby said weakly, lifting the dog down to take the cup. It was making her feel sick looking at that mouth and breathing in the awful stinking breath.

Bobby couldn't get her finger through the tiny cup handle so held it like a bowl, scared of dropping it. There were lines on the carpet from the hoover — it looked like a well-mowed nylon lawn. She thought about the ancient, threadbare carpet at home with its garish swirls of mustard and brown, its fag burns and stains. She carefully sipped the weak tea, terrified of dropping the cup or knocking something over.

'Let's go upstairs. We can play some records,' said Matt briskly; more of an instruction than an invitation.

Bobby looked at the Hi-Fi cabinet in the corner of the room, and the records neatly stacked next to it, but said nothing and followed obediently. Her feet made prints in the lush cream shag-pile and she felt her tights crackling with the static. Walking up the stairs, she held the saucer in both hands, the cup chattering.

She had never been in such a tidy bedroom. Her room at home was the opposite; the single bed wedged against the black-speckled damp wall, the window with the peeling sill, and the tatty psychedelic curtains. The curling posters pinned onto the woodchip wallpaper. Clothes dumped on the chair and a tiny desk, which doubled up as a dressing table, piled high with schoolbooks, makeup, records and mugs of half-drunk cold tea.

Matt's bedroom was immaculate. There was nothing on the smooth walls except for a poster of the Periodic Table and a team poster of Manchester United. Everything looked so controlled, as if it had been designed to be observed. It was almost like a cell.

'Please, can I use your toilet?' Bobby asked.

She was feeling awkward, not like boyfriend and girlfriend. Were they that? She didn't need to ask where it was. This house layout was an exact copy of the Armstrong's. Bobby locked the bathroom door and breathed in the overpowering, cloying floral air freshener smell. This room was done in pink: paintwork, lino, bath, bog, frilly blinds, nets, pink fluffy mat around the sink base, and a pink piss mat around the toilet.

On top of the cistern was a Sindy doll with a black beehive hairdo, holding tiny maracas. There was a red plastic rose stuck in her hair. She had a full shiny polyester flamenco skirt hiding a petticoat which covered a toilet roll. Bobby lifted her up and a miniature pair of feet stuck out from under the cardboard tube. She was wearing black plastic high heels, but no knickers. Her crotch was perfectly smooth, and Bobby grimly reflected that life would be a lot simpler if humans were like that too. She fiddled about with some of the stuff on the windowsill, almost knocking over a bottle of Panache.

Over the bath was something very different to the bathroom in Bobby's house; a shower. Its white head perched proudly off the wall like a plastic swan, partially hidden by its curtain of pink roses. Bobby thought of the daft shower contraption Mum had bought off the indoor market — a rubber hose with two attachments that were supposed to fit on the bath taps but blew off if they were turned on too hard. When you eventually balanced the water pressure and temperature, somebody downstairs would turn on the kitchen tap, and you were either scalded or frozen.

In the end, everyone gave up and used a saucepan or a jug to rinse their hair, and the shower thing just sat curled up in the airing cupboard like a yellowing, unloved snake in a towelling nest. Bobby looked in the mirror, expecting to look different, somehow. But her familiar, thin olive face with its black eyes looked back at her. She washed her hands and dried them on a soft pink towel.

Matt was stretched out on the bed like Lord Muck, an arm behind his head. Bobby perched on the edge of a chair by the desk. It was stacked with chemistry books and a holder with pens, all with their unbitten lids firmly attached. Directly on the wall above the desk was a calendar with a revision timetable filled out in different colours. He saw her looking at it and nodded importantly.

'I'm doing A-levels this year. I have a place at Leeds University.'

You've already told me that half a dozen times, thought Bobby.

He did that slight sniff again, and inclined his head.

'Do you have to get certain grades or is your place unconditional?' The enquiry was light. Bobby smiled, smoothing down her skirt over her laddered knee, wishing she had something more interesting to say.

'I need three B's, which I'll get, no problem. I'll almost certainly get A's,' he said it as if it was fact.

Bobby made a small sound which she hoped sounded approving and impressed. Secretly, she thought, *you're a complete dick to be so arrogant, but isn't this part of being in a couple? This is normal. The man says something you don't agree with, but you just smile and nod because it's easier than disagreeing. That's what living with Mum and Ray did, warped your sense of how to behave. Wouldn't it be so much easier to be with someone you could disagree with and it didn't become a drama?* There couldn't be a discussion, a rational disagreement, which didn't end up in tears and shouting at Bobby's house.

She cleared her throat and a silence stretched out between them for a few seconds. Bobby's eyes wandered around the room and she looked back at Matt, who was still sprawled out on the bed. She was already thinking she'd rather be at home.

'I think James Robson off Pennine Road is going to Manchester Polytechnic to do something to do with engineering. He's a friend of our Davey.' She kept her voice bright, trying to find some kind of common ground.

'No, he'll be doing a BTEC or something like that. Not a degree. And anyway, Manchester Poly isn't a *university*.' His tone was dismissive and final. There was to be no discussion or debate. He didn't ask her if she was applying to university, or college, or looking for a job after she finished school.

'Come over her and sit with me.' He patted the bed, as if encouraging a small dog to jump up next to him.

It wasn't a suggestion, it was an order, but it was nice to be given some attention, maybe? Bobby couldn't help thinking of Grandma Alice and how she would have probably told him to piss off and grow up. She didn't move straight away and looked away from him. There was a record holder for 7" singles next to the desk, sitting on a small record player. There were only about five or six records, all disco, except for one Elvis.

'What sort of music do you like, then?' She felt herself smiling and the familiar excitement inside when she talked about music or books. She could spend hours with Wendy or Davey listening to records or the radio, talking and listening, and dancing.

He made a slightly dismissive, scornful face. 'Nah, I'm not really interested in music that much.'

Bobby felt bitterly disappointed. How could she have a boyfriend who didn't like music? Maybe that's just how it was? Maybe that wasn't everything in a relationship? Like Mum said, all that really mattered was to have a man to look after you. In women's magazines the articles said it was important to have some different interests to your boyfriend, it made for a better relationship.

A small voice, talking exactly like Grandma Alice, again popped into her head and asked what was wrong with looking after yourself, and not having to rely on anyone else. Bobby ignored it and heard herself saying okay when Matt told her to sit next to him and she said little after that — she let him do the talking and the touching.

He smelled of sweat and Brut aftershave. He pushed her back on the bed and she awkwardly put her feet up, whilst he pressed her down and kissed her in a practised way, pushing up her school jumper and shirt and unfastening the clasp on her bra with rough efficiency.

She focused on the Periodic Table and wondered how she was supposed to feel.

Is this it? Am I supposed to be enjoying this? Because I just feel hot, and it hurts. She kept still, arms rigid at her sides. It felt a bit like being at the doctors with none of the reassurance or kindness. Matt was trying to peel down the waistband of her tights when Bobby sat upright like a mummy rising from the dead, pulling her jumper down.

'I think I need to go. I'll be late for me tea,' she said flatly. Her face was burning.

Matt sighed, looked petulant and said, 'Okay then,' in a stroppy but controlled voice.

It didn't matter that much to him if he didn't get what he wanted with Bobby. He was shagging a girl from school and she was really keen on him. But this one was different; her diffidence was intriguing, and it was always good to have someone on the back burner if the other one didn't work out. The sky was clouding over when Bobby passed the gnome and his mates on her way down the garden path.

Matt stood at the door. 'Why don't you come round tomorrow after school? Mum and Dad will be back on Saturday.' The suggestion was light, casual. He made a slight shrug as he spoke.

What you mean is you want to have another snogging and groping session in your room before your mum and dad get back as they won't want an Armstrong in the house. But the voice was silenced again as Bobby smiled and agreed.

Chapter 9
May 1982

Midge decided she needed another source of income. She had worked a paper round Monday to Friday for the past couple of years for Mr Crown, who ran the newsagents and post office on York Street. It was a nice enough job but the pay didn't make up for the early starts in all weathers, vicious dogs, and complaints from miserable sods who reckoned Midge had torn the front of their *Daily Mirror*, trying to feed the paper through a letter box the size of a fag packet.

Gregory Crown was one of the few adults Midge really liked. When she had first gone into the shop to start her paper round, she hadn't met him before, and nobody had warned her what he looked like. When he turned to greet her, she saw that one side of his face was a regular old man's face — clean shaven with a strong jaw and thick eyebrow, a wave of Brylcreemed blue-black and silver hair swept back. The other left side was a burned, puckered, rippled mass of plastic-like flesh. The skin was shiny in parts, an eye fused shut, and scarring reaching down to his neck. There was no left ear, just a wrinkled hole without a lobe. Mr Crown's left hand was a livid, melted paw.

Midge was utterly shocked. She pretended a second too late she wasn't surprised by his appearance, rearranged her own face, and explained she was here to take over from David Prendergast, a neighbour who had decided early mornings and hard graft were not for him. Gregory Crown admired her gentle courtesy and hired her on the spot. He held out his good right hand for her to shake, and she grasped in firmly. He was the only person who called Midge by her birth name; Amanda. They liked each other immediately and struck up a friendship. There had been a lot of men in and out of Midge's short life, and he was one of a tiny number who treated her with kindness and respect.

Grandma Peggy told Midge that Gregory Crown was once a very handsome man who used to sing in the church choir and in the pubs round town. In 1940, he had been flying back from Germany in a Lancaster bomber when the Luftwaffe had put paid to his RAF film star looks and beautiful young voice. After the first shock of seeing his disfigurement, Midge never gave it a second thought. Mr Crown wore his scars with a quiet grace. Much as Midge would have liked to have asked him about the war, she never did. It was something unspoken between them that didn't need to be voiced. A quiet understanding.

They had a nice little routine going, Midge and Mr Crown. He would be there when Midge arrived with Baz at 6.30 am, having marked up all the papers in his elegant, cursive script, slotting them neatly into two canvas delivery bags. She would push the door open with its sharp tinging bell, and Mr Crown would be there behind the counter like a quiet sentinel, looking up with his tight half-smile.

In the winter, a pool of golden light from the unshaded bulb hanging low over his head would illuminate him and the stacks of papers. Midge often reflected that the damaged side of his face was always in shadow. Framed like this, an observer would never know he was scarred, as if the war had never happened to Gregory Crown.

In the summer months, the job was easy. The light mornings made all the difference, and Midge liked to roam the streets before everyone was up and about. It was her favourite time of day, nobody about to bother her and there always seemed time to daydream and make up stories about the people who lived behind all the letter boxes. She could find a wall to sit on to read the paper, flick through magazines she would never buy, eat some sweets, and talk to Baz.

This April and May, Mr Crown had been listening to the radio a lot more when she came in, usually Radio Four or the World Service. It always seemed to be the same monotone posh man's voice seeping out of the speaker, sounding serious and strained.

'What's happening today, Mr Crown?' Midge twitched her head to the enormous old wireless on the counter.

Next to the radio, Jaggery, the shop cat, was purring like an engine, almost drowning out the sound of the newsreader. Fast asleep and tightly curled on a stack of the *Woman's Own*, Midge realised she had never actually seen the cat awake.

'War, love.' He glanced up at her, his eye filled with sorrow. 'We are at war with Argentina, over a few daft bits of rock in the South Atlantic. And it will get a lot worse soon. We have sunk one of their ships; The *Belgrano*. There will be hell on now. They will want revenge for that. All those lads of theirs, dead.' Mr Crown sighed flatly. He passed his hand over Jaggery's back in a gentle, repetitive motion, and Midge saw that just for a moment he was far away, back to a place he would rather not recall.

Midge didn't know much about the Falkland Islands, and had never heard of South Georgia. She had seen a lot of stuff on the front of the papers about the war and was embarrassed to think she had originally thought the Falklands were off the north coast of Scotland. She sat down and properly read the paper one day and realised they were eight thousand miles away. Midge opened an atlas at school and her small stubby finger with its bitten nail had traced the route of the British taskforce, travelling from England down the map, an impossibly long way. Past southern Europe, the west coast of Africa, the east coast of South America. Dropping further south before tapping her finger on the microscopic lump that was Ascension Island as it slid to the South Atlantic at the bottom of the world.

'Right shug, here you go,' Mr Crown rasped out in his soft Potteries accent, lifting the paper bags onto her slight frame, bandolier style across her chest. He popped a Crunchie into the bag and winked solemnly with his one bright, sky-blue eye.

'Thank you,' smiled Midge, and staggered out into the street, followed by Baz, her canine chaperone.

Midge had the round whittled down to fifty minutes, except on a Thursday, which was local paper day, and it took an hour. It was a big round, mostly taking in the tight rows of terraced houses on the west side of town. It was straightforward though; this was almost exclusively *The Mirror* and *The Sun* territory, the odd *Racing Post*, comics, and magazines. She pitied Shane Atkinson, who had the round of posh houses branching east off Victoria Road. All long paths up to big, bay windowed detached houses taking the broadsheets like *The Times*, *The Telegraph*, and the odd *Guardian*.

The worst bit of her round was Gritstone flats. A big 1960s block with broken lifts used as toilets, packs of stray dogs roaming the concrete walkways, and a lawlessness that permeated every piss-stained stairwell.

The forecourt in front of the flats was littered with broken tellies flung over the balconies in rage or despair, used nappies, broken glass, and litter. There always seemed to be someone screaming, somewhere. The front of the flats was a kaleidoscope of graffitied walls and boarded-up windows.

Once, Mr Crown had asked Midge to knock on a door with an unpaid bill going back weeks. A young lad, already pissed at ten in the morning, had answered the door. Midge held the envelope out in a shaking hand and the man had ripped it up in front of her and screamed,

'If yer want money, yer can take it out of that,' and pointed to his crotch. Midge had turned and run like the clappers.

When the flats were done, Midge flew through the rest of her round. Her favourite houses had a big letterbox with a loose flap, no dog, and a long hallway. It gave her the greatest satisfaction to roll up a paper into a tight cylinder, pushing it into the letter box, and banging the end of the paper so hard it flew like a missile down the hallway. She always did a little dance on the spot and a cheer if she could get it to hit the kitchen door.

Every now and again, if a paper boy rang in sick, Midge would be called in to do a weekend shift. She didn't much like it; the papers were too big and unwieldy, and the magazines slipped out onto the floor, or got mixed up in the bag. It was more interesting though, and she didn't have the time pressure to get round before school. During the week, the only people Midge saw were the milkman and people going to work. At the weekend, there were always a healthy number of people staggering home from a night out, which livened up proceedings.

One Sunday, a beautiful, warm, silvery May morning, not long after the sinking of the *Belgrano,* Midge decided to cut through the park. The gates were locked, but the fence at the side was smashed down to facilitate a shortcut. Midge squeezed through, hoiking her bags through the snagging green chain-link fence. Just by the tennis court was a line of benches which looked out over the bowling green and a row of clashing bedding plants in psychedelic colours. Midge figured she would take five minutes to sit on a bench, pull a paper out, eat her Crunchie and read her stars. It didn't happen though, because lying on one bench was a body.

Midge wasn't frightened, more curious, mentally wondering whose door she would have to knock on to tell them to call the police. Baz took no notice. He was off sniffing in the flower beds, squatting for a crap amongst the petunias. Midge approached the bench slowly, hands outstretched, fluttering slightly before realising it wasn't a dead body but a sleeping girl.

A bride, still in her long, frothy white nylon dress, a wreath of plastic flowers encircling her long blonde hair, was fast asleep on the bench. Her hands were curled gently on her flat white stomach, cradling a small bouquet of wilted yellow roses and a packet of cigarettes. Beside the bench was a pair of white high-heeled shoes embellished with plastic butterflies. The shoes were placed neatly together with care, as if the girl had put them outside a hotel room or under a bed.

Clapping her hand to her mouth to stifle a laugh, she stood watching for a while. The bride's chest slowly rising and falling, thinking she really had seen it all now then decided she should wake the girl. She dumped the bags on the floor and spoke to her softly,

'Are you okay?' She held her hand above the girl, hesitating to touch her.

The sun was warm on the back of her neck, and it sparkled off the bride's shiny makeup. Her eyelids were painted bright blue and she had two slashes of crimson up each cheekbone. There was no response, and Midge eventually touched her shoulder gently, then more vigorously, as the girl showed no sign of waking. In the end, one intensely blue bloodshot eye opened and a croaking voice rasped in irritation,

'What?'

'Are you okay? I mean, you must be cold?'

'Nah, I'm fine. Leave me alone,' she huffed, sounding offended, as if she had been disturbed from a comfortable bed with feather pillows, a deep mattress and soft, clean silk sheets.

'Where's your…husband?' Midge sounded like an outraged maiden aunt.

The bride swung her legs around and sat upright, pulling the crown of flowers firmly onto her head. Her legs were bare, mottled white and blue, almost translucent. She was younger than Midge first thought, maybe eighteen. It was the makeup that made her look older.

'I don't know, and I don't fucking care.' She cried, threw back her head, and let out a raucous, rough bray of laughter. Her voice sounded tired, papery from fags, drink, and shouting. She lit a Silk Cut and took a deep drag, closing her eyes and exhaling with force, staring at Midge with raw intensity.

'What a fucking night that was, and not in a good way.' She rubbed her face with a shaking hand and started plucking at the folds of her wedding dress. A thin, bright gold band glittered on her left hand, catching the sunlight. One knee juddered up and down under the rustling taffeta. She peered at Midge intently, head on one side like a blonde sparrow, and said sharply,

'You're Wendy's little sister, aren't you?'

Midge rubbed her chin and nodded slowly, thinking to herself, *our Wendy seems to know everyone.*

'Well, she was right about that dickhead. I shouldn't have married him.' The bride sprang up and smoothed down her dress, adjusted her headdress and in a huge, haymaking arc threw her bouquet over the bowling green as if to an invisible bridesmaid.

'Right, I'm off,' she announced. She picked up the butterfly shoes and marched over to the shortcut, scrambling over the broken-down fence in her filthy bare feet and strode up Silver Street like a slender ghost.

Midge stood open-mouthed, staring after her, wondering if everyone in this town was completely round the twist. It was definitely time to start looking for another job. She sat down on the bench, dumping the half full paper bags on the ground, sighing contentedly. She selected a copy of *The Sun* to be delivered to the miserable old bitch at the top of Silver Street and flicked to the astrology section, unwrapping her Crunchie, which was melting in the warmth of the sunshine. *Pisces: Mercury is in Retrograde. A good week for exploring business opportunities but be cautious of strangers. Change is afoot. Lucky colour: turquoise.*

Midge idly watched Baz starting to dig a hole in the middle of the bowling green, arse in the air, front paws scraping furiously. She giggled to herself. The parkie was going to go mental. She shoved the remainder of the Crunchie into her mouth and folded up the paper, leaving chocolate fingerprints on the front page as she returned it to the bag. She crossed the bags over her body and stood up, whistling for Baz as she followed the path out of the park, the sun on her back.

Chapter 10
Alice: May 1942

It was dark and cool in church, and Alice was hungry. It seemed she was always feeling hungry these days, even though her family ate better than most, supplementing the ration with fruit and vegetables grown on the windswept plot next to Flint Cottage. She sat between her mum and dad, in their usual place — on the left, three rows from the back. James was thinking about starting haymaking soon, maybe at the end of the month, if the weather held. Rose was worrying about a couple of hens that were off colour, possibly going broody. Alice fidgeted; the waistband of her tweed skirt itching.

Going to church was the only occasion where she wasn't in trousers. She held her hands in her lap, on the coarse, green-brown fabric, resisting the urge to scratch. Her eyes wandered over the dim interior of St Francis'. The Stations of the Cross, the faded curtain on the confessional box, were all as familiar to her as the backs of her hands. The stained-glass windows, protected from bombing raids by a lattice of tape and thin battens of wood, allowed little light, and the blackout curtains pulled to one side made the interior even gloomier.

Father Dolan's voice was a soft drone, and Alice could see a couple of older people nodding off. She smiled at Peter Brown, the altar boy, who was rocking back on his heels, dying to get away to play football. She let her eyes and mind wander up and down the mostly empty pews, willing the priest to hurry and finish. There were new people in church today. Everyone sat in the same seats, week after week, making it obvious when strangers came to Mass. Alice idly examined them one by one, head on one side, trying to appear absorbed in Father Dolan's sermon, thinking, *Oh, will you just get to the point so we can get out into the sunshine?*

The strangers were sitting two pews in front. Four men, all in unfamiliar uniforms. A red-headed man in an officer's uniform, two tall blond soldiers and on the end of the pew a smaller, slight man with very dark skin and hair. Alice saw him turn. She had never seen anyone with as dark a complexion before. Where the sun penetrated through the window to the right, it turned his hair into a wavy cap of navy blue, exactly the colour of a raven's wing. Alice noticed he had a prominent nose and bad skin, and he looked too thin.

The men were part of the group of American servicemen stationed near town. It wasn't a surprise to Alice to see some of them in a Catholic church. Hundreds of them were stationed all over the north of England and they had become a common sight in the pubs, tearooms, cinemas, and dance halls when they were on leave.

The Americans in town had caused a great deal of excitement amongst the women and a good deal of resentment amongst the men. Wild stories were circulating about local girls selling themselves for cigarettes or the new nylon stockings. In the case of Peggy Kenny, she didn't want any of that. She was quite happy to have sex with a strange soldier for pleasure alone, and if he gave her a bar of chocolate or bought her some drinks, then it was a bonus.

The girls who went out with the American soldiers were called 'Yankee Bags', but they didn't care. The men were friendly, generous, had good teeth and knew how to enjoy themselves. And why shouldn't the girls too? Life in town during the war was uneventful. They were manufacturing parachutes and other textiles for the war effort, but there wasn't a good deal else to do other than go to the pub or the Alhambra to watch a picture or a news reel. Life was short and most of the men were away.

Mass finished and the congregation filed out onto the street. Father Dolan was talking to the red-headed officer, his soft Irish accent drowned out by the American's loud voice. The other soldiers stood clustered in a group, lighting cigarettes and chattering amongst themselves. Alice turned her face to the warmth of the May sunshine, breathing in the sour smell and the dull chatter of the mill opposite. Now there was a war on, there was no quiet Sunday feel to the town, and she was glad to follow her parents as they turned away from church to begin the uphill walk out of town to Flint Cottage. She tucked her arm through her mother's and listened for a few minutes to her dire predictions about the sickly hen.

'Well Mum, if they're dead when we get back it'll be roast chicken for dinner, so it won't be all bad,' she reasoned, yanking up her stockings and grinning at Rose.

Almost a week later, she saw the dark-skinned American man again. It was a Saturday afternoon, and Alice was walking along the old drover's lane above Flint Cottage. She liked to come up here and find a dry-stone wall to sit on, to look over the town and the Cheshire plain beyond. On clear days, you could see the Welsh mountains and the smoke haze of Manchester in the distance. On a summer's day, the sky was filled with the sounds of birds and insects and the smell of fresh cut hay, or the coconut fragrance of the gorse.

These hills were as familiar to Alice as the muck and noise of the mills and streets below. She knew plenty of people at work who had never been up here in their whole lives. Folk who lived a couple of miles away in the town and had never breathed in this clean air. Or watched the wind making the grass ripple across the fields. Or heard the rough mother's call of an ewe to her lambs.

He was walking up the steep lane, which gave out onto the moorland at the top of the hill, where the fields stopped and the open rough country began. Alice sat on the wall by the side of the lane, above the wildflowers and the cow parsley, and watched him. She felt slightly annoyed that the peace of her afternoon was going to be disturbed. Her hands rested on the warm stones, hair lifting in the breeze away from the damp nape of her neck. The sky was clear except for a few high clouds, delicate as feathery shaped combs, promising a late spring heatwave. She sat and waited as he reached the brow of the hill.

The American trudged slowly, face sweating and mouth slightly open, khaki jacket over his arm. He saw her and looked startled. Alice raised her hand, feeling slightly foolish, and quickly folded her hands together in her lap. She didn't know what to say, but she couldn't really ignore him. The soldier looked wary, offering a slight nod as he sauntered up to her, smoothing his hair down and squinting in the sunshine.

He made a brief comment about the heat, and what a lovely place it was up here, away from the town. Alice nodded in agreement, watching his discomfort with some sympathy. She couldn't imagine what it would be like to be sent to another country, far away from home, never knowing if you would ever be able to go back. The soldier had the oddest voice she had ever heard; she thought all Americans sounded the same, but that was just from watching films, she supposed. There was something about him. He just looked *different*.

Alice didn't really mix with the men in town. She had been to a few of the dances organised at the mills, but mostly kept her distance. She felt awkward around them; her place was in the hills. The soldier gestured in admiration to the crags and tors to the east, blue and grey in the heat shimmer. Alice nodded and named them one by one with pride. The words round and loving in her mouth as she pointed to each in turn, laughing as he struggled to repeat the familiar names in his American accent. She noticed he had good teeth and an open, kind smile.

There was a small spring running from the hill at the side of the wall. Cushions of vivid, emerald green moss grew like sponges out of the cracks between the stones. He bent and cupped some of the cold water into his mouth, drinking greedily and noisily. When he raised his head, the front of his shirt was soaked. Alice was amused; it was the sort of thing her dad would do. You wouldn't see a town person doing that. They would only think water came from a tap or a pump. He sat down next to her on the wall, uninvited but not unwelcome. Close enough to make her surprised.

She suddenly thought few of the town men would ever do that. Alice looked away, feeling her neck and face becoming clammy at the proximity of his hand on the stones next to her. They watched the swallows swooping, their satiny spitfire bodies darting and dogfighting for insects high above them.

Alice carried on answering his questions about the sheep and the landscape, the stone walls which he had never seen before, the barns and farms hidden in the folds of the rocky hillsides. Then there was just a companionable silence, not awkward at all, just the sounds of the wind and birds, the trickling of the spring.

Eventually, she asked him if he wanted to have a brew and see the orphan lambs she had reared by hand. He frowned at this and shrugged, and she suddenly realised with inward amusement that he didn't know what she was talking about.

'Tea. I mean, a cup of tea.' She spoke slowly, miming the action of drinking.

He laughed with sudden embarrassed recognition.

'Oh *tea!* Yeah, they told us you British people are tea drinkers. That would be great, thank you.'

They walked back down the lane to Flint Cottage, the sun hot on their backs, Alice pointing out the lambs clustered by the yard, calling for her. They rushed towards her and she picked one up, burying her face in the soft nubbly fleece. She smiled as he bent towards them, rubbing their upturned faces and whispering something to them in Italian. She was surprised and confused at how pleased she felt that he liked animals.

They started meeting up when they had free time. Alice had never had a boyfriend. But this didn't feel like courting as such. It was just a natural friendship with someone her age. She learnt the soldier was an Italian American. His parents were from Sicily, but he was born in San Francisco. His father had African heritage from way back. Sicily had been invaded by everyone over the centuries, and the evidence was in the faces and skin colour of its people. He didn't know why he had been posted to England; the soldiers had been told little. They were waiting to do whatever was instructed.

Most of Alice's questions were met with a shrug and, 'I don't know.'

Until now, Alice hadn't really taken much notice of the war. There were changes at work, bureaucratic annoyances, forms to fill in about the animals, the blackout, and rationing. But Alice had no personal experiences to connect with. James was too old to be called up, and she had no siblings who might have been in the services. This was the first person she had spoken to who had been sent here — to be a part of something much bigger happening somewhere else in the world, spoken about on the wireless or read in the newspaper. It was all so abstract.

One warm evening in early June, she was steadily and rhythmically grooming Edward, the working pony, while the soldier sat on the low stone wall in the yard, watching. She passed the brush over Edward's dark brown coat, smoothing out the dried sweat from his day working in the fields. She moved to comb out his mane, teasing out the knots and tangles, plucking out burrs and prickles. She released the handfuls of hair and grass, allowing them to be carried away on the breeze.

'Are you afraid?' She was surprised at how the question burst out from her, unplanned. And how the words sounded; thick in the back of her throat.

She couldn't see his face due to the sun setting behind him. There was a long pause, and Alice carried on passing the comb through Edward's coarse black mane.

'Of dying? Yes, of course.' His voice sounded strong and young, practical. 'But there's nothing any of us can do about it. We have no say in it.' She heard the shrug in his voice.

Alice untied Edward and, without speaking, led him into the barn for his feed. She was glad that the soldier stayed in the yard, not wanting him to see her trembling hands.

It was the start of a hot summer in the hills and it was easy to forget the war. The hay was cut and baled; the stubble burned to bronze in the scalped fields by the cottage. Away from the wireless and the newspapers, life continued as it had for centuries. Alice would walk up from town after work and stand at the stone circle, watching for the soldier's black brilliantined head as he climbed the hill to Flint Cottage. Sometimes they just watched the sky and the sheep, listening to the sound of the rising, bubbling call of the curlew or the soft baby's mew of the buzzard.

They walked to the upland streams and drank from the ribbons of water cascading from the rocks. The soldier holding Alice's hand as they climbed the tors and crags fuzzy in the heat haze, following the footpaths, coffin roads and drover's paths that she knew from earliest childhood. They lay on the tufted grass and heather and watched the skeins of cloud racing above. Alice's head resting on the rough fabric of his shoulder, his arm around her, hand buried in her thick soft hair. Sometimes they would lie as the sky turned from blue to deepest violet. The first pinpricks of stars emerging as dusk deepened and Venus appeared, like a lamp in the western sky.

The soldier would cover her mouth with his, blotting out the night sky, and Alice would forget about the war because at that moment nothing else mattered. He disappeared before she knew she was pregnant. One day, towards the end of the summer, he didn't turn up for their arranged meeting to walk in the hills. She just assumed he had been held up, had his leave cancelled for some reason.

A few days passed, and then she heard a woman at work remark above the clatter of the machinery. 'The Yanks have gone.'

The Yanks have gone.

It was as simple and as shocking as that. As if the radio had unexpectedly been switched off. Or she had found a previously perfectly healthy sheep dead in the field, an unexplained, sudden event. Maybe it was a mistake and the woman was talking rubbish. But no, the days passed and became two, three weeks, and a subtle enquiry at the post office confirmed it. The American soldiers had moved out, to be replaced by others. Nobody knew where they had gone. Mrs Robinson, the post office manager, looked up from a stack of telegrams and frowned at Alice over her glasses.

'There's a war on, lass. They would never tell us where they have gone to. Were you sweet on one of them, love? Not to worry, plenty more where that one came from.' She turned away from Alice, who left the shop like a sleepwalker and began walking home blindly, heart hammering wildly in her chest.

She never heard from the soldier again and obsessively wondered if he had been killed, or if he had been wounded and had been sent back to San Francisco. Or had he just forgotten about her and moved on to another girl? She started a letter but didn't know who or where to send it to. James and Rose were philosophical. Anything could have happened, they reasoned. Privately, they thought he was a wrong 'un, but they said nothing to Alice.

Lying in her narrow bed in the tiny, whitewashed bedroom under the eaves, she often dreamed about him.

Of his voice and how they had lain together in the centre of the stone circle. But she couldn't picture his face as hard as she tried. In the dreams, his head would be above hers, the sun behind him, his features in shadow. The weight of his body and smell of the hot summer grass vivid, overwhelming, and she would wake, panicked and bathed in sweat.

She wandered the hills as usual, seeing him everywhere like a ghost. A shadow she couldn't quite reach. As summer slid into autumn, she occasionally sat on the wall above town. Sometimes thinking she could see him coming up the hill towards her, as he had done on that first afternoon. She was always mistaken. It would be a farm worker, or a neighbour, or even the shadow from a cloud across the sun making a shape on the lane. It didn't stop the lurch of her heart inside her chest, though, like a hopeful bird trying to take flight within her. *It doesn't take much to change a life forever,* she thought, shrugging. And she would make her way home, wrapping her jacket around her tightly.

Alice had no intention of hiding the baby. She carried on working and ignored the whispers, nudges and the glances at her belly. Shrugging off the insults, sometimes shouted across the street, or in the mill. She delivered her baby girl on the floor of the family kitchen, on a freezing winter's night. Staring out of the window as she laboured, by the time a slim crescent moon had appeared in the window's frame, it was over, and Rose passed the tiny screaming infant to her. Now she didn't even think about the soldier. The pain was hers alone and her reward was this perfect baby girl. She watched the small dark face look up at her with her father's eyes.

James and Rose looked after Stella and Alice went back to work. No comment was passed in judgement by them. The child was looked after with the rough, practical love of the lambs James reared by hand. Stella was as dark-skinned and dark-eyed as her father and wasn't allowed to forget it. The 'nigger's bastard', the 'Eyetie's kid', the 'black bastard'. By the time she was out of primary school, she'd heard it all. She cried and railed at Alice, who told her to ignore them, to carry on and stop being mard.

Alice didn't care what people thought and had no intention of marrying for respectability or settling down. She worked; she kept her kid. Alice was independent and kept roaming the hills as if nothing had happened, collecting her bones and feathers. Tracking the year by the stars and the trees and the endless cycle of tupping and lambing. She didn't need anyone, she had all she wanted.

Chapter 11
Midge: June 1982

It was the beginning of June, when Wendy came home from work one night and flopped on the settee next to Midge, who was trying to watch the latest Falklands War update on the teatime news. She had her feet up on Baz, using him as a furry canine footstool, a plate of egg and chips balanced on her knees. Mr Crown had been quiet of late. Several British ships had been sunk, and last week she had seen him in the shop standing still, oblivious to Midge — listening to the news on the radio that the *Galahad* had been hit, and many British soldiers had died or been badly burned.

Midge had watched the news so she could talk to Mr Crown about the conflict. He never spoke about his own war, but seemed very preoccupied with this one. By the end of May, Midge knew the names of the stricken British ships, *Ardent*, *Antelope*, *Sheffield*, *Coventry*, and *Atlantic Conveyor*. The paper round was taking longer now. She was stopping to read the news, studying maps of the Falkland Islands, the diagrams of military engagements.

Midge could tell anyone who cared to listen where Ascension Island, Mount Tumbledown, South Georgia, Goose Green, and Stanley were located. She now knew the difference between a Gazelle, a Hercules, and Harrier. She wasn't sure how old Mr Crown was, but she was sure he wouldn't have been much older than her during the Second World War, and Midge couldn't imagine having to do the things she had seen and read about these past few weeks.

Wendy pulled off her shoes and threw herself full length behind Midge, groaning with satisfaction as she lit a fag and pulled a cushion under her head.

'Christ, are you not sick of watching this boring shit?' she grumbled, rubbing her eyes.

The picture on the telly was of burning ships and a footage of soldiers trudging over barren green-grey open moorland, not unlike the fells above town.

'They're the Paras,' announced Midge, 'at Bluff Cove.' Her eyes never left the screen as she shovelled in golden coloured chips.

Wendy frowned and made a goggle-eyed face. God, Midge could be so weird. Why didn't she watch *Top of the Pops* or *Coronation Street* like normal people?

'I've seen a job for you. Are you still looking?' Wendy said idly, flicking ash into the saucer balanced on her chest.

'Of course I am. Where?' Midge turned to face her; the news reader had started on a feature about the World Cup.

'In the pet shop. They want a Saturday person.' Wendy sighed flatly, scratching her nose with an electric-blue thumbnail. 'Though why you'd want to work somewhere like that is beyond me, you could easily get a job in a café like Bobby, instead of mucking about with animals and cleaning up shit.' She drew on her fag and picked up a tattered copy of *Jackie*.

'That's ace, thanks Wend. Brilliant.'

Midge put her plate on the floor and stood up, snapping the telly off. She did a little dance, stepping over Baz, who was on his back now, spreadeagled with his freckled belly and balls on show.

Wendy stared at her flatly, shaking her head with pity. 'You're such a dick,' she drawled.

This was it. Midge's heart started racing. She was obsessed with animals, and if she could get paid for looking after them and learning about them, even better. The shelf between her bed and Wendy's was crammed with her small collection of wildlife books and animal stories fighting for space with Wendy's avalanche of ashtrays, records, clothes, and makeup.

'Right, I'll go there after school and ask.' She could hardly keep the excitement out of her voice. She pulled her thin brown hair into a ponytail, imagining herself opening a cage and confidently taking out a rabbit, showing it to a customer and explaining in detail its husbandry requirements. Midge ran out of the room, thundering up the stairs to see if she had anything remotely clean and smart to wear when she visited the pet shop tomorrow.

Boston's Pets was located in what had once been two terraced houses. Just like many of the businesses and pubs in town, the front doors and windows had been changed at some point to make a shop. Customers stepped straight in off the street. What had been the main front rooms was now a darkish room with a counter at the far end, and behind that, a kitchen and storeroom.

Midge stood for a moment on the threshold, took a deep breath, and composed herself. Opening the door slowly, she entered cautiously. She didn't come in here often. Jean couldn't afford the prices. All their pet stuff came from Kwiksave or from the stall in the market.

Boston was busy helping a man choose some budgies, so she had time to look around. The two men glanced over when the door opened, but turned back again. It was only a child, so they carried on their conversation without acknowledging her presence. Fish tanks lined one wall from floor to ceiling. Lit from within, they bathed the side of the room in an eerie green light. Midge nervously watched a fat orange goldfish drifting soundlessly through the eye socket of a plastic skull. Another hovered on the prow of a sunken galleon, observing Midge impassively.

On the opposite wall was a bank of cages, like a block of flats for animals, housing mice, rats, rabbits, and guinea pigs. The smell was powerful, but not unpleasant — a combination of sawdust, animal shit, and fur. Midge walked over to watch them, entranced as a couple of rats wrestled on the floor of their cage while another straddled a cardboard tube, reaching for its drinking bottle, whiskers vibrating. Other shelves above the small animals were stacked with pet food, small packets of hay and straw, food and drinking bowls, toys, and treats.

There was a small carousel with books on pet care, cat collars, and dog leads. She rotated it slowly, pretending to read while the bloke buying budgies started talking about cuttlefish. She had a little daydream about life working here, filling up the wire rack with new stock and arranging the collars so they wouldn't get tangled up. As she shoved a book on gerbils to the wire shelf, her thoughts were suddenly interrupted.

'Get out,' rasped a bored smoker's voice.

Midge jumped violently and turned around to see Jacob, the infamous scarlet macaw holding court in the middle of the shop. He was housed in a tall cage and was gripping a small log with his grey talons. Jacob was well known in Gritstone for his foul-mouthed tirades and sarcastic asides. Midge watched him in wonder, smiling as he rattled off a torrent of abuse. He was as beautiful, glamorous, and foul-mouthed as Wendy.

Notorious for lacerating the fingers of the unwary and insulting everybody, Jacob had lived in the shop since before Boston was born. Legend had it that old man Boston had won him in a card game from some travellers in Stockport, but the truth was long lost. He was the most gorgeous and exotic creature Midge had ever seen.

Mesmerised, she watched him spread his red, yellow, and blue wings. He dipped his head, spun and arched, like a model on a catwalk.

'Hello,' whispered Midge, walking closer, careful to keep her hands in her pockets. She was suddenly filled with the pity and rage she always felt when she saw a caged bird.

Jacob looked over his shoulder as if checking nobody was listening and shuffled closer to Midge along his log — his scaly feet moving slowly like a mechanical toy. He tilted his head conspiratorially and opened his beak.

Midge could see his leathery grey tongue as he whispered carefully, 'Just go home.'

The man with the budgies was leaving. He handed over some cash to Boston and left with a small cardboard box with perforations on the lid. Midge approached the counter with a cautious air of confidence she didn't feel.

Thomas Boston was a proper oddball. He was about forty, with a potbelly and drooping handlebar moustache, protruding eyeballs with irises the colour of porridge, and a mousy head of permed hair. His eyelashes were almost colourless and crusty, and they moved slowly, like the fringes of a Venus flytrap.

Thomas had taken over the shop when his dad died. He had no interest whatsoever in animals, but he looked after them with an obsessive care. What he lacked in love for living creatures he made up for in his love of money. Boston had a raging gambling habit and liked a drink.

He didn't like the look of this kid. She looked poor, rough. Off the estate, he reckoned. Thin, eyes too big for her head, hair scraped back into a ponytail, a once-white Aertex shirt tucked into too-big jeans and trainers that had seen better days. She appeared clean, though.

'What d'you want?' he demanded; arms folded across an orange nylon pot belly.

Midge stood up straight. This was her moment. She needed to look responsible, reliable, grownup. Her family was none of these things, but he didn't know that, and this was her chance.

'I would like to ask if the Saturday job is still available?' she croaked.

'What experience do you have?' His voice was dismissive, scornful. He passed a hand over his permed curls.

Midge was ready for this. 'I've got a cat and a dog. I look after them; feed them and take the dog for walks.' She drew herself up, trying to look more confident than she felt and pushed her shoulders back.

She didn't tell Boston that they might as well be wild animals for all the care they got from Jean and Wendy. They came and went as they wished, roamed the estate, and were fed whenever they chose to turn up. Jasper was fed by at least three other families on the estate. He was as shameless as a stray, and Baz was often seen rifling through the bins at the back of the chippy, and shagging anything that moved.

'Never seen you in here before,' he challenged, narrowing his reptilian eyes.

Midge didn't know what to say. It was true, Jean would buy nothing in here. She said he was a greedy bastard and charged over the odds. Midge had probably been in here half a dozen times at the most. She stayed silent. There was a long, uncomfortable pause, and then something seemed to shift in Boston's face. He made a weird clicking sound in the back of his throat and stared at her. Midge felt instantly uncomfortable. *What a weirdo.*

'Alright, you can start on Saturday, nine until five. On trial. If you turn up late, you're finished. There's plenty more kids around here looking for work.' His voice was expressionless, staccato.

Midge was ecstatic. 'Thank you so much, I won't let you down,' she burst out breathlessly and left the shop.

She sprinted up Skein Street, clutching her arms around herself so the good luck wouldn't run out. She was halfway home before she realised she hadn't asked how much the pay was.

Everything went okay in the shop for a while. Midge was reliable and hardworking. She turned up for work on time and did everything asked of her. She was quiet and respectful with the customers and didn't steal anything. Boston checked the till and the stock like a hawk and would know if so much as a halfpenny or a chew stick went missing. He showed her how to clean, feed, and water the animals, and how to use the till. She learnt quickly and didn't make mistakes. She stood behind the counter with quiet pride, engulfed in her oversized overall, pressing the keys on the cash register with solemn deliberation, carefully counting out change into the palms of her customers.

Midge noticed he was weird with the customers. Almost monosyllabic with the men and older kids, but he turned on the smarm when women and girls came in — smiling and giggling and cracking lame, embarrassing jokes. Standing a bit too close to them when they were looking at the animals and offering advice in a different voice than normal. He adopted a pretend-posh voice and assertive posture, sometimes touching their arms or giving them a friendly, conspiratorial nudge.

Midge didn't like the way his eyes followed them when they came in; watchful, greedy, predatory eyes, blinking like a lizard. She expected a giant tongue to flick out suddenly and wrap itself around them, dragging their soft bodies into his greedy wet mouth.

Some women responded to his clumsy flirtatious ways, and then he moved up the gears, ramping up the banter. It would start off a bit harmless and if there were no objections, Midge would see him pushing it further. Telling a few dirty jokes, commenting on their clothes or bodies, openly looking down their tops and asking if they had boyfriends or husbands. Sometimes it worked, sometimes it didn't. Some stopped smiling and shut him down with a look or an abrupt comment. Others went along with it, flicking their hair and pushing out their breasts, enjoying the attention. Midge watched him silently as he smirked and licked his lips.

There were a couple of women who let it go a lot further. Midge had watched him sliding his hand up the skirt of one older girl while she stood looking at the rabbits. They both carried on talking while his hand crept further over her bottom and between her legs. It made her feel sick to watch his well-practised routine, the calculation, the weighing up of which women would be willing and which would rebuff him.

There was another older woman who came in most Saturdays and would stand behind the display carousel while Boston kissed her, his hands under her top, rummaging around in her bra. The woman stared at Midge over the top of Boston's head, and she went to hide in the storeroom. She would stay there until the doorbell rang, and she knew it was safe to come out.

Boston started to leave Midge to look after the shop on her own, taking himself off to the bookies for an hour or so, sometimes all day. He would open up and do a bit of bookwork, then disappear and come back to cash up, pay Midge, and lock up the shop. Midge always knew when he'd had a big win. He came back all smiley and almost chatty. She knew when he'd lost too — he would be monosyllabic and snappy, and she would keep out of the way. It wasn't like working for Mr Crown, but it was okay. It was money, after all.

One late, hot afternoon at the end of June, he turned up about four and shuffled around in the shop front for a while. Midge was doing the weekly job of cleaning mouse cages in the back room. She would place a cage of mice on the bench to her left. On the right-hand side would be a clean cage, filled with an inch of clean sawdust, a cardboard tube, and a ball of paper nesting material. Midge would scoop up the mice and transfer them to the new cage with a pinch of their soiled bedding.

She had noticed that male mice would fight when they first went into the clean cage and realised it was because it didn't smell right. A pinch of the old bedding made it familiar and they settled down straight away. The water bottle was emptied and put into the sink for washing, and a new full bottle was attached to the cage. Fresh rodent food was added to the feed hopper, and the cage was placed back on the shelf in the front of the shop.

Boston came in, turned the shop sign around to *Closed* and locked the door. He wandered into the storeroom and started shifting boxes around. Then he suddenly came up behind Midge. She felt his hands on her, around her middle, between her waist, and her non-existent breasts. Pressing on her narrow ribcage.

She froze feeling saturated with shock, fear, and embarrassment. She could hear the soft clicking sound in his throat. They both stood immobile for a few seconds.

It was as if he was testing her reaction, and because she didn't do or say anything, he moved his hands up higher, under her Snoopy t-shirt. Midge clamped her arms together and tried to move away, but he was too strong and pushed her to the floor easily. He said nothing, and didn't look at her at all. Her heart hurled itself against the bony cage of her chest, like a small wild animal desperate to escape.

It didn't take long. Midge was aware of him unfastening his trousers, then he pulled her shorts down and got on top of her, forcing himself between the fork of her body. She screwed up her eyes, aware of his hot, wet breath on her skin. She tried to clamp her legs closed, but he held her down with one forearm and prised them apart with his other hand, his filthy long nails digging into the soft, thin skin of her thighs.

She could smell him, sour, his body and his breath seeping over her. Her mouth opened in shock, but no sound came out. It felt as though her entire throat had closed up and was lined with thick, choking dust. It was over in less than a minute. Midge was aware only of intense pain, his breathing, and awful protruding eyes. She focused on the skylight above her. An aeroplane was tracking across the brilliant blue sky of its picture frame. He had finished before the plane had vanished from view; the contrail floating behind, gauzelike, marking its progress.

Boston got up and walked away. Saying nothing and without looking at her, he strolled back into the front of the shop, leaving Midge on the floor in the sawdust. With ragged breath, she silently scrabbled her shorts back on and stood up, her face burning and whole body trembling violently. For a few seconds, she thought she would vomit, and had to hold onto the edge of the bench. The mice she had been cleaning out continued to patter around their cage, clustering around the nozzle of their drinking bottle to taste the fresh, cold water.

Boston didn't have to tell her to be quiet about what had just happened. He didn't threaten. He didn't need to. They both knew she wouldn't say anything. Men like Boston have a nose for girls like Midge. An unerring eye for those too quiet, too shy, too easily shamed to say anything. Men like Boston could single out a girl like Midge in a room of a hundred. They have a finely tuned antennae for vulnerability.

She stood in the storeroom's doorway, mute, then inched out into the shop, uncertain how to leave and still unable to speak. Her pumps made a slight squeaking sound on the lino. He turned to the till, pinged open the drawer, took out her wages, and left them on the counter.

'You can go early,' he said casually. He looked her straight in the eyes, blandly.

His face was completely normal. It was as if nothing had happened and this was just a transaction. Part of her job — his complete and absolute right to do as he wished with her, her status exactly the same as a guinea pig or a goldfish. And that was it. Midge slid the money off the counter and into her narrow, trembling clammy hand and left on legs that felt like wobbly, disjointed stilts.

She didn't remember walking home. She played out what had just happened in disbelief, frame by frame, as if it had happened to another person, in a film or in a book. The sun was still orangey late-afternoon hot, and Midge could feel it drying the sweat on her face. There were some kids playing on the patch of parched yellow grass in front of the flats. They were riding bikes over a homemade ramp made from a pallet and a square of plywood. Midge was vaguely aware of Baz sitting watching them, curled up on someone's jumper near the bins. Normally she would have found that funny, but she carried on walking, head pounding, trembling uncontrollably.

Nobody was in when she turned the key and walked into the cool of the hallway. It was tatty and familiar. The peeling wallpaper and smell of chip fat and fags. The sun shining through the glass in the door onto the dusty telephone table, and the phone directory with numbers scrawled over the ripped cover, stained with coffee rings. Midge leant against the wall for a minute, listening to the ticking of the clock and the thundering of the blood in her ears.

She tried to steady her breathing, inhaling raggedly to suppress the need to scream. She rubbed her arms. They were covered in goosebumps despite the heat and she realised she was shivering with cold. She glanced at herself in the dusty mirror, seeing a small, thin white oval looking back, sweat shining on her brow. Then she ran upstairs, relieved nobody was here to guess what had just happened. She rubbed her face violently.

It never occurred to her to tell anyone, to call the police, to tell a grownup. All she felt was a terrible rage and disappointment that this job, this opportunity, had been spoiled. Midge locked herself in the bathroom and ran the bath. The immersion hadn't been on, and she only ran a couple of inches of hot water before it ran cold. She stepped in and sat down, a residue of Vim scratching her bum, suddenly feeling a stinging sensation between her legs. She rested her burning face on her knees and sobbed. Crying in great hitching gulps, trying to calm down, she focused on the limescale-frosted tap, slowly dripping water onto a yellow skid mark of years-old stained enamel.

She picked up the dry, fissured bar of green soap from the edge of the bath. There was a stubborn pube stuck to the top. Dunking the soap in the water, she mechanically made a thin lather. Midge ran through the day again, trying to think of a single occasion that might have encouraged Boston to do what he had just done, but couldn't think of a thing. She hadn't flirted with him like the women he carried on with in the shop. She didn't know the first thing about that kind of behaviour.

Have I done something wrong? She knew that was bollocks even as the thought entered her head. Her first instinct was to tell her mum, but Midge dismissed it at once, thinking of the embarrassment, the fuss that would result. When Jean lost her rag, she did it big time, and Midge just wanted what had happened to just go away and be forgotten. She ground her knuckles into her temples, kneading the racing thoughts. Jean would make it twice as bad. She closed her eyes and pressed her face onto her knees again, wrapping her arms around her legs as the water cooled.

Sometime later, there was a noise on the stairs and Wendy's voice. 'You'd better not have used all the water, Midge,' she cried.

'It was nearly cold when I got in. You'll have to switch it on,' Midge answered, surprised at how normal her voice sounded.

'Fucking hell,' hissed Wendy through the door. 'I'm meeting Bobby in an hour. Hurry up!'

There was a loud click in the cupboard outside the door as Wendy switched the immersion heater on, then a tuneless whistling. Midge stood up and rinsed off her thin boy's body with the plastic jug that lived upside down on the taps. She noticed with revulsion that there was mouse shit and sawdust floating on the grey surface of the bathwater. Pulling the plug out quickly, she shivered, using the flat of her hand to swill the debris down the plughole.

She wrapped herself in a grey cardboardy towel. Without drying herself, she went to the bedroom and sat on her bed. Her feet curled up beneath her like a shell. Wendy was downstairs, frying something to line her stomach before she went out on the piss. The crackling sound floated up onto the landing. Sunlight was still streaming through the curtains, making a hot, bright square on the covers. Midge lay down, heart hammering, hair soaking into her pillow.

She couldn't get her head around what had just happened and why. Boston was a grownup. Midge was a child. She wasn't daft and knew things like this happened. But to her? She didn't even look like a woman. Why did he want her? She had given no encouragement, not like the women in the shop who went along with his games. Not like the girls at school with boobs and makeup who flirted and had boyfriends and grown-up clothes.

Stinging tears came as she tried to think about what she could have done wrong. She pressed the rough towel to her face, not wanting Wendy to see that something had happened to her. She would just badger until she had to tell a lie and that would make everything worse. There was another week to go before she had to be in the shop. Maybe it was a one-off. Maybe it wouldn't happen again. *Yes, maybe if she just kept going on as normal, everything would be okay. Boston might think about what had happened and realise it was wrong and would stop? She could carry on with her job, being with the animals, put this behind her and pretend it never happened.*

She quickly dragged her pyjamas on and got under the bedcovers, even though it was stiflingly hot in the bedroom. Picking up *Charlotte's Web*, she opened the book where she had left it this morning, a lifetime ago. Her eyes followed the lines on the book, but the words didn't register. Some time later, she heard Wendy thundering up the stairs to get in the bath.

The thought of people finding out. The shame and embarrassment made her skin prickle with sweat, and made her feel as if she would vomit. Midge turned the book over and stared at the cover, suddenly thinking it looked silly and childish with its picture of the little girl, the pig, and the spider. Staring at the ceiling, she tried to think sensibly and calmly. She had to keep going to the shop. She loved the animals, and her mum and Wendy would know something serious had happened for her to give it up. Telling people was out of the question. Her family was notorious on the estate.

Midge wasn't stupid; she knew what people thought about the Kennys. Her mum was a fat, old whore. Her sister going the same way, that's what they thought. She would be seen as a troublemaking little slag. When her dad had lived at home, the coppers were always at the door, or a moneylender, or the bailiffs. No, she had to keep her trap shut. She pressed her bitten nails into her cheeks; the blood whooshing in her ears again, and closed her eyes, trying to calm her breathing.

Wendy burst into the bedroom to get ready for her Saturday night out. 'What the fuck are you doing lying in bed, yer nutter?' She rolled her eyes at Midge and leant over her to open the window. 'It's boiling in here. Are you poorly?'

'Nothing, just a bit tired, that's all.' Midge pushed the book to one side, wrapped the covers around herself, and sat up.

Telling Wendy was out of the question, she would be as bad as Mum. Wendy shrugged and shook her head, gathering her stuff to get ready. Midge watched the familiar routine without seeing it. Wendy had bought the new ABC album, *The Lexicon of Love* and popped it on the record player turntable while she did her makeup and got changed. She chain-smoked while she ringed her eyes with kohl, applied mascara, and shimmery lipstick. Then white plastic earrings, a vivid green mini dress, and white plastic shoes. The music was so loud Midge could feel it vibrating in her chest. Wendy sprayed her body with a gallon of Limara's Green Summer and her head with half a can of Elnett, and smiled at Midge through the thick, toxic, Saturday night haze.

'Right, you divvy, I'll see you later.'
She blew a kiss at Midge, shoved her fags into her handbag, and was out of the door with a slam.

Midge listened to the feet thundering down the stairs. She lifted the needle off the record and slid down the bed, under the covers. The house was silent, just the sound of fear and shame ringing in her ears. She wished Jasper was here.

She lay awake until it became dark, watching car headlights like searchlight beams tracking across the walls and ceiling as cars drove onto the estate. Listening to Jean's wet, rattly cough in the room next door. Her mum had come home from the pub relatively early and alone. Midge longed to get up and walk the few footsteps across the landing, to get in bed with her mum and tell her what had happened — but she couldn't make her limbs move to do it. The shame kept her pinned to the bed, as though a slab of concrete was holding her down and paralysing her.

The next morning, Midge woke up stiff and sore. Her limbs were heavy and felt bruised. She lay for a while, watching the sunlight ripple on the peeling wallpaper. It made different origami-like bird shapes as the curtains moved in the draught from the open window. A blackbird was singing its head off somewhere. Wendy was asleep on top of the covers of her bed, face down in her clothes. She had one shoe on and there was a can of lager on its side, leaking into the carpet.

Midge felt an overwhelming sensation of tiredness and anxiety. She wrapped her arms around herself like a straitjacket, hugging herself until her ribs ached. Slowly, she peeled back the covers and got out of bed. The quicker she got moving, the quicker she could chase the thoughts from her head. She nervously rubbed her hands over her face, wiping gunk from her eyes and pulled on her clothes.

The difficult part was not saying anything and carrying on as normal. Midge went to school the next day, almost dreading the school holidays coming up, because there wouldn't be the distraction of lessons and the zoo-like atmosphere to keep her thoughts at bay. The summer term was almost finished, just a few more weeks to go.

That week, she sat in her classes like a polite zombie, making all the right comments and sleepwalking through her days. She ran round the athletics track in PE, small and ungainly. She smiled at her mates' daft comments and jokes, handed in her work, answered questions and took her exams like a robot. At dinnertime, she sat on the bank overlooking the football field with the others and ate her butties mechanically — they tasted like cardboard in her mouth.

The Saturday after she was raped, Midge went to the pet shop as usual. In a state of embarrassment and anxiety, well hidden from Boston. She crept from the till to the animals and back again, willing herself to be as small as possible, completing her jobs in total silence. He said and did nothing out of the ordinary that day; it was as though it hadn't happened. Midge left at 5 pm in complete relief. Maybe that was it. Maybe nothing would happen again. Maybe she could start to forget.

Relief soared through her body as she walked home, the evaporating tension leaving her body weak as she turned her face to the early evening sun. *That's it, it's over,* she thought, turning into the estate, almost blinded by the reflection of the sunlight on the windows of the houses opposite.

It wasn't a one-off, though. That summer, sometimes Boston repeated the assaults. Raping her during the shift as absent-mindedly and routinely as he did any task. Midge was just another animal, to do with as he wished. After he attacked her, he would go back into the shop as if nothing had happened — ready for when one of his lady customers came in and he would fawn and giggle, playing the cheeky devil-may-care shop keeper — all elaborate courtesy and pervy jokes.

Behind him, a thin wraith of a girl in a white shop coat would drift past, going about her business. Ghostlike, invisible. Sometimes, after he had raped her, he would leave extra money with her wage on the counter and look at her with hardened eyes; a bribe and a warning. She never took the extra money. She would separate it from her wage and slide it away with her fingertips, as if it was contaminated.

Midge learnt to isolate it. To live her life in the shop as a different life. A world that was shut out and re-lived again at night, when she would lie awake listening to the sound of Wendy's steady breathing, wondering why she couldn't bring herself to say anything. Knowing she wouldn't say anything. Wondering how to a make it stop. All it would take would be to reach out her hand across the gap between the beds, shake Wendy awake and unleash hell. She even practiced the speech to her big sister, explaining everything.

She could smell Boston on her body, even when she got out of the bath. Could see his globular eyes and hear his wet breathing. She could feel his hands on her, forcing her to the floor, pressing her legs apart. Gouging. It was like a film clip playing constantly, making her catch her breath.

It was just one sentence, she thought. *A few words could fix this. 'If you don't stop doing this, I will tell someone.'*

It was that simple, and that impossible. She stood next to people. At home, sitting on the settee next to Jean and Wendy. At school, looking at the familiar faces she had known since forever. Once she even thought she might be able to tell Gregory Crown. Building up the courage to tell them, the words were there, in her mouth. Powerful, shocking, simple words that could save her, but they wouldn't come out. It was as though something held the words by an invisible rope that ran down her throat and into her chest.

She couldn't release the rope; the words wouldn't come.

Jean knew there was something wrong, but couldn't pinpoint it. One night, Midge was curled up on the settee watching a nature documentary when Jean staggered in. She'd gone straight from work to the shops, then to Stella's to collect the catalogue money. She shoulder-barged through the door with four bulging Kwiksave bags, the handles cutting into her swollen sausage fingers like wires. Dumping them in the kitchen, she rubbed the feeling back into her purple hands, forcing the knuckleduster sovereign rings round the right way.

'I'm shagged out, love, I don't know about you. I'll brew up. What are you watching?' she asked.

'David Attenborough. It's a documentary,' muttered Midge. Her eyes never left the telly as she mechanically ate a packet of Hula Hoops.

Jean stood with her hands on her hips, looking at the screen as a chimpanzee absentmindedly scratched its balls. 'Well,' she observed tartly, 'he's better behaved than a lot of men I know,' and rooted in her bag for her fags.

Instead of laughing, Midge made a choking sob, and two large tears suddenly appeared, spilling down her cheeks. Jean narrowed her eyes. Midge never cried, ever. It was other people that created dramas in this house, but never Midge.

'Hey, what's up, love?' she whispered softly, sitting down heavily next to her youngest child, putting her arm around the narrow, heaving shoulders and kissing the top of her head.

Midge shook her head, shrugged, and carried on staring at the telly through a film of tears. 'Nothing,' she whispered, a thin line of mucus running onto her upper lip. She wiped it away with her sleeve.

Jean didn't believe her for a minute. But when Midge didn't want to say anything, no amount of badgering would change her. It was like trying to break open a pebble. 'It's hormones love, we all feel like that sometimes,' reasoned Jean. She shook Midge reassuringly and heaved herself off the settee to put the kettle on. 'I'll make us a brew and some fish fingers and chips. That'll make you feel better. You carry on with yer monkey programme.'

Midge didn't hear her. All she could think about was what was going to happen when she walked into the pet shop on Saturday morning.

Chapter 12
June 1982

It was the Barnaby holidays. All over the North West, the factories were closed and most of Gritstone went to Blackpool. It was a mill town tradition going back generations. Families loaded themselves onto buses and trains, and even the local paper sent a photographer down to the railway station to take pictures of the holidaymakers boarding the trains to the coast for a few days.

Wendy was beside herself with excitement. It was her first Barnaby as a fully-fledged mill worker. Bobby had just finished her exams. Sod it, they would both have a brief holiday for a couple of days — it would be a laugh. Wendy had booked a B&B just off the front. They would share a room, more money for drinks and dancing.

They got a free lift in the back of a neighbour's van. He was going up to Blackpool himself for the full Barnaby holiday, but it meant sitting in the back on bags of Blue Circle cement and listening to his World Cup predictions, while his wife stared straight ahead, silently chain smoking with the windows up.

Wendy pulled a face and whispered to Bobby, 'Miserable cow. She's got a face like a melted welly.'

Then they got the giggles and were told they had to behave, or they'd be chucked out and have to get the bus. The back doors of the van eventually opened, and they stepped out into weak sunshine onto the fabled Golden Mile with their small suitcases. Wendy had the address of the B&B scribbled on the back of an envelope; it was in a street behind the Tower.

She strode off, looking at her badly drawn map and within a couple of minutes, they were standing in front of *The Seashells,* one of a row of shabby Victorian villas, all with *No Vacancies* signs, and the same net curtains and weedy gravel front gardens.

The pair stepped over a green oyster of phlegm lying in front of the step and Wendy knocked sharply on the door. It was opened by a large woman with a massive piled-up canary yellow beehive. Bobby instantly thought of Bet Lynch. The landlady stared down at them with disapproval — she had the psychological advantage of being on the top step. She looked at the girls and frowned. Her enormous breasts stretched the front of a shiny pink blouse into ovals where the buttons strained across the fabric, exposing a grubby grey bra. Wendy and Bobby glanced at each other, desperate not to laugh out loud.

'How old are you two? You said eighteen on the phone.'

The woman's teeth didn't fit properly when she spoke, they moved independently of her lips. Bobby thought she was going to start properly laughing and had to look away, covering her mouth and pretending to examine a seagull disembowelling a bag of chips in the gutter.

'We are,' sighed Wendy in a drawling, bored voice. It was almost true — they were both over seventeen.

The woman jacked up her tits with crossed arms and continued to stare at them both. Wendy lifted her chin and shifted her handbag onto her shoulder assertively. The standoff continued for a minute or so, and Wendy shrugged and gave her the *take it or leave it* face. The landlady tutted and weighed up the alternative, which could be a couple of lads, possibly Scottish, who may or may not trash the room, piss in the wardrobe, and make a lot of noise.

'Alright then, but no bother from the pair of you. No mess, and no bringing lads back. No drinking in your room. No monkey business.' She pointed directly at them both in turn. 'Breakfast is at eight and you're to be out of the room by ten sharp.'

The girls nodded mutely before she turned as slowly as an oil tanker, and they followed her up the steps. Wendy gave her the double vees behind her back as they went. The steps led into a narrow corridor with dirty striped wallpaper and an ancient carpet covered in a bobbly plastic hall runner. They descended some more steps, then into a small bedroom with two narrow single beds. It reeked of damp and stale fag smoke. Wendy jerked her head at Bobby and made a pretend gagging motion with her fingers in her mouth just before the dragon turned around with more instructions.

'The bathroom's down the hall. Showers are on a meter. You'll need change. I haven't got any.' She handed a key over to Wendy with a slow, deliberate motion, as if it would unlock a suite at The Ritz. Wendy gave her the benefit of a dazzling smile as she took the key with elaborate courtesy. 'And that front door is locked and bolted at midnight. A minute later and you'll be sleeping on the Front.' Her eyebrows vanished up into the mass of sprayed hair and she glared at them both as though it was a crime to come on holiday.

Bobby nodded gravely, looking down respectfully at the floor. She closed the door as the landlady waddled back down the corridor. They both clutched each other and started shrieking with laughter.

'What a shithole! No mess, what bollocks! If we trashed the place, it would be an improvement,' snorted Wendy, scoping out the room like a burglar. 'Auld witch. Midnight my arse! I'll leave the catch off that window when we go out, and we'll come in that way tonight.' She rubbed her hands in anticipation, threw her case on the bed, flicked open the catches, and rooted out a bottle of cider. 'Right then, no time to waste.'

After a few swigs of Woodpecker and a reapplication of makeup, they headed out. Wendy's pay-packet burning a hole in her handbag, and Bobby looking to eke out her Minerva money.

The town was heaving. Half of Gritstone was there. Groups of lads roaming around, eyeing up the talent, and looking forward to a few days of boozing. Colourful flocks of girls with pale sun-starved legs in thin summer dresses wandered up and down, arm in arm, eating candyfloss and exchanging banter.

After a visit to the rock shop, they wandered into the Tower Ballroom to giggle at the old people foxtrotting around the dancefloor to the depressing nasal sound of the Wurlitzer. They headed for the Pleasure Beach and the amusement arcades, breathing in the smells of hot sugar, and the unmistakable body odour waft of cheap hot dogs. Feeling queasy after the Grand National and the Revolution, they headed to the beach, watching the tatty little donkeys listlessly trundling up and down.

'Shall we go for a paddle?' suggested Bobby.

They were huddled in deckchairs in their coats, pale legs exposed to the sun shining weakly through grubby cloud, drinking hot Vimto. They were both regretting the over consumption of rock. Bobby ran her tongue over her teeth. They felt as though they were coated in fur. She pushed her bare toes into the cold grey sand and unearthed a ring pull and a few fag ends.

Wendy squinted at a faint brownish line on the horizon. 'I would if I could see the water, but I can't be arsed to walk that far. Shall we go and have our fortunes read? Or the waxworks. What d'yer reckon?' She elbowed Bobby in the ribs.

'Fortunes. The waxworks were shit last time I went with Mum and Davey and I can't see they'll have improved much.'

South Pier was the usual chaos of light, noise, and Saturday afternoon crowds. Amongst the arcades, side stalls, and carousels of dirty postcards, crappy hats, and beach balls, were a few fortune tellers. Wendy chose one that was in a covered alleyway between an ice-cream shop and a bingo hall. The opening was a grubby purple net curtain and a curved sign saying *World Famous Gypsy Rose, Palmist, Clairvoyant to the Stars*. There was a faded picture of Tom Jones and one of Tony Bennett propped up by the narrow doorway. A small dog busily scratched itself in front of the curtain. Wendy parted it and said tentatively into the darkness,

'How much?'

Gypsy Rose was a handsome older woman with brown teeth, wearing a lot of sparkly scarves over a bobbly polyester jumper and slacks. There wasn't much room in the little shop. It was more of a lean-to, really. Bobby and Wendy hovered by two folding chairs. The gypsy sat behind a small table covered in a greasy velvet cloth, crowded with a crystal ball, packs of tarot cards, and a smouldering cigarette in an ashtray.

'Now then, lasses, come in and sit down.'

Wendy and Bobby ferreted in their purses for coins while the gypsy indicated a small copper coloured bowl with a price list. They sat down on the chairs, knees crammed together. As soon as the girls had coughed up the cash, she seized Wendy's hand and started stroking the palm with her thumb. Bobby observed her quietly. The gypsy's fingers and nails were nicotine stained and dry, crowded with rings. Her earlobes were wrinkled and elongated, stretched down with clusters of gold hoops. The whites of her eyes were tinged yellow, with fatty white deposits at the corners.

'You're a bonny-looking lass. There'll be a lot of men in your life.'

'There have been already. Almost all of them arseholes, to be honest,' reflected Wendy, her fox eyes smiling.

The old woman ignored her, a dirty nail scraping the young pink palm. Bobby snorted and fidgeted in her seat.

'You'll meet one who will be different. You'll marry young, have two babies, both girls.'

Wendy watched and listened intently, eyes never leaving the gypsy's face, entranced. Bobby zoned out while the gypsy told Wendy what she wanted to hear. A big house, a handsome husband, plenty of brass. She listened to the rise and fall of the bingo caller in the shop next door. The 'Oohs' and 'Ahhs' when someone called 'House!' and the shadows of the holidaymakers passing the curtain. The little dog pushed through the fabric and drank noisily from a plastic washing-up bowl in the corner before curling into a ball on a shopping bag with a soft sigh.

It was Bobby's turn. The gypsy asked to see one, then both palms. She rested the backs of them on the small table in front of her and exhaled, still holding her fingertips. Bobby looked alarmed, her eyes widening. She was spending a lot of time just looking, but not saying anything. It suddenly seemed boiling in the little room and she could feel her dress clinging to her back with sweat.

'I can see a dark man.'

That's hardly surprising, thought Bobby, inwardly sighing. She thought of her mum and Davey and their colouring; the Sicilian grandad she had never seen. She looked blandly at the older woman, giving nothing away.

The gypsy stroked her hands repeatedly. Turning her palms over. It was making her feel uneasy, and the little shop was clammy and airless. Wendy lit a cigarette and narrowed her eyes, watching the gypsy like a hawk.

'I can see flames and a coloured bird,' the woman intoned quietly.

'A phoenix? That's a bird that comes from a fire. Is that what you mean?' demanded Bobby.

'Perhaps. The bird is flying near someone you know. A woman, an old woman.' She shrugged and placed Bobby's hands back on the table.

There was no mention of a husband or babies or big houses. Other than that, it was the usual stuff, more or less the same spiel that Wendy had been given, but minus the happy ending. They didn't want to pay extra for a tarot reading. They left, Bobby slightly miffed and unsettled by her experience. Wendy pointed to a chippy and they wandered towards it to fortify themselves for the night ahead.

By the time they had gone back to *The Seashells* to get changed and tarted up for their night out, the light had softened and even though it was still broad daylight, a ribbon of illuminations was stretching up the Golden Mile. The Tower, gilded against the early evening sky, was glowing with thousands of lights, and the air was fragrant with the smell of chips and hot vinegar.

With time to kill before the clubs opened, Bobby and Wendy strolled arm in arm along the Front. Wendy in her new minidress, white with black polka dots, and Bobby in an identical version but in blue and white stripes. They had both been chosen from Jean's catalogue, especially for the occasion. Wendy knew she looked fabulous and danced along, twirling around lampposts and singing.

Bobby shook her head. She loved her new dress, but she needed a drink before she was going to do any singing. They worked their way from pub to pub, ignoring the stares and catcalls of gangs of lads and men, an entire night of laughing and dancing ahead of them.

Eventually, they wandered past a club called Coconuts. The doorman greeted them with a lewd wink.

'Ey up, girls, are you coming in? Free entry tonight for ladies and some drinks vouchers.'

They looked at each other and shrugged. 'Aye, go on then', said Bobby.

They were ushered through the entrance with a flourish and clattered down some steep steps in their heels, deep into the sweaty darkness of a cellar club. It was a real dive, with plastic palm trees and foil on the pillars instead of mirrors. It stank of cheap perfume and aftershave, body odour, and fag smoke.

Wendy strutted up to the bar, jostling her way through the crowd, Bobby squeezing in behind her. The music was deafening, Bobby could feel the vibrations of it fluttering in her chest. She couldn't hear what Wendy had ordered but she pointed to something on the wall, some sort of drinks menu. Within seconds, she was handing Bobby a plastic pineapple filled with something blue, with a straw and a pink umbrella sticking out of the top.

'What the fuck is that?'

'A cocktail, you daft cow. Get it down yer.'

The club started filling up with gangs of sunburned girls. The music was pumping. There was a raised walkway above the dancefloor ringed with men eking out expensive pints. They watched the girls dancing below with predatory greedy faces, as though observing animals in a pen — waiting to be selected, bought, eaten, used up.

Bobby and Wendy stood at the side of the dancefloor to finish the blue cocktails before they started dancing. Within ten seconds, a pair of men had sidled along to chat them up.

Both were old creeps, and Wendy dealt with them quickly. Bobby didn't hear what she said to them, just saw her mouth moving close to one of the men's ears. He was smiling and nodding and suddenly the smile froze, then faded from his face. He recoiled and stepped back, pulling his friend along by the sleeve, and they disappeared into the crowd.

'What did you say to him?' laughed Bobby.

'You don't want to know. Drink up, I like this song.'

She disappeared into the sweaty crush of sunburned shoulders on the dancefloor, waving her arms in the air to 'Hungry Like the Wolf'. Bobby necked her drink and followed, laughing at the DJ, who was dancing on the stage like an electrocuted scarecrow in a nylon glitter wig.

They danced relentlessly for a couple of hours, sweat trickling down their backs. Stopping occasionally to order more drinks and then were back out again on the dancefloor, into the mob of greasy-faced girls and sweating lads — shirts stuck to their backs, the lights tracking across the wet faces of the crowd.

Bladder bursting, Bobby left Wendy getting down to Kool and the Gang and went to queue for the toilets. When she finally got through the doorway, it was like a scene from hell. One basin was clogged with vomit. A girl was sobbing, mascara running down her face, someone trying to comfort her by patting her arm like a dog. One cubicle was jammed shut, a woman hammering on it and shouting through the door.

Another girl was applying lipstick, fluffing her hair in front of the cracked mirror over the sinks, oblivious to the chaos. She blasted her hair with a jet of spray from a can, then smacked her lips together, smiled at her reflection with approval and snapped her bag shut, stepping delicately over the clots of wet toilet paper and broken glass on the floor.

Bobby slid into the only working cubicle when it became vacant, opening it with her elbow and kicking it shut with her heel. She yanked her knickers to one side and hovered over the bowl, anxious not to let any of her skin touch the toilet. The floor was swimming in God knows what. There was no toilet paper, so she fished around in her bag for a tissue and read some of the graffiti as she peed. *Linda the slag, Terry is a prick, Tracey loves it up the arse.* Phone numbers were scrawled at an angle on the door.

When Bobby reeled out of the toilets, she couldn't see Wendy anywhere on the dancefloor. Glancing around, she spotted her deep in conversation near the bar with a dodgy-looking older man with a drooping Mexican moustache. She was stabbing her finger towards his face and gesturing to the holdall he had between his feet. The man was looking truculent and waving his hands around.

He pushed Wendy with the flat of his hand against her upper chest. She took a couple of steps backwards, then he pulled a bundle out of the bag. It was something wrapped in a towel. Some girls joined them and even above the music, Bobby could hear the girls screaming as he unwrapped the towel and revealed a python. He draped it over the neck of the nearest girl and brandished a camera. Wendy shouted something in his face and stormed off, almost knocking over a glass collector. Bobby chased after her and grabbed her arm.

'What the fuck was all that about? Did I just see a bloke pull a snake out of a bag?' yelled Bobby, trying to make herself heard over Shalamar.

'Yeah, the cruel twat. I told him snakes are sensitive to noise and vibration. But he just told me to fuck off. People pay to have their picture taken with that snake and then he chucks it back in the bag and goes to the next club.' She glared back at the snake man, surrounded by the shrieking girls, and shook her head.

'How did you know all that stuff about snakes? I didn't think you liked animals?' Bobby steered her towards a small table away from the dancefloor.

'Our Midge. She knows all about that sort of thing. Weird little kid.' She shrugged and threw her drink back.

'Speaking of reptiles, it's my turn. Pint of snakebite?'

'Go on then.' Bobby forced her shoes back on her swollen feet.

Later, they danced with two lads from Burnley who were on a stag do, but it all went wrong when one of them started feeling Wendy's arse and she threw her drink over him. They disappeared through a fire escape before the bouncer could grab hold of them and ended up in a ginnel full of people fighting and spewing. Bobby glanced at Wendy's white face, hair stuck to her forehead with sweat, mouth and lips stained blue.

'Shall we get some chips and go back? It's nearly two. I'm starving.'

'Aye, go on then. I'm knackered, to be honest.' They linked arms and staggered like two shipwreck survivors to the mouth of the ginnel.

Next morning, still fully clothed and woken by the relentless screaming of seagulls, they felt like death. Bobby had ripped her dress climbing through the window and there was curry sauce on Wendy's candlewick bedspread. She moaned softly as she turned over, massaging her forehead and focused on the fluorescent orange stain.

'That'll never come out. Fucking hell, I feel like shit.'

Bobby was up. Dressed in just her knickers and bra, she was trying to scrub her makeup off in a small cracked handbasin basin using the wet corner of a towel and a desiccated, ancient shard of soap. The floor was littered with shoes, crushed newspaper, and the remnants of the chips they had brought back.

'We might feel better after we have a brew and something to eat,' whispered Wendy. Her feet were sticking out of the end of the bed, soles filthy, heels blistered red raw.

'Well, I couldn't feel worse.' Bobby gave up trying to scrub the Blue Bols stain off her lips and turned to Wendy, who was upright now, rubbing her head.

What time did we get back?' she croaked, voice hoarse from singing and smoking.

'No idea, but it was light. Three-ish? I was surprised we found that chip van.'

They dragged some clothes on and wandered down to the dining room at the front of the house. It was full of silent, hungover faces. The pair sat down at a table by the window. A small, pinched looking ancient Irishwoman in a flowery tabard came over with two teacups and a stainless-steel teapot that leaked when Wendy tried to fill their cups with a trembling hand. The girls didn't get the opportunity to order anything and the woman disappeared, then reappeared shortly with two plates, each containing a slice of toast, an incinerated sausage, one slice of flabby bacon, and what appeared to be a folded over beige flannel but was in fact scrambled egg.

Wendy picked the scab off the top of a plastic tomato and squirted ketchup over her plate. Bobby made a soft groaning sound.

'I don't think I can do this, Wend,' she whispered.

'Course you can, don't be mard. Get it down you, you'll be fine,' she said briskly.

Bobby sipped her tea and closed her eyes. 'I think I'll just have a brew and a fag.'

Wendy speared the sausage with her fork and pointed it at Bobby, bloodshot eyes dancing. 'You'll need more than that, chuck, cos we're doing it all over again tonight!' Then shoved the lot in her mouth in one go.

Chapter 13
1964

Stella had started work at Earnshaws aged sixteen and had been immediately pursued by most of the lads working there. She had gone out with a few of them, but didn't take any of it seriously, thinking she could do better and held out for someone with money. She was keeping herself single for one of the mill managers or the textile reps from Manchester or Leicester in their posh cars and nice suits. Stella didn't want a knitter or a weaver wearing a cloth cap covered in lint. She relished the power she had over men — it was the only power Stella had. After spending her childhood as Alice Armstrong's bastard, now the tables had turned.

Away from Flint Cottage and the muck and repetition of rural life, Stella enjoyed the factory environment. She started off as a dogsbody, like most of the school leavers. And over the years, worked in different departments of the mill: on the factory floor (moved as she was too much of a distraction to the men), the sewing room (moved as she was hopeless with a machine), the lab (removed because she was slapdash and lazy and bored with the precision required of the job). Stella now worked part in accounts and in the cavernous warehouse, checking off the rolls of fabric.

One wintry day in January, a buyer came in from a prestigious department store in Nottingham. There was a kerfuffle in the factory before his visit; everywhere tidied to ensure a good impression. He was to have coffee and cake in the manager's office instead of stewed tea and a dry Eccles cake in the canteen like every other visitor. The buyer wanted some sample dresses made up from Earnshaws jersey to place a big order that would be worth thousands.

Wearer trials were common practice in the rag trade, and the girls in the office usually wore the samples for a few days, washed them at home, and reported back on any problems. The dresses would then be examined in the lab, and the fabric analysed for shrinkage or stretching, pilling or sagging.

The girls in the sewing room made up the sample dresses and they were distributed amongst a handful of women in the mill. Wearer trials always caused a great deal of excitement if the outfit was fashionable. This one was a straight, shift dress in a burnt orange colour — a popular style at the time with older women.

There was a lot of chatter as the finished sample dresses were shoved into bags in the clocking off queue. The big shot from Nottingham disappeared for a few days before returning to check out the fabric. People were told to put on clean overalls and the junior members of staff were warned to be on their best behaviour. This could be a big day for the mill if he liked the way the dresses looked.

That rainy morning, the girls were made to walk up and down the factory floor between the offices and the lines of the knitting machines to the familiar whistling and catcalling from the lads. The noise from the machines was tremendous, and none of the girls could hear what the buyer was saying to Gibson, the factory manager — they could just see their mouths moving. Mr Nottingham was standing with his arms folded, tall, elegant and slightly built, skin clean and pinkish.

Gibson was short, thickset, and balding. His navy overalls covered in cotton fluff, under the pale light filtering through the skylights, he looked as though he was going mouldy. Eager to make a good impression, Gibson ushered the girls to one side of the office wall, glaring at them as if they were an unruly flock of hens.

Mr Nottingham had them all line up like a police identity parade as he looked at each dress. The women were chuckling and elbowing each other as he studied the fit of the dresses and asked them to turn around. Jean Kenny, Stella's friend, rolled her eyes and made an exaggerated arse waggle as she took her place in the lineup. Gibson reprimanded her sharply, looking exasperated. The buyer remained expressionless, making notes on a pad with an expensive-looking pen.

They were a motley crew, and even though the machinists had made the dresses in different sizes, they weren't especially flattering. Jean was a big girl, and hers stretched across her breasts and backside. Stella's was a bit too big, but the colour and the length suited her, and she strode arrogantly up and down the factory floor with a bored, blank expression, as though she was walking for Dior.

On closer inspection by the girls, it was generally agreed that Mr Nottingham was a good-looking bloke. Expensively dressed in a navy-blue wool suit and a dark red silk tie, shiny leather shoes, and fashionably cut light brown hair, worn longer than the local lads. He stood out like a sore thumb in the mill. Everyone else was in dusty overalls, hair covered in caps, and feet shod in thick soled work boots. He stopped in front of Stella who, unlike the other women, didn't look at her feet. She looked him right in the eyes with an insolent expression. She hated the wearer trials and felt like a cow at the mart, being herded up and down for inspection.

'How does the dress feel? Is it comfortable? How did it wash?' He had a pleasant voice, a soft Midlands accent, when he said how it sounded like aah.

'Fine.' She shrugged and carried on staring. She could see Gibson out of the corner of her eye, looking flustered and annoyed at her rudeness. He shifted irritably on the spot, moving a clipboard from his hands to under one arm, about to intervene.

The buyer took the sleeve between his fingertips and rubbed the fabric. Stella could see the skin on his hands was office-soft and he smelt clean, like lemons. She put her head on one side.

'Not the sort of thing I'd normally wear.' She crossed her arms and rocked back on her heels, head back.

He smiled up at her with his good teeth. 'What would you normally wear?' He was gently mocking her.

She looked straight at him. 'Something more up to date, shorter,' she snapped.

'This'll cost twenty pounds if we decide to have it made, so I doubt you could afford it, anyway.' He smiled again, showing the excellent teeth.

Gibson brayed a too loud, relived laugh. He was glad it wasn't just him trying to put this bunch of bloody troublesome women in their place. Stella could feel her cheeks burning. *Arrogant prick*, she thought. Mr Nottingham walked off with Gibson, and they all went reluctantly back to work, the excitement over.

Later on in the afternoon, Gibson took Stella aside and bollocked her for being unfriendly and rude. Stella didn't give a shit, but kept her trap shut, nodding in the right places. She didn't want to lose her job over a frock. Mr Nottingham came back two weeks later and placed an order. Stella saw the paperwork when it came through. There was a great deal of excitement in the factory, as this meant overtime and bonuses for the lads.

When Stella clocked off that night, she was one of the last to leave. She had made a mess of a despatch note and had to add everything up again, then have it checked by the manager before she went home. The accounts office was a modern building, built in the 1950s as an add on to the 18th century main mill building and chimney. When the factory was empty and the machines had been put to bed for the night, Stella found the mill creepy, like a sleeping beast. She walked across the yard past the clocking machine, punching her card and slotting it by her name on the wall rack. She strode across the yard, past the wagons parked neatly in a row, all wearing the maroon and cream Earnshaws livery.

Mr Nottingham was sitting in the visitor's car park in his shiny Rover as she made for the main gate. Stella was still pissed off about his remark, and passed his car, staring straight ahead. Aware of her laddered tights and crappy raincoat, she knotted her headscarf tighter under her chin and pretended to look in her handbag for her cigs. The car door opened, and he got out, smiling.

'I hope I didn't get you into trouble.'

She shrugged. 'Wouldn't be the first time.' She lifted her chin and stared at him blankly.

'Can I give you a lift?' he offered, tilting his head towards the car.

Stella perked up. It would be one in the eye for the net twitchers in town if she drove past in this nice shiny car. 'Aye, go on then,' she conceded, as though doing him a favour. She felt a lurch of excitement in the pit of her stomach as she folded her long legs into the Rover. He looked at her with a small smile and started the engine.

They didn't go home just yet, though. Vincent, (Mr Nottingham's real name) was a bit of a smooth operator, and Stella was soon ensconced with a glass of sherry in the lounge bar of the Pole Star, the only pub in town that served food. When he dropped her home that night up at Flint Cottage, Alice watched her with wary interest.

'That was a nice motor that just dropped you off.' She tilted her head at the window as the car left.

'Yes, just a friend. A man I met at work.' Stella's tone and face were neutral.

Alice said nothing. She couldn't understand Stella's obsession with getting a man, and a man with money at that. There had been plenty of lads calling for her over the years. Nice, hardworking men, but none of them were ever good enough. She was never satisfied.

Jean didn't say anything when Stella told her she had been out with the buyer to the Pole Star the next day during their morning break. They were sitting in a corner of the canteen, watching the rain pouring down, turning the red brick of the mill a dark orange.

'Probably wants to get in your knickers, but there you go,' she observed, offering Stella a cigarette.

Stella shrugged. 'He looks like he's got a few quid and has a lovely car.' She put a lit match to her fag, inhaling deeply.

Jean smiled, scratching her head with a teaspoon. 'Stella, that's all you bloody think about.' She coughed, a wet, ratchety sound, and flicked ash into a small tin ashtray, slurping at her tea.

Stella jerked her head at the group of sweaty, scruffy lads at the end of the long Formica table. They were smoking and laughing loudly at a dirty joke one of them had made. They had their papers out on the table; someone was doing the crossword, others looking at the racing page.

'I can do better than that lot. They think I'm a stuck-up bitch, anyroad.'

'I can't think why,' sighed Jean, grinding out her fag and hauling herself to her feet. 'Come on, better get back or Gibson'll be whinging.' She gave Stella a little shove, and the lads nudged each other as she strutted past, tits out, nose in the air.

It was all a novelty to Stella and she thought she was on to a winner. *If I play my cards right*, she daydreamed, she would be married to a textile executive, live in a nice house and be able to give up work. She might learn how to play tennis or ride a horse and holiday abroad. She had visions of a long, sunlit lawn sloping gently down from a beautiful Victorian villa surrounded by rhododendrons and a gravel drive.

It wasn't going to happen, though. Vincent had a blonde, tennis playing, horse riding, sherry-drinking wife at home who was one of the director's daughters.

Vincent courted Stella ruthlessly and methodically. She never knew when he was going to turn up to collect her for a night out; always from home, never from work since their first meeting. They went to lovely pubs and even a Chinese restaurant in Manchester. He gave her a beautiful wool coat and some high heels that were made of such soft leather, Stella didn't even know she was wearing them.

She knew it was getting serious when he asked her to go away with him for the weekend to a hotel in London. This was it; he was going to propose. She spent two weeks' wages on new underwear and a scratchy nylon transparent nightie. He gave her a small red leather case for her things to go in. Stepping out of the car in the West End, she felt like Elizabeth Taylor — her dark hair coiled under a smart felt hat and her handbag in the crook of her arm, she thought she would burst with excitement.

He didn't propose, but there were more weekends away, more gifts. Stella badgered him to see his house in Nottingham, but there were always excuses. Sometimes she didn't see him for a couple of weeks, and often he didn't phone up when he said he would. They went to the races at Haydock Park, the theatre in Manchester, and afternoon tea at Betty's in York. Travelling first class on the train and Stella always receiving gifts.

Alice told her to be careful, and Stella rolled her eyes. Alice had never met this man, only glimpsed him from the window of Flint Cottage. It didn't sit right with her that he didn't want to come in and say hello. It was bad manners. Jean was quiet, sceptical, and missing her friend. Stella dropped her when she started going out with this bloke. She noticed the nice new things: the wristwatch and the coat, good stockings and a scarf. She envied Stella, but something wasn't quite right.

In April, Stella realised she was pregnant. It was a shock, but she hoped this would be the incentive for Vincent to marry her. She would have her prize. Stella sat in the toilets at Earnshaws, locked in a cubicle, looking at her slim, brown outstretched hands, and imagined what her engagement ring would look like. A nice fat solitaire glinting on her slender finger, catching the light.

She smiled as she imagined the jealous faces of the women in the office who called her a stuck-up bitch behind her back. Imagined their fury as she walked into the office and showed them the ring and said she wouldn't be back. She was marrying Vincent and wouldn't be coming to work anymore. She couldn't wait to tell him; he would be so excited. She shuddered with the anticipation of the life that was waiting for her.

He had been clever; she didn't have his phone number, or his address. She only knew the company he worked for, and his name. After not hearing from Vincent for a couple of weeks, Stella casually mentioned to the accountant that she hadn't seen him around the factory for a while. Looking from side to side to check nobody was within earshot, he muttered quickly out of the corner of his mouth.

'I heard he's left the place he was working. Don't tell anyone, but there was a big scandal there. He had been carrying on with one of the director's wives and it all came out. He's disappeared.' He shook his head slowly and theatrically 'I knew he was a wrong 'un when I first clapped eyes on him. Apparently, he owes them a lot of money as well. He had his hand in the till.' He opened his eyes wide to emphasise the severity of the crime and repositioned the stack of invoices he was carrying to rest across his chest.

The dinnertime hooter went, and he nodded quickly at Stella to indicate the conversation was closed, walking past her briskly. Leaving her standing in the middle of the corridor, shock and panic rising. Stella felt sick. The blood rushed to her ears, the noise like a shell held to her head at the seaside. For a moment, her legs felt boneless, weak. A weight of utter panic and disbelief settled itself on her chest like a stone. She had been a complete fool and was now in exactly the same position her mum had once been in. She had ended up, by her own arrogance, in the situation she had most wanted to avoid. All that want and greed. For a few seconds, she felt breathless and on the edge of passing out.

What a stupid, bloody idiot she had been.

Slowly, she walked back out onto the shop floor to give herself some breathing space, oblivious to the whistles and remarks as she sleepwalked past the machines. Everyone was rushing towards her to go for their break. She opened the filing cabinet, which stored the sample folders, and pretended to look in it, face burning and heart racing. She thought about her beautiful clothes and shoes, the hats and weekends away, the food and drink and all the rest of it. All probably paid for with stolen money. And now she was up the stick.

One lad who had once asked her out walked past and ignored her, and she felt like crying. He had an open, earnest face, covered in sweat and lint. She remembered making fun of him at the time and laughing at his hurt and embarrassed expression when he turned away from her, humiliated.

She thought of the stream of hard working, honest lads who she'd dismissed without a backward glance after their clumsy attempts to court her. They wouldn't touch her with a bargepole now. Feeling her temperature rise, her stomach heaved. Slamming the filing cabinet shut, she ran across the shop floor and into the toilets. Stella stayed in the cubicle for a long time, smoothing her hand over her flat belly, wondering how long it would be before everyone knew her business and started talking. Before they started saying like mother, like daughter.

One thing Stella wasn't was a mardarse. She didn't tell anyone for a couple of weeks because she hoped Vincent would contact her and it would all be a mistake, a vicious rumour. But he didn't turn up, and she realised she hadn't really believed he would.

'When summat is too good to be true, it usually is,' Alice used to say.

Jean was unsympathetic, but practical. 'I thought he was a smarmy shit. Flash as a rat with a gold tooth.' She exhaled two jets of smoke from her nostrils, shaking her head; a bleached blonde dragon in a nylon tabard.

Jean leant across the table, scanning the room for eavesdroppers. Stella could see the open pores on her cheeks, lipstick congealed on her mouth as she hissed,

'Are you going to get rid of it? How far on are you? I know someone in Jacquard Street who might be able to sort you out, but you haven't heard her name from me.'

Stella shook her head. 'No, I'll have the kid. It's my fault. I should have known better, really.' She exhaled, sitting up straight in her chair, hands folded in her lap. Maybe if she carried on speaking with confidence, everything would be fine.

Jean shrugged and ground out her cigarette, picking up her mug of tea. She could never work Stella out. But one thing she knew; she was as hard as nails if she set her mind to something.

Alice wasn't surprised when she found out the news. She pitied Stella in her situation, but she had been a silly, vain, and greedy young woman. Now she had a nipper on the way. She would just have to get on with it, as she had done.

Chapter 14
1967

Because Ray had washed up in town as a stranger, he could reinvent himself and his past. He'd chosen to bullshit Stella and the kids, and anyone who cared to listen. No one knew what he had been up to before he rolled up, and nobody much cared. People soon saw him for what he was; a big, handsome gobshite who drove wagons, beat women, and drank too much. He turned up in town one day in the late 1960s looking for work. He'd been sacked from the last place; a haulage yard in Manchester. He'd got greedy, creaming off a few too many loads of timber and selling them on. Some arsehole had grassed him up. It was time to look further afield.

Cleanly shaven and in his best suit, polished shoes, and newly cut hair, he cut an impressive figure — lean with glossy gold hair and pale blue eyes. He didn't mention a wife and kids he'd left behind, though. They were the last thing on his mind when he parked up his car and looked for the nearest pub. Thirsty and wanting to get a feel for the place, he dropped into the first pub he saw, the Carders; a typical mill town boozer. He glanced around. There were a few couples in the lounge.

With filthy windows and an ancient crone behind the pumps, there wasn't much promise.

Then he spotted a cracking bird sitting on a high stool at the bar with long black hair; beehived at the front and rolling down her back in inky-blue curls. Her legs crossed and her white Go-Go boots shining, pale pink lips like pillows. She was wearing a purple and green paisley minidress and looked completely out of place amongst the flat capped and head-scarved mill workers. Ray slid through the rest of the punters and stood at the bar next to her, pretending he hadn't seen her, smoothing his hair down and standing tall.

He ordered a pint of bitter and looked sideways at Stella, handing over a crisp new banknote to the ancient barmaid. It curled upwards like a pale leaf between his index and middle finger. He could see the bird looking at him with open admiration. Ray had been handsome then, before the booze and fags had got to him. Glancing at her briefly, he noticed her huge brown eyes — so dark, he couldn't see the pupils under the spidery false lashes. Her olive skin was faintly pink on her high cheekbones. She smiled at Ray and turned back to her Babycham.

He took a packet of cigarettes out of his jacket and offered her one, smiling. She accepted it, lowering the fringes of her lashes as she thanked him. Ray moved in with the lighter and suggested they sit somewhere else to talk. He flicked his head at a corner table and Stella slid off her stool obediently. Grinning to himself, he followed her. He was in.

The evening Ray walked into the Carders, Stella was waiting for her best mates, Jean and Lynne to get the train into Manchester for a night out. Alice had the kids, and they would go drinking and dancing at the Twisted Wheel or the Ritz, then some soft lad would drive them back home again in the small hours on a promise that wouldn't be kept. The girls turned up full of booze and laughter, and Stella sent them away. Jean and Lynne wandered off to get the train without argument, wondering how long this bloke would last.

Stella was never short of casual boyfriends. As she grew to her late teens, she changed status from being Alice Armstrong's 'half-caste bastard' to a glamorous object of admiration and desire amongst the men in town, provoking suspicion and envy amongst the women. Settling herself on the stool, Stella gazed at Ray through the thick false eyelashes, quickly making an assessment. Older than her, by a good stretch, but that didn't matter, not if he was handsome and tilled up. She scanned his broad shoulders and thick hair, good suit, and cleanly shaven chin.

Ray was performing the same appraisal. He glanced quickly at her left hand out of habit and saw with a little stab of satisfaction and surprise that the third finger was naked. He was amazed this little diamond in a shit heap was single. His eye roamed over her body. The skirt ridden up high on her thighs, the length of slim long legs in fishnet tights. She was completely aware of him sizing her up and sat up taller, pushing out her chest. Dragging on her fag theatrically with what she hoped was an elegant air of nonchalance, Babycham glass in the other hand, held out in her fingertips by the stem.

Silly cow, he thought, grinning. *This is going to be easier than I thought.* 'Do you want another one of those?' He drained his pint and pointed at the daft glass saucer with the picture of the fawn dancing on the rim.

Stella gave another bat of the eyelashes and tilted her shoulder towards him, smiling. 'That would be lovely, thank you.' She put on a pretend little girl's soft voice and smoothed the dress down over her hips.

Ray nodded and got up wordlessly to walk to the bar, slowly, so she could assess his height, broad shoulders, and swagger. Ray was in his forties when he courted Stella, and she was in her twenties. The kids were toddlers and she was struggling. While she worked, the twins were looked after partially by Alice, and whoever else was free. Stella had moved away from the cottage and down into the town to a house on the estate, and there she stayed, aloof and proud. The kids were passed around her female neighbours between shifts, living on jam butties and lukewarm tea, grudgingly cared for by a battalion of well-meaning unpaid mill women.

Alice's parents, James and Rose, were dead, and Alice had inherited Flint Cottage. She had given up mill work as soon as she was able, taken over the small holding and scraped a living with the sheep, glad to be away from town. An unconventional grandma, she let Davey and Bobby run wild when they visited. As they got older, they roamed the fells with her, learning about plants, animals, and the wild moors. They soon learnt which birds nested on the ground and which in the trees or barns, their calls and songs.

They helped deliver lambs, mended walls, collected eggs and foraged the hedgerows — listening carefully as Alice taught them what they could eat and what would give them a bellyache at best, or kill them at worst. She had tried to bring Stella up this way, the life she loved, but had failed to interest her in folk medicine, animal husbandry, astronomy, and wildlife. But Bobby and Davey adored Alice and were proud of her eccentricities and endlessly curious nature.

Ray had grown up in poverty in Manchester, the youngest of a big family. He rarely went to school and was stealing food almost as soon as he could walk. He lived off his wits and was well known to the police by the time he was a young teenager. Sometimes he picked up work labouring, but always seemed to end up fighting, stealing, and moving on. He had spent most of the war in and out of military prisons, mainly locked up for thieving and fighting. He had been safe and far away from the enemy. The most action he had witnessed was mopping floors and sorting mail.

Once the war ended, he absorbed himself into the mass of demobbed young men and women trying to pick up life where they had left it in 1939. He never admitted this to anyone, and became skilled at dodging difficult questions, inventing stories at a moment's notice. He could have just been vague about his time during the war, but he craved approval and as time went on, the stories and his invented past became more and more elaborate and complex.

Ray quickly realised opportunities and sympathy were more freely available if people thought he'd experienced conflict and suffering. His greatest weakness was his vanity. The most commonplace conversations after the war amongst men were questions on where he served and with which regiment. To save the embarrassment, he started making up small white lies that then grew into bigger lies. He could have kept it simple, said he was a miner or a farmer in a protected industry, but he liked the admiration of the women, and the camaraderie of the men with a shared experience.

Once he came to court Stella, he had honed his alter ego of the war hero. He had shyly admitted to seeing active service, but not in too much detail. He would start a story, dropping the name of a country or battle, speaking softly and hesitantly, looking into the distance, or down into his glass. Stella would go all misty eyed and speak sympathetically. He soon had her hooked.

Over time, he had extended his resume, changing regiments regularly and magically appearing to fight in different conflicts simultaneously, in different countries at exactly the same time. He had fought as a one of Monty's desert rats in El Alamein, rescuing comrades from a burning tank under heavy shelling from Rommel's troops. In the steaming, fetid jungles of Burma and Malaysia, he had outwitted the Japanese, sweating in his concealed foxhole, avenging his dying comrades with fearless charges through the dripping jungle.

Stella listened open-mouthed while he described in terrifying detail the night he had parachuted into a sunbaked, parched Sicily as part of Operation Husky. Blown hopelessly off course and fighting for survival, almost dying of thirst in the mountains.

When he'd exhausted that story, he talked of his exploits in mainland Italy. He had dug into the freezing mud and rain of an Italian hillside, waiting to take the rubble that had once been the abbey of Monte Cassino. Ray found time to fight in India in the Battle of Kohima. He had taken part in the brutal struggle for control over the Kohima-Imphal Road. He vividly described to Stella the hell of the hand-to-hand fighting on the flank of Garrison Hill. His voice trembled as he described the monsoon breaking as he and his fellow soldiers brought out the wounded under cover of darkness.

Composing himself, he would talk of the withering gunfire, of recapturing the district commissioner's bungalow in the Battle of the Tennis Court. He recalled his terrible thirst as drinking water ran low, the brutality of the Japanese and the heroism of the Indian and British troops. A vivid and accurate picture, but he simply hadn't been there. He would pause sometimes, taking a deep breath, looking at Stella with a barely controlled quiver in his voice. She would stretch out a sympathetic hand and stroke his arm, comforting him, murmuring softly.

D-Day saw him struggling ashore on Sword Beach with his comrades, dodging the German defenders on the clifftops. He'd been particularly busy during this time, capturing Pegasus Bridge, fighting hand-to-hand in the villages of Normandy. Hiding in the bocage with his comrades, ambushing hapless German soldiers as he single-handedly led the allied advance into France, he described a vision of hell to an open-mouthed Stella.

He was careful who he bragged to, mind. There were still old people in town who had seen both world wars. Old men from the First World War with an empty jacket sleeve pinned up where an arm should be or on crutches, the result of a badly mended leg, set hurriedly under lamplight in a field hospital. It was these men who often said nothing. They wore their scars inside and out without gobbing off about it.

Once or twice, Ray had come unstuck when he was pissed and telling his tall tales. Geoff Wickham, a fellow wagon driver, had quizzed him one night about his exploits in North Africa and Ray had to do some serious backpedalling when he found out the missing fingers on Geoff's right hand had resulted from a genuine firefight in the desert. Geoff started asking Ray where he'd been during the war, genuinely wanting to reminisce, and Ray was forced to bluster and cut the conversation short.

Within a few weeks of their meeting, Ray was living with Stella and the kids in her little house on the estate. He got a job driving wagons and was a hard worker. Initially, he treated Stella like a princess, new clothes, a new hoover, no worrying about coins for the gas and electric. He pretended to like the kids as well, buying them a few cheap toys and listening to Stella rattle on about how beautiful they were and how clever they would be when they got to school.

It didn't last long, though. Ray loved a drink, and so did Stella. Ray had a vicious temper on him, and Stella was volatile and easy to wind up. He loathed the kids; some other bloke's little bastards. He hated the way they looked up at him warily with their giant, suspicious sloe-like black eyes.

Within six months, he had his feet properly under the table, and Stella was on a tight leash. No more dancing in Manchester or weekends in Blackpool with her mates. He stopped pretending to like the children. The fake smiles dissolved into blank stares and indifference. He liked his women where he could monitor them.

Ray expected a clean house and a cooked dinner on the table. He was doing her a favour, after all. She needed to do as she was told and be grateful. Slowly, without realising, her energy and confidence dissipated as Ray began to assert complete control.

He didn't keep an eye on his wife, though. He had left her in Stockport a year ago with two broken ribs and three kids under five. He didn't mention that to Stella. She didn't need to know, and what she didn't know wouldn't hurt her.

Within a year, they were locked into a pattern of drinking and fighting. Stella was kept to a strict timetable. Work, then straight home, tea on the table when he came in, then he would start the boozing. She was expected to sit there, keep her trap shut, and look pretty. He didn't always go to the pub. He liked to drink at home in front of the telly where he could monitor that carping bitch.

Ray didn't want to leave, though. He was living rent free with the best-looking woman in town. All he had to do was give her a bit of money and attention now and then. And if she got mouthy, or looked like she might want to get shut of him, he would give her a good belting and get her to see sense. He was the man; he was the boss. Ray had a simple philosophy where women were concerned: *Behave yourself, love and everything will be fine. Cross me, and you won't know you're born.*

Chapter 15
July 1982

Matt pulled a face and curled his lip when Bobby said she was going to a Kenny family wedding. They were sitting on a park bench in the late afternoon sunshine. Bobby had her bag balanced on her knees. She was on her way home from school and only had a week to go before the end of term. Matt had now officially left sixth form. His exams had been taken and he was waiting for the results, which he was confident would take him off to university.

'Why would you want to go to something like that? They're all trash.' His voice was slow, scornful, mock-amused.

Bobby felt intensely irritated and focused on a small patch of eczema under his eye. It was pointless defending the Kennys. Everyone had the same opinion except the Armstrongs, and a few other families who moved in the same social and economic orbit.

'She's my friend and it's her cousin's wedding.' She spoke slowly and deliberately, annoyed at even having to explain. 'She's asked me. I'm her best friend.' She held her hands, palms up, in a shrugging gesture. Her voice sounded tired even to herself.

She readjusted her bag as it tried to slide off her knees. Hugging the books to her chest and resting her chin on the top, she stared straight ahead at two kids on bikes, pulling wheelies across the bowling green, and making gouges in the velvety turf.

'Yeah, but they're not real friends, though, are they? They're cronies,' he pursued, voice exasperated, patient, as though he was speaking to a child.

Bobby had a habit of this; questioning him, pushing her luck, asserting herself. He pushed his hair out of his eyes and started drumming his fingers on the warm surface of the wooden bench. It crossed Bobby's mind that she never saw Matt with many friends, or *cronies*, whatever the difference was in his head. The only people she saw him with were the smartarses he was at school with. The ones who came into the café, but that was it.

Bobby thought it better not to say that, instantly reflecting that she did that a lot with Matt — thought about what she should or shouldn't say depending on what she his reaction would be. She shouldn't have to explain. She could go anywhere, with whoever she wanted, whenever she wanted. Couldn't she?

'Who else is going?'

'Dunno.' Bobby shrugged. 'Me, Wendy, Mum, Lynne, Peggy, far as I know. There will be others though, family.'

He made one of his sniffing head jerks and smiled derisively, looking even more disapproving. Bobby looked straight ahead, staring at the kids again. They were being chased off by the parky now. She made a movement to get up, hitching the bag onto her shoulder.

'You don't want to be going to something like that. I'll take you out somewhere nice instead,' he wheedled, in the special singsong voice he used when he wanted her to do something.

Bobby wasn't like other girls he knocked about with. She wasn't as easy to control or bribe. Sometimes he could feel a rage rising in his body that made him long to slap her or grab her by the throat.

Now that they were supposed to be boyfriend and girlfriend, they didn't go anywhere nice, not really. Not like when they had first met. Matt's plans could change at the drop of a hat and there were times she was waiting on the corner of Ribbon Street, or outside work, and he was late with a half-formed excuse or didn't turn up at all. Wendy told her she was a mug and he was using her. Bobby knew it was true. But with all the shit that was going on at home with Mum and Ray, he was a distraction. She would deal with the Matt issue after school finished for the holidays at the end of July.

Bobby rose, flicked her hair back, and stared at him with blank, black eyes. 'But I'm going to the wedding, and that's all there is to it.' She walked away quickly without turning around.

The wedding was a weekday registry office do because it was cheaper. The reception afterwards was to be held in the Pennine Social Club's function room, a desperate-looking place on the edge of the estate with fag-burned Formica tables and metal bars over the windows. It was a cool day for high summer. A fresh breeze blew up Broad Street while the wedding guests stood outside waiting for the bride. The groom was there already; a fat lad with a greasy red hungover face, looking like a sea lion stuck in a shiny Burton's suit. He was nervously chain smoking and simultaneously polishing his plastic shoes on the back of his trousers.

The best man was a rake thin lad in a blazer and slacks that looked borrowed and slept in. A crushed pink carnation clung on to his button hole. He had two missing front teeth and tiny red raw eyes, like a rat with conjunctivitis. He was wringing his hands nervously, smiling, and nodding as the small group of guests huddled together on the cobbles.

A white Triumph Herald swung round the corner from the Co-op and pulled up outside the registry office to a thin cheer. An elderly man clambered out and walked around to open the rear door and help the bride-to-be and her father out of the car. She was heavily pregnant, in a shiny, clinging white dress with giant puff sleeves. White fishnet tights clung to her thick, shapeless legs like caul on sausages. A pink plastic handbag on a chain was slung over one arm and in the other she held a small bouquet of salmon-coloured carnations and twenty Bensons. A livid yellow love bite was visible on her throat. She wore a small white pillbox hat at an angle; the net pulled over one eye, well crammed down on a crispy permed yellow frizz. Her face, a mask of orange foundation, eyes ringed in electric blue eyeshadow, and mascara. A thin slit of a mouth, painted frosted coral.

'Ah, gorgeous,' said a woman next to Stella. 'She looks like Princess Diana in that hat.'

'Not as long as I've got a hole in me arse,' muttered Jean, dragging on a ciggie and rooting in her bag for a miniature Johnny Walker.

Lynne let out a cracked bray of laughter. She was still applying makeup with a shaking hand and a small mirror. She had been on the hen do last night and wasn't feeling too clever. Stella, on a rare trip away from Ray, was already sweating in a fake fur jacket, Jackie Kennedy hat, and sunglasses, looking like a Mafia wife. Jean frowned at the sunglasses and realised she must have a black eye. The fur coat was odd for July, but that was Stella for you.

Wendy, as always, made everyone else look scruffy. She looked like a slim copper beech in a green dress and gold dangly earrings that caught the sun when she turned her head. Midge was at school and said she might come to the reception, but Wendy knew she wouldn't. Peggy was looking smart in a navy-blue old lady suit with gold-coloured buttons and her dead cat hat, smelling of Charlie perfume and setting lotion. She was muttering something about them being heathens as it was a registry office do.

The bride-to-be stumped over to Jean, Stella, and Lynne on her spindly stilettoes, dragging on her fag and rubbing her swollen belly.

'Ey up, girls, did you enjoy last night?'

'I'm feeling rough, to be honest,' rasped Lynne, unwrapping a stick of chuddy and slotting it into her mouth. She was wearing an imitation leather PVC dress that hung off her scrawny frame like a crow trapped in a bin bag.

'Aye, me an' all. They should never have gone along the optics with that pint pot. I think that's what finished me. The baby's been kicking all morning.'

Probably got a raging hangover, the poor little bastard, thought Bobby. She peeled the cellophane off a new packet of fags, shaking her hand to free it from the clinging static. A harassed-looking clerk wearing a frilly blouse came out with a clipboard and told them it was time to come in. She needed to move things along. This was the last wedding of the day.

Everyone took a last drag on their fags, chucked them into the road, and trooped dutifully into the building — an ugly 1960s structure with the dole office on one side and the driving test centre on the other. It didn't take long. Within half an hour, the newly wed Kennys came out into the road and were pelted with confetti. Photos were taken, including one for the local paper, and they all walked up to the club in the late afternoon sunshine.

The club steward saw the procession coming up the street and unlocked the function room doors with a flourish. A smell of old carpet, stale beer, fags, and bleach wafted out. He propped the door open with an empty Double Diamond barrel as the guests swarmed in. The room had been decorated with balloons and streamers. A sagging *Just Married* banner hung limply above the stage where the DJ was untangling a nest of cables. At right angles to the bar were two trestle tables covered in a white sheet, various lumps and bumps underneath suggesting the shape of either a dead body or the evening buffet.

A scrum developed by the bar as everyone queued for their first drink and the music started cranking up. Thin beams of late afternoon sunshine filtered through the dirty, barred club windows, lighting up the clouds of cigarette smoke and dust in the function room. Two little girls in party dresses were the first on the dancefloor, jacked up on pop and Monster Munch, giving it all they had to Buck's Fizz, while the DJ introduced himself with a series of crackly lame jokes about the World Cup and was ignored by everybody.

The evening followed the time-honoured tradition of most Pennine Social Club weddings. The single men and hardened boozers standing up at the bar getting steadily pissed as couples, women, and children danced or sat the small tables near the dancefloor.

The couple were toasted with some warm Lambrusco, the cake was cut, and the bride and groom took to the floor for their first dance, stumbling around awkwardly in a circle to The Commodores 'Three Times a Lady'. Bobby and Wendy danced with each other, giggling at Lynne who was smooching with the rat-eyed best man, his hands roaming absent mindedly over her arse.

At 8 pm, The DJ announced the buffet was open and someone whipped the sheet off the trestle tables like a conjurer. There was a stampede to the food. Piles of butties on white sliced bread already curling at the edges and a skin forming on something grey in a glass dish that looked like meat paste. Lots of stuff on cocktail sticks, impaled on a cabbage wrapped in tinfoil. Bowls of crisps going soft and a Battenburg with a bread knife next to it. A Matterhorn of ham barm cakes shared its own side table with a monster jar of piccalilli.

Bobby queued up with Wendy, her paper plate bending as she loaded it with a big slice of pork pie and a pile of crisps. The DJ was behind them, humming to himself. Wendy giggled and pointed to the buffet table; someone had already put a fag out into half a tomato.

'It's hardly Studio 54, is it?' said the DJ, piling butties onto a plate and jerking his head towards a minor scuffle that was taking place near the bar.

Two teenage lads were being swiftly ejected through the fire door by a skinhead with a tattooed face.

'That's a Gritstone wedding for you,' deadpanned Wendy. 'It's survival of the fittest.' She fixed him with her best terrifying blank stare, mechanically chewing on an Eccles cake.

Nobody spoke as the food was demolished before the next shift on the dancefloor began. Bobby came back from the toilets and sat down at a table. She watched Stella, Lynne, Jean, and Wendy dancing together after their feast. She felt overwhelmed with loneliness. This was the natural order of things in Gritstone. You left school, went to work, met a lad, got married, came here for your reception. You would get a house on the estate or in one of the tiny terraces in town. Then babies would come along and it would all start over again. It was like they were programmed to do the same thing, whether you liked it or not. Like a dog chasing a ball and returning it dutifully to its owner, not really knowing why.

Wendy was dancing like a girl possessed, head thrown back, shimmying in her sparkly green catalogue dress, shrieking with laughter in the middle of a circle of clapping women. Bobby had never felt as bored in her life. What was wrong with her? She didn't want all this, but she didn't know what she wanted.

'Have you not got yourself a nice fella, Bobby?' screamed Peggy over the music, plonking herself down in the seat next to her and shoving her glass onto another table that was swimming with spilt drinks.

'No, not really,' Bobby howled back over 'Tainted Love'. Her throat was sore from the smoke and having to shout to make herself heard. She shuffled her chair nearer to Peggy so she could hear her better.

'It'll be Wendy next. Although she wants all the fun and none of the mither. I was the same at her age. And Jean was the same. She's never cared what folk think, not like your mum. I still carried on going to Mass. You can still be a decent person, you know. You just have to do what's best for you.' Peggy took a sip of her half of bitter and looked at Bobby, whose face looked like she was at a wake, never mind a wedding. She patted Bobby's smooth brown arm with her wrinkled hand and smiled at her. 'You'll be alright, love.'

Bobby smiled and took a sip of her drink. The lager had turned warm and her head was aching. Stella was up dancing now. She looked about twenty; face pink, laughing her head off. Her thick black hair swinging, jiving with the best man who was, for all his physical shortcomings, a great dancer. The DJ was playing a 1960s set and the older people were up.

Peggy jerked her head at the bride and rolled her eyes at Bobby. 'Would you look at the belly on that girl!' They both burst out laughing.

Wendy ran over and dragged Bobby up by her arm. 'Come on, you miserable cow, get up and dance with me!'

It was after twelve when the party spilled out into the street. Wendy was shrieking with laughter and tottering on her heels, spinning Bobby round. Bobby was already dreading getting up for the Minerva tomorrow, but it had been a funny night in the end — a classic Gritstone wedding. It would be worth the bad head in the morning. And her mum had really loved it, dancing with Jean and Lynne. Having a laugh, being whirled around on the dancefloor to all the old records of her youth.

Further down the alley, between the club and the yard where the beer barrels were stored, a man slipped into the darkness of the car park. He had seen enough, watching through the window while that stupid bitch made a fool of herself with that young lad. This was why she shouldn't be let out without him there to supervise. She just couldn't help it. Couldn't control her behaviour. It wouldn't happen again. He was going to have to start laying the law down. She was getting above herself, letting him down — he would be a laughing stock.

He watched the shrieking, dancing women again, and almost blacked out with rage. That skinny young ginger slag of Jean Kenny's was whirling around a lamppost now, making a show of herself. Ray could feel the sovereign rings biting into his palms when he clenched his hands and strode off quickly. He needed to get back before Stella and that gobshite bitch of a daughter of hers got home.

The walk home sobered them up. Wendy was barefoot now, her heels rubbed raw by her shoes. They walked past the closed-up chippy and Stella was getting anxious. She looked at Earnshaws clock as they passed the mill and was horrified at the time.

'You'll not turn into a pumpkin,' mocked Wendy, swinging her shoes and singing at the top of her voice.

No, thought Bobby, *but her face might look like one if Ray's still up and had too much to drink.* He'd agreed to this night out, but he would probably have expected Stella back early, and not pissed. Davey was out for the night, staying at Chris's flat, so there were just the two of them to go back and face Ray. Bobby started to internally berate herself for not keeping track of time, not cajoling her mother out of the club earlier. She sped up, dragging Stella along, stumbling in her heels like an overgrown puppet.

They left Jean, Wendy, and Lynne on the corner of Ribbon Street and walked in silence to their own front door. When Bobby slid the key in the lock and pushed the door open softly, the house was in darkness. Although neither of them said anything, they were both thinking the same thing: *he's gone to bed.* Stella was thinking she could curl up on the couch in her coat and in the morning say that she had got in early and fallen asleep.

Bobby closed the door with a soft click, pushing Stella wordlessly into the front room without turning the light on. Bobby was about to breathe a sigh of relief, but then she saw Ray. Sitting in his chair in his boiler suit, upright, just his outline visible in the light filtering through the nets. Her first instinct was to burst out laughing. He looked ridiculous, like a taller, slimmer version of Alfred Hitchcock.

Stella gave a small, shrill scream, and shouted, 'What the hell are you doing?' Then started giggling.

Bobby felt sick with fear. Stella was plastered, and Ray was absolutely raging. She placed herself quickly in front of her mum, hands up as though she were submitting to a gunman. He didn't bother putting the light on; he didn't need to. He lunged forward and shoved Bobby out of the way, as easily as if she were a child. Ray caught Stella by a handful of her hair and twisted it, her head was forced up at an awkward angle and he pushed his face up close to hers, spit spraying her cheeks.

'I don't know what you're fucking laughing at. You had to make a show of me, didn't you? This is why you can't be trusted. You stupid, stupid bitch.'

His voice was low, controlled, and slow. For a second, Bobby thought that would be it. He would just shout and shake her a bit, and then storm off. But then he slapped Stella quickly, hard across the face, with his other hand still holding her by her hair. And when she flung her hands up to protect her mouth, he punched her in the ribs, pushing her backwards so she fell against the armchair. Then he marched upstairs, slamming the bedroom door.

Bobby spent the night with Stella, drinking tea and passing her cold flannels as she held them to her head and face, screwing her eyes at the pain and trying to smile at her daughter. Sometime towards dawn, she fell asleep. Bobby watched her pale swollen face propped up on the settee arm, the red bruises from Ray's sovereign rings making three large circles on her cheek.

I can't stay here and keep watching this, she thought, then had to push it out of her head. She had lost count of how many times she'd thought that over the years. And now, it just made her angry because Stella wouldn't take any notice. She wouldn't listen. Or she did listen, but was paralysed either with fear or whatever. Bobby couldn't leave her mum looking like that. She phoned the Minerva at six and told a furious Maria that she had a migraine. Bobby hung up as Maria continued to squawk that there were plenty of other kids looking for jobs.

At seven, Ray got up and came downstairs. He walked into the front room to get his keys for the wagon and ignored them both. It was business as usual and he was off to work as though nothing had happened. Davey came back from Chris's to get ready to go to work. Bobby heard the key in the door and he took a moment to register that Bobby was home on a Saturday, which was unusual. Then he saw Stella's face and guessed the rest.

'I'll put the kettle on,' he muttered quietly, and left the room. Bobby could see by the set of his shoulders he felt like her. They were coming to a point now that a decision would have to be made. Something had to happen.

Once, when they were younger, they'd been talking about Ray and what could be done. They'd thought about reporting him to the police. The police had been called many times over the years by neighbours when Ray had been really kicking off and Stella had run into the street screaming at him. But they weren't really interested. They would come in the house, tell Ray and Stella to keep it down and go easy on the booze. The estate was used to it. The police were used to it. Nobody was bothered enough to change anything. It was the Gritstone way.

Davey brought in brews and a plate of burnt buttered toast for everyone and opened a window. Fresh summer air and birdsong flooded the room. He sat in Stella's chair and pushed the mop of black curls out of his eyes, his face expressionless. He looked at them both crouched there together on the settee; Stella with a swollen face, bruises, and a small, bald, raw patch of scalp above her left temple. They reminded him of two injured animals huddled together for protection. Bobby smoothed Stella's hair away from her white clammy face, the way a mother would to a poorly toddler. Stella, deflated, looked up at them both through swollen eyes.

Davey tried to lighten the mood. He nudged Bobby and smiled. 'Hey kid, home on a Saturday! It's like old times. When does the wrestling start?' He crunched on a carbonised piece of toast, wincing as it scratched the roof of his mouth.

Bobby, eyes gritty with lack of sleep and dried on mascara, smiled tiredly and couldn't help chuckling, remembering the wrestling matches in the front room.

One day, Davey had body slammed Big Daddy style on top of her, and one of Stella's ornaments, a little girl holding a lamb, had fallen off the mantlepiece onto the fireplace and her head had come off. Davey had glued it back on, but Stella saw it straight away when she got in from work and went mental. The wrestling reenactments stopped when Davey dislocated Steven Cassidy's shoulder in a Boston Crab and they spent an afternoon and evening in casualty with his mother screeching she would have the police on them.

As young children, they all loved a Saturday when Ray was working. A whole day to themselves to watch telly, dance in the front room, play records and do whatever they wanted without him bullying, mocking, and laying down the law. It felt like a little holiday. How could Stella not see this? How could she not want this? Every day could be like this if she only told him to fuck off. Bobby remembered the countless times they had challenged her over his behaviour. She sat stroking Stella's hair, and they ran like a series of repeated films through her head.

'But he puts food on the table and pays for your things...'

'No. No, he doesn't!' Bobby would interrupt. 'That's not true. You pay for it, and we pay for it. He pays for himself and what he wants, and lives here for free. It's your name on the tenancy, Mum.'

She would dance in front of Stella with frustration; eyes wide, wringing her hands, and pleading for her mother to see reason. She recalled waving her arm in a wild circle, taking in all the crappy, tired furniture. The dent in the plaster where a missile had taken a chunk out of the wall. The cheap ornaments and the nicotine-stained net curtains.

'He lives here for free, like a fucking cockroach or a rat. A parasite who's draining the life out of all of us. Just tell him to fuck off!'

Fear and defensiveness always kicked in with Stella and she would scream at them to shut up and that they were ungrateful and Ray had been like a father to them.

'Yeah, but one day Mum. One day, he's gonna kill you.'

She remembered standing in front of Stella holding her and shaking her by her soft fleshy upper arms, thin fingers digging in, trying to get her to understand. Stella's head wobbling like a puppet, watching the tears run into the eyeliner creases around her eyes.

'Why don't you love us enough to leave him? Why won't you do this for you and us? Why don't you get it?' Her voice would fade, tired of repeating itself uselessly. 'He doesn't love you or he wouldn't do these things to you. He only loves himself. Ray doesn't give a fucking shit about anyone but his own bastard self!'

But Stella would plaster another layer of Constance Carroll foundation over any bruising, open a fresh packet of Silk Cut, and everything would go back to normal for a while.

Stella drifted off to sleep again, and Bobby stood up. Her legs were stiff and she felt grubby, still in last night's party clothes. Her teeth felt furry and her head woolly. She went to put the immersion heater on to run a bath.

Davey followed and caught her arm. 'You okay?' He whispered, 'What happened? Just the usual?'

She rubbed her face, smearing the rest of the eye makeup and pinched the bridge of her nose. 'Yeah. We were at the reception up at the club and were late back, I suppose. Arsehole hadn't said when he wanted her back. It was after twelve and when we got home, he was waiting for us, in the dark, the daft twat.' She stared blankly up at her brother. 'You know what he's like. Misses nowt. He's got eyes like a shithouse rat. Anyway, he belted Mum in the face and punched her in the belly then just went to bed and fucked off to work this morning as though nothing had happened.'

Davey looked at her, shaking his head slowly, voice weary, he spoke, 'I know I've said it till I'm blue in the face, but it's got to the point where we have to do summat to stop him.'

Bobby shrugged. 'I don't know what we can do. It's up to her. The coppers aren't interested. What do we do, kill him? *She* has to do it. She has to leave him. He'll never go, it's too cushy here. And if or when we go away to university, or college, or wherever we go to, then there will be nobody to protect her.'

Davey set his mouth in a bitter line. He spread his hands out and then looked down at them and back up at his twin. 'I'm not staying in this shithole after I finish school. I'm sorry, Bob, but I'm out of here and if you have any sense, you'll do the same. This is going to carry on whether we are here or not. You know that, don't you?'

She pushed her hands into the small of her back and leant from side to side, stiff from being awake all night. Catching her lip in her teeth, she spread out her hands and looked at them, thinking of the fortune teller in Blackpool. The daft old crone had said nothing about this being her future.

'Aye. It's just the guilt, I suppose. Of leaving her here with him. But yes, you're right, we can't stay here. We've tried and tried. Grandma would have her in a flash, but no, she's too awkward.' Bobby started to climb the stairs, then turned around, 'If Matt phones or calls, I'm not in.'

Chapter 16
August 1982

Jean grunted, lifting the settee higher. The mottled, crepey skin on her triceps flapped as she hooked her hands under the PVC arms, eyes screwed up against the smoke from the fag clamped between her teeth. Wendy tottered backwards in baby steps, gripping the other end. Baz was circling behind her, excited that the front room furniture was being relocated to the garden.

'Come on, Mum, give it a shove. It came in this way, so it's gonna go out. Get out of the bloody road, Baz!' Wendy shouted over the noise of the twin tub spewing grey water into the kitchen sink.

They tilted the settee sideways and it scraped out of the kitchen, through the back doorway, into the garden.

'Christ, I've got a sweat on.'

Jean put her end down and Wendy swung the settee round to face the sun. Jean flumped down on it and stretched out. The garden was a wilderness of waist high grass, willowherb, and ragwort. Bordering three sides were high, unkempt privet hedges. Hidden in the grass were long-lost toys and balls, a lawnmower that hadn't seen the light of day for decades, and the remains of a motorbike. A flotilla of butterflies danced above the mass of overgrown vegetation.

Midge was sitting on a cushion balanced on an upturned mop bucket, reading from her stash of library books. She had started the *Observers Book of British Butterflies* and a copy of *Jackie,* that Gary had nicked from the paper shop in the precinct rather than fork out the 16p. Midge briefly wondered what *Cathy and Claire* might make of her own personal dilemma. She strongly suspected it wouldn't be printed alongside the usual stories of period pains, acne, and two-faced friends on the problem page in the back of the magazine.

It was a scorching late summer afternoon. The school holidays were in full swing and Wendy and Jean were both ecstatic to be off work for a week. Jean settled on the settee with her fags, lager cooling in a washing-up bowl of water, and a stack of magazines and the paper. She tilted her face to the sun, the dry riverbed of her cleavage exposed above a too-tight vest.

Wendy stripped down to her bra and knickers and flattened a patch of weeds to stretch out on her bath towel with *Smash Hits.* Jean peeled herself off the sweaty vinyl settee again to drag a folding table into position for crisps and more cans of lager. Midge had a bottle of dandelion and burdock, keeping cool in the shade.

Bobby and Stella turned up to return the catalogues, closely followed by Lynne. She was swinging a carrier bag of lager cans, wearing shorts over a swimming costume,

Lolita heart-shaped sunglasses, and a towel draped around her shoulders like a flyweight boxer. The small table was cleared of crisps and lager and the catalogues opened for general perusal. Jean was the local agent for two of them and seemed to spend hours knocking on doors all over the estate, collecting money or organising orders.

'Let me tell you about that dirty bitch, Tracey Henderson.' Jean wrinkled her nose in disgust. 'She returned a top and a dress after a week and said they didn't fit. The top had deodorant in the armpits and stank of perfume, and the dress had a fag burn. Swore blind she hadn't worn them. I'll never be able to return them. Cheeky cow, must think I was born yesterday.' She furiously wriggled in the settee and reached for her fags.

'Who's she?' interjected Wendy, looking up from her magazine, squinting into the sunlight.

'The skinny blonde one who lives above the dry cleaners. Thinks she's the bee's knees. She's got a little dog with a posh name.' Jean clicked her fingers, trying to recall the breed. 'It's a Lapsang Souchong, I think. Summat like that anyroad.'

Midge collapsed into giggles. 'Mum, that's a type of *tea*. You mean a *Lhasa Apso*.'

It was the first time Wendy had seen her laugh in weeks, and she smiled back at her little sister.

'You know what I mean, Miss Know-It-All,' shrugged Jean, and went back to the catalogue.

'What do you think of the yellow boob tube?' she said to nobody in particular.

Lynne flicked through the tissue thin pages with a spit moistened finger, periodically stopping to say, 'That's nice. Ooh, I like that…' until she reached a lime green leopard print dress. 'That's the one, please Jean.'

Jean took out her order pad and a biro and started scribbling. The afternoon wore on and the drink took hold, Jean was getting a bit maudlin. She'd had her hours cut and so had Stella, so this afternoon was something of a work wake.

'So, I went to the Labour Exchange.' Jean inhaled deeply on her fag and then exhaled skywards. She scratched the dry skin on her shins.

'It's called the Job Centre, Mum,' said Midge, without looking up from her book.

'Whatever. So, I went to the *Job Centre* and it's all partitions covered in carpet with little postcards on. Secretarial, clerical, driving, whatever. I looked at them and thought, I can't do any of these fucking jobs. Not one, except delivering the free paper.' She threw her head back; a cackle of sarcastic laughter. 'There were hardly any of them; jobs, I mean. God help us all if they lay more off as there's bugger all work in this town. Unless you are about to leave school. They put kids on a YTS now. They won't count as unemployed, see?'

She took another drag on her fag and shook her head. 'They're asking for *skills*. All I can do is overlocking. The lad, not much older than our Midge, in a suit that was hanging off him, face covered in spots — he said,

"How many O levels do you have, or CSEs?" or whatever. And I said, "I don't know what you're talking about, love. I left school at fifteen. I left on the Friday and started work on the Monday.'"

She shrugged and looked at Stella and Lynne, who nodded assent and murmured, 'Aye, we did.'

'It's a good job Wendy is in work and our Midge has her little job, otherwise we'd be knackered. The family allowance only goes so far. I've got to fill in a form about getting some dole money. Never in this world did I think I'd be relying on a Giro.' She shook her head again.

Midge glanced up at Jean and felt sick. Did this mean her mum expected her to stay working in the shop? Was she relying on the money? She put her head back down to her book again, reading without seeing the words.

Wendy rolled over to toast her front. 'Summat will come up, Mum. Don't worry. It's not like none of us knew this was coming. They've been talking about cheap imports for ages.' She peeled the bra straps off her shoulders so she wouldn't get tan lines.

Jean shrugged and opened another can. The weather was too nice to get upset; what would be would be. She had just had a postcard from her older sister, Carol. She'd emigrated to Canada years ago and was planning a visit back to Gritstone next year. That would be something to look forward to. She passed the card around; a photograph of a navy-blue lake, mountain and pine trees.

Baz dragged himself into the shade, panting, and flopped next to Midge with a groan. She rubbed his head, afraid to look at anyone. A string of iridescent drool dangled from his tongue and he screwed up his eyes in contentment.

Lynne suddenly looked up from the newspaper and over at Bobby and barked, 'I knew what I meant to say, Bob. I saw Matt Thomas the other night, coming out of The Gem, chewing the face off a blonde girl. Didn't know you'd finished with him.'

Jean glanced at Bobby and murmured, 'Nor did she, by the look on her face.'

'The twat!' Wendy shrilled, shaking her hair out of her eyes and jumping up, shoulders red and freckly from the sun.

'It's alright, Wend, honestly.' Bobby placed her cool, clammy hand on Wendy's hot pink arm. Keeping her voice level, unconcerned, she felt her stomach plummet like a descending lift with rage and humiliation.

The women exchanged glances and Stella made a warning face and shook her head. Jean screwed up her mouth and made a dismissive flapping gesture with her hand. The sunlight flashed off her sovereigns.

'They're all arseholes, love. Never you mind; you can do better than that little shit.'

Everyone went silent. The only sound coming from blackbirds squabbling in the hedge, and the creepy tinkling of an ice-cream van playing 'Greensleeves' on the somewhere in the estate. Bobby feigned nonchalance, heart racing, flicking through the catalogues, aware of everyone's eyes on her bent head. She spotted Midge's pile of books; this was the perfect distraction. Midge was engrossed in one. A slim book with a white cover and some sort of symbol or simple illustration on the front in black text. Bobby handed the catalogue to Stella and moved to sit next to Midge, rubbing the imprint of the gravel on her thighs, and pointed at the book.

'What's that you're reading? It looks like Chinese writing.'

Midge closed the book and smoothed her hand across the cover. Her fringe flopped over her eyes, and she brushed it out of the way. The sun had moved around and was burning her head. She pushed her bucket further into the shade and Bobby joined her, dragging a cushion to sit next to her on the edge of the path, among the dandelions and dock leaves sprouting through the cracked concrete. Midge raised her face, dappled green like a sprite in the shade from the hedge, eyes ringed with black shadows. Her voice was soft. She rested the book on her bent summer-holiday scabby knees.

'It's Japanese writing. They call them *characters*. It's about nature in Japan. Well, it's about an ancient calendar, really. Instead of four seasons, they have seventy-two short seasons based on what's happening in nature at that time of year. It changes every five days or so. It tells when buds are opening or leaves are falling. Or animals are being born, when crops are ripe, that kind of thing.' She paused and shrugged, then lowered her dark grey eyes to the page.

Bobby smiled. She never really saw Midge this animated. 'What's happening in Japan today then?'

Midge leafed through the pages and traced her grubby forefinger down a column. 'It says now is the time of "minor heat" and that in the next few days, "the young hawk begins to fly."'

Wendy looked over and rolled her eyes, holding her hand up to her mouth and stifling an imaginary yawn. Bobby ignored her, fascinated by the intensity of Midge's voice and the weird calendar.

'So, what about, say…' She looked up into the white-hot sky and picked a date at random. '…The first week in March?'

'My birthday,' whispered Midge. She bent her head, flicked through the pages, found the date, and looked at Bobby with a rare smile, showing small, crooked teeth.

'That's early spring. That week is when hibernation ends. It's the time "when the small creatures wake."'

The shadows were lengthening in the back garden and the mood had lifted by the time Bobby slunk away from Jean's. Wendy had her tape recorder playing and she and

Lynne were dancing to some tinny hissing music. Jean was pissed, cackling in the depths of the settee, sharing a joke with Stella. Nobody but Midge saw her drift away, slipping down the ginnel at the side of the house. It took less than five minutes to get home. When Bobby opened the front door, the house was cool, still, and silent. Davey and Ray were still at work, and Tiger was asleep on the ironing board in the kitchen. She put her hand on the banister and saw it was shaking. Letting out a furious, ragged sigh, she galloped up the stairs.

Carefully and methodically, Bobby searched the bedroom for anything Matt had bought her. She felt like she was performing some kind of decontamination procedure. She wasn't interested in questioning him or looking for an explanation. Bobby believed Lynne completely and realised she had probably known what he was like all along. It was just a matter of time, she just hated being made a fool of. She should have listened to her instincts back in the café when he came in with his mates, looking for a bit of sport at her expense.

Bobby shoved everything into a bag as quickly as possible, as though the items were dirty. Into the Kwiksave carrier went a couple of books; both authors she didn't like, but he thought she should. Next was a shitty plastic heart-shaped picture frame with a photo of them both taken outside the park, her eyes squinting into the camera. She bagged up a bangle and a pair of earrings, a scarf which had shrunk in the wash and two cassette tapes. Scanning the room, Bobby checked she had eradicated everything relating to him, rage gently abating. Abruptly, she sat down on the bed and wiped the sweat off her forehead, realising she had to return everything right now.

It was still hot when she rounded the bend at the top of the estate and she saw the Thomas house, glowing like a miniature palace in the early evening sun. The gravel drive and the garden were as mental as ever, if not more so. Bobby thought there were additional gnomes and plastic animals populating the lawn. Bobby walked swiftly up the path, kicking the gate open and swinging the carrier bag. Not ringing the bell, instead, she hammered on the door as hard as possible, trying to control her breathing and look calm.

Fury was draining out of her now, apprehension thickening in her throat. Her hair was plastered to her face like black seaweed and she could feel sweat running down her chest, trickling between her breasts, and soaking the band of her bra. A figure moved behind the patterned glass and a middle-aged man in overalls and socks opened the door. He looked nothing like Matt. He was short and stocky, with coarse ginger hair and an open face with a kind smile.

'Hello love, can I help you? I think the *Avon* lass has already been this week.'

'I'm looking for Matt. Is he in?' snapped Bobby.

'Well, no love, he isn't, but come on in anyroad. I'm Keith, his dad.' He looked slightly confused, but his voice was friendly.

Bobby was ushered into the lounge. Despite the hot weather, the fire was on. The heat, overpowering; the gas fire like a raging orange grid on the wall. Angel, the poodle, was sitting in front of it, panting.

'Marg, there's a young woman here looking for our Matt. D'you know where he's at?'

Marg Thomas was on the settee reading *Woman's Own*. She was the dead spit of Matt, but with dyed black hair. Her face was set in an expression of disapproval. *Mouth like a cat's arsehole*, thought Bobby.

'What's your name, love?' asked Keith, his voice low and hesitant.

Marg knew exactly who it was. The jet-coloured eyes, the slim build, and dark olive skin. It was Stella's kid. She looked just like her; scruffy, skinny, black-eyed cow.

'I'm Bobby. I'm Matt's girlfriend.'

Bobby looked at her feet and thought she must have dog shit on them by the expression on Marg's face.

Keith looked embarrassed and confused. He made a handwashing motion. His palms made a dry rasping sound like sandpaper being rubbed together and he waved to a chair.

'Well, I'm very pleased to meet you. I do apologise. I didn't know our Matt had a girlfriend. Sit down, love.'

Bobby was hovering near one of the armchairs, but a look and a raised hand from Marg stopped her. The older woman stood up and smoothed down her pink nylon housecoat, speaking crisply and correctly in a pretend posh voice, like someone impersonating the Queen.

'That's because he hasn't got a girlfriend. I don't know where you got that idea from, but never mind. We'll tell him you called.'

There it was, the sniff, the jerking back of the head, just like Matt.

'Well, not to worry, love. Do you want a brew?' Keith offered in a soft voice.

Marg didn't have to say anything else. Bobby knew the score. Her face was burning; the hot, humiliating flush travelling up her neck. She held out the carrier bag as though it was toxic.

'No thanks, Mr Thomas. I've got some stuff here from Matt. Things he gave me, presents. I don't think I should keep them because I won't be seeing him anymore.' She kept her arm extended, head tilted back.

Marg looked momentarily taken aback by the bag, and Bobby smiled sadly. *He hadn't told them. She had been such a silly cow.* It all fell into place now; being told not to ring the house or call around. Never being asked over unless they were away. They didn't have a clue who she was.

'I really think you have the wrong idea; Matthew isn't interested in *relationships*. He will be going away *to university* soon.' She paused as she said it, pronouncing the word as if it was some strange and exotic place in a faraway land, outside of Bobby's understanding.

Bobby rolled her eyes; she was sick of this shit. Marg clocked the cheeky young bitch pulling a face and decided it was time to put her back in her place. Where she belonged; in the roughest part of the estate. Stella Armstrong's little bastard.

'*Actually*, I don't want you in my house a minute longer.' The fake posh voice went up a couple of octaves and she made another small shake of the head and a sniff. 'Like I said, *he's not interested.*'

She was talking to Bobby as if she was trying to get rid of a persistent Romany hawking lucky heather, or the lad with cerebral palsy who sold tea towels and pegs door to door. Bobby suddenly lost her rag and started stabbing the air in front of Marg's face, scarlet with rage.

'He was interested enough when you were away on your holidays, dancing the fucking fandango in Blackpool. Or tanning that ugly, hard handbag of a face in Benidorm. He was interested enough to fuck me on your bed, and on your posh settee, even on your stairs. I have been here countless times. I have pissed in your toilet and drunk tea out of your daft china. I've even had to sit and pat that ugly little dog that stinks like a potter's donkey.' She pointed at Angel, who stayed in her basket, looking slightly offended, gazing at Bobby through crusty eyelids.

Marg's face was goggle-eyed, thin eyebrows halfway up her forehead now. They had been plucked away and the brows pencilled in above them, much too high up. What with the brows and the black curly perm, Bobby thought she looked just like Gary Glitter, or Ming the Merciless. Despite her fury, she almost laughed. Marg made a scandalised whinnying sound, moved forward, and pushed Bobby in the middle of her chest.

'Get out, you dirty little bitch. You're just like your mother!' She'd lost the posh accent now, talking broad, rough Gritstone.

Bobby thrust the bag at Marg and it fell to the floor. The tape unspooling across the carpet, coming to land at Keith's feet. He bent down to pick it up, mouth hanging open in surprise.

'There's his stuff back. He's a lying, bullying twat, and you're welcome to him, yer stuck-up bitch.'

Bobby stormed towards the door, followed by Marg, Keith hovering behind like a spare part, still kneading his hands together. Bobby wrenched it open, cool air spilling into the hallway.

'Go on, get away from here!' Marg was screeching at her, face puce with rage.

Faces appeared at the windows of the house opposite. A couple crossed the road casually to watch the drama. Marg clocked them. She quickly shoved Bobby onto the doorstep and slammed the door behind her.

Trembling, Bobby marched down the path, and turned to see Marg staring at her through the parted nets. Giving her the vees with both hands, she kicked the head off the gnome that was laughing at her the most, slammed through the gate, and walked away from the estate. By the time she was halfway up Victoria Avenue, Bobby had calmed down and her heart had stopped racing. She realised she really wasn't remotely bothered about Matt and the other girl, if she was completely honest with herself. All she was narked about was having the piss taken out of her. She actually felt elated that she had one less thing to be mithered about.

Her breathing slowed and she became aware of the coolness under the enormous mature trees that lined the avenue. The paving stones were smooth, even and weedless. This was one of her favourite streets in town. The vast Victorian and Edwardian villas were originally built for the wealthy mill owners. Stretching west out of town, they had long lawns and gravel driveways with arches into courtyards that had once housed carriages and horses and now kept gleaming expensive cars.

Front gardens were planted with well pruned laurels and cherry trees which flowered with pink blossom in the spring. They didn't, reflected Bobby, have any boarded-up windows, graffiti, or rotting cars, slowly being consumed by waist high grass and nettles. These were the houses who employed window cleaners, gardeners, and house cleaners — the families who paid people like her to do their dirty work. The people who counted the silver when the cleaner left and wrinkled their noses up at the smell of stale cigarettes, cheap clothes, and poverty.

Some of the girls from school lived on Victoria Avenue and the satellite groves and crescents which led off it. All had lovely, restful green-sounding names: Elder Avenue, Larkspur Crescent, Larch Grove. Further still, and even more desirable, were the posh houses on the new estate which backed onto the golf course, all pampas grass and daft house names instead of numbers.

These girls weren't like Bobby and Wendy. They were girls who went skiing on holiday and visited the dentist. Who joined the Brownies, had ponies, and went to ballet classes. These girls had shiny clean hair and went to school with wicker baskets covered in big nylon covers like shower caps on cookery lesson days. They didn't get their clothes from the Freemans catalogue or have their hair cut by a neighbour sitting on a stool in an unheated kitchen, hands in their armpits to keep warm. They didn't do PE in shorts from the lost and found box — they had blinding white Aertex shirts and spotless pumps, glossy hair fastened up in ponytails.

Bobby reached the end of Victoria Avenue as it curved to join Elder Avenue at the top of the estate. She had come full circle. She could see Matt's house from here; it looked as if nothing had happened. For a second, she contemplated throwing a brick through the lounge window. Crossing onto the estate, she was back on home territory. The light was harsher here; the trees were skinnier and unhealthier. The pavements cracked and weedy, front gardens scrubby. Houses changed abruptly to identical red brick council boxes lined up like dirty Lego.

Ahead of her, she could see Davey wandering back from work. She could tell he was tired by the way he stooped as he walked. Bobby couldn't face going back to Jean's; the sympathetic comments, histrionics and the whinging about men and work. She was almost looking forward to going back to school in a few weeks.

This time next year, Bobby would have finished her A-levels, and would have to think about what she was going to do. Even the prospect of a job looked uncertain now. She'd always dreaded the idea of going to the mill like Wendy, but now it was looking as though she wouldn't have to worry about that. After Jean and Stella's litany of work woes today, it sounded as though there wouldn't be any jobs anyway.

Chapter 17
September 1982

The summer was almost over. School would start next week. Above town, the fields looked yellow and dry, stubble silver in places. On the higher ground, up near Alice Armstrong's cottage, the heather was still vivid in patches of purple.

Midge walked south from the estate, out towards the flat fields on the edge of town, where the railway track followed the course of the river. She was almost hidden from view by the tall grasses on one side and the sweating, stinking bulk of the council tip on the other. The sun flashed off a pile of rusty bikes and twisted scrap metal as seagulls shrieked above. Her T-shirt was already plastered to her body with sweat, and her thin brown ponytail hung limply down her back.

Midge could feel the pebbles and lumpy ground through the thin soles of her pumps as the coarse, dry grass scratched her calves. She followed a narrow footpath known only to the kind of kids who came down to the back of the tip to smoke, shag, sniff glue, and smash stuff up. It was a place away from interfering adults and older teenagers. Weighing down one shoulder was a thin cotton bag with a cartoon picture of the

Roadrunner printed on the front. Inside this was a bottle of pop, already getting warm, a bag of crisps, a smashed-up Chorley cake, and a cheese buttie wrapped in a Hovis bread bag.

Only a few days to go and then back to school. Normally, she would dread it, having to put a uniform on and submit to being told what to do and when to do it. Swapping the freedom of days spent reading on her bed or wandering around with Baz for the classroom and the chaos of school life. This September she was looking forward to. It meant fewer days in the shop and maybe an opportunity for change.

Just as the railway line started its lazy, gentle curve away from the river, a small brick outbuilding with a smashed window came into view. It squatted, half hidden in the long grass and dusty shrubs. This had once housed equipment for the men who maintained the railway, but it was long since abandoned. Now, ivy half covered the structure with rotting planks leaning against the asbestos roof. The floor around it decorated with shards of broken glass, dog shit, cigarette ends, and litter.

Midge made for the entrance, which once had a door, smashed open years ago and now hanging from one hinge, its peeling green planks blistered and parched. She saw movement in the doorway and a white face appeared with a lank fringe. She stepped into the hut and for an instant couldn't see anything in the dark coolness. As her eyes adjusted to the dim interior, she saw the familiar red brick walls gouged and covered with graffiti, and suddenly the smell of piss was overwhelming.

'Alright, Gary?'

Gary Butler was sitting on a pile of rusty fencing which was stacked in a corner. He was smoking with one hand and holding a small brown dog and a Kwiksave carrier bag with the other. He nodded and smiled slowly.

'Hiya Midge. It's boiling out there, but I think it's better to be burned than put up with the stink of piss — I don't think Butch likes it.' He looked down at the little dog, who was staring up at him, one trembling paw raised, waiting for a treat.

Gary was as slim and small as Midge, with white-blond hair and a badly fixed hare lip. His high-pitched nasal voice echoed around the walls. The little brown dog continued to look up, with his overbite and grizzled face, hoping for some food from the bag. Midge bent down to stroke him. His fur felt like a greasy Brillo pad.

'Yeah, it's horrible. Let's get out,' she agreed, kissing Butch on the forehead.

She hitched up the bag again and turned away from the stinking cool of the building and into the white-hot heat of the day. They moved round to the back of the hut where there was a very slim bar of shade slowly growing on the sparkling carpet of glass. Gary dragged two car seats from a pile of rubbish and positioned them against the wall. They sat down, bare legs sticking to the vinyl. Butch crawled underneath them into the coolness with a content grumble. Gary opened the carrier bag and held it out wordlessly to Midge. Inside lay a big bottle of Tizer, two Milky Ways, something in a square of tin foil, a packet of chewing gum, half a packet of Kendal Mint Cake, and a bag of Monster Munch.

Midge nodded approvingly. 'You've brought more than me.'

Gary lived with his dad in the Gritstone flats and they had been friends since primary school. They often met up for a picnic or a smoke, like two old people enjoying each other's friendship in companionable silence. Gary's mum had disappeared when they were in the last year of primary school. She was an enormously fat woman who hadn't left the house in years. Midge used to see her when she called for Gary, peering round the edge of the curtains like a large zoo animal kept in captivity.

One day, Gary had come home as usual, and instead of making his tea, he found his mum standing in the kitchen in her slippers and underskirt with a bread knife, trying to carve handfuls of flesh from her sides. The ambulance that attended took her to some unknown place referred to by the adults as, 'A Special Hospital'. Gary's dad, whippet thin and surly, took over rearing his son alone, moving like a shadow through Gary's life, silent with grief and self-pity. They moved to the flats at the other side of the estate; two grim fingers of pebble-dashed concrete poking into the thin Pennine air. Gary occupied the same social strata at school as Midge.

These were part of the group of kids who never had the right PE kit or the correct uniform, who were targets for the nit nurse and Sister Philomena — the RE teacher who despised all children, but particularly the poor ones. She doled out the free school meals vouchers like an SS officer handing out yellow stars, patrolling the corridors with her metal ruler, and her rosary beads.

Gary emptied the bag onto the seats in the space between them, opening the tin foil to reveal a sweating ham barm cake that he ripped in half. Midge wordlessly did the same with the cheese one and they swapped halves. The shade was covering their upper bodies now, the sun blinding on their white skinny legs.

'What's happening, owt?' mumbled Midge through a mouthful of bread.

Gary shrugged, 'Nothing really. I've got me auntie staying at the minute. She's a pain in the arse, but always gives me some money when she comes. What about you? Haven't seen you much since you started at Boston's.' He glanced at Midge, thinking she seemed quiet. *Probably dreading going back to school, like me*, he thought.

Midge didn't look at him, shrugging, and mechanically chewing the ham buttie. She focused on a small flock of brown birds landing on the tall grasses opposite the shed. This was her time to say something, but her tongue was welded to the roof of her mouth.

'They'll be off soon. Maybe to Africa for the winter,' Gary reflected, jerking his head at the birds.

I wonder what it would be like to sprout some wings and go with them? Midge thought suddenly. *That would be bloody amazing.* She exhaled and closed her eyes.

'Are you okay? You're miles away.' He stopped eating and shook his head at her.

'Aye, I'm alright.' She ripped off a piece of sandwich and put it in her mouth, chewing slowly. She turned to face him, swallowing the dry bread down. It was like eating a ball of cardboard.

'Sorry, what were you saying? About the holidays?'

If there was one person in the entire world, she should be able to tell it was Gary. Midge had got out of bed this morning with that sole intention. She would tell him and then, by magic, everything would be resolved, and she could get back to normal. Telling Gary would be a like saying a spell out loud that would make the past few months disappear. It would be like Doctor Who, like time-travelling magic.

'I've not done much, really. I went to Rhyl with Mum and Wendy. We stayed in a caravan, someone Mum used to work with, but it was a bit boring,' She paused to pick at a scab on her knee. 'Wendy was whinging the whole time.' Her words felt thick, like glue in her mouth.

Gary nodded knowingly. 'We went to Llandudno once to stay with someone Dad knows. Half of the town were there. I spent all my money on the first day in the arcades. I don't think Dad wanted to be there, to be honest,' he shrugged as his voice faded away.

They finished the food and pop in silence. Butch was chewing exaggeratedly, his back teeth gummed together with Monster Munch. Midge threw a piece of bread in front of her, and almost immediately, a large glossy raven with a shaggy beard swooped down. He strutted about for a second or two, fixing them both with a quick eye, ate the crumbs, then waited. Midge crumpled up the Hovis bag and spread her empty hands to him.

'I've nowt left,' He flapped away with a dry caw.

'Right then, shall we get on?' Gary said decidedly, rummaging around in his pockets and pulling out a handful of two pence pieces.

Midge nodded and they shoved all the rubbish into the Roadrunner bag and wandered down to the railway line. Butch was gathered up under Gary's arm to save his paws from the broken glass. The land was completely flat, in contrast to the hills to the east. Local people said a Roman road was under here, close to where the railway line passed on its way to London. Gary and Midge had often searched the dusty surface looking for treasure, but they only ever found ring pulls off empty pop cans and fossilised dog turds.

Just as the train line finished its sinuous curve, straightened out and headed due south, Gary squatted and lined up a couple of two pence pieces a foot apart, balanced on the centre of the rails. Midge touched the hot metal rail with her palm. Gary bent his head to the smooth silvery surface, as if listening for a heartbeat.

'It's coming,' he announced decisively, to nobody in particular, and shivered in anticipation — widening his eyes as he smiled at Midge.

In the distance, they heard a low whistle and backed off to lie on the grass in the bushes, right by the rails just their heads sticking out, flattened on their bellies. Butch was tucked under Gary's arm, his face placid. They watched the train approach, accelerating rapidly. Sun glinting off the windows of the driver's cab, the destination sign to Euston a momentary blur. Suddenly, it was on them, the ground shaking beneath them. Midge squinted and squeezed her fists and eyes together, stomach tensed hard. Gary was laughing and shouting. The noise was tremendous, overwhelming, like a giant metal scream.

Just for a couple of seconds, Midge wondered what it would be like to spring up, to run right under the avalanche of noise and metal. How quick would it be? Would it be so quick it wouldn't hurt? What would she look like afterwards? Just a smear of meaty redness on the gravel between the train tracks, like mince? The thought was over in a flash, and she looked over at Butch and giggled. He had watched the train shrieking past but just gazed at it with indifference, one ear twitching.

'He's just not arsed, is he?'

Gary nodded and laughed, the livid scar from nostril to lip standing out on his pale freckled face. 'No, he doesn't give a shit. He's hard as nails, our Butch.'

They sprung up laughing, running over to the tracks as the train receded. The coins were transformed into flat copper discs, worn completely smooth by the train wheels, hot and wafer thin. Gary handed one to Midge and she examined it, smiling, and put it into her pocket, running her fingers over the warm surface. He plucked at the front of his T-shirt to shake off the shards of broken glass sticking to it, throwing his coin in the air and catching it. The euphoria of the coin flattening session drained away, and they walked in silence away from the tracks, the sun hot on their uncovered heads.

The pair wandered through a small grove of tired silver birches, headed for the river. In the tall trees above the water, herons had built a scruffy shambolic nest. As they walked towards the bank, one took off from the branches, ungainly pterodactyl shape dark against the sky as it flew away with a loud krrk.

Gary chucked twigs for Butch, who made a half-arsed attempt at catching them. Midge ran her fingertips through the tops of the grasses, peeling the seeds from the stems and throwing them like brown confetti. They came to a small, pebbly, muddy beach sloping into the water with a rope swing hitched to a tree on the nearside bank and took turns sitting on the knot and swinging across. Midge looked into the dark green depths as her shadow passed over, wondering when she could talk to Gary; what to say, how to start the conversation. She watched the insects dimpling the water and decided the time wasn't right. She would wait for later, when they went back for their stuff. A dragonfly hovered, wings trembling.

They wandered back through the shrubs for a while, dawdling and throwing stones in the river, listening to its blue-green song as it moved over the stones. The afternoon was losing its heat, and the trees were making longer shadows on the surface of the water. Midge was filled with the melancholy late summer feeling of waiting to go back to school. A knot of anxiety hardened and curdled high in her stomach.

As they walked back to the hut, they paused to look at the remains of a bonfire. Amidst the blackened and crushed lager cans was a lot of half-burned paper, pages of a porn magazine ripped into shreds, the edges charred. Pink flesh, a breast, a woman's mouth, open in a square shape which looked to Midge like pain. A triangle of black fur. Gary stirred the fragments of paper with the toe of his trainer.

'Dirty bastards,' he scoffed. 'Slags.'

Midge shivered, looking away. Suddenly, she wanted to go home. The day was spoiled. Nothing was the same anymore. Everything had changed. She couldn't tell Gary now. He would think she was like the paper woman, with her legs open — her dirty body torn up like rubbish on the river bank for everyone to see.

Chapter 18
October 1982

It was almost Halloween. The clocks had gone back and crispy brown leaves were rasping along the pavements of town. People had their fires going, and on an evening, the air smelt of smoke and sharpness. Every now and then, a firework would scream off when it got dark, as kids started warming up for Bonfire Night.

Midge decided that if she didn't tell someone about Boston, she would leave the pet shop before Christmas. People would think it was weird, because she always said she liked her Saturday job. It was a great opportunity to make money, learn about animals, and well, jobs were scarce. Plus, it was nice that she could help her mum out.

It was half-term. Jean asked Midge to take the catalogue over to Grandma's, as she was going to buy a new carpet sweeper. Peggy had a sort of non-electric vacuum cleaner, which she called the Ewbank. She had used it for years, but had decided she was going to splash out and treat herself to a new one.

Peggy lived in one of a row of flats above the shops on the main road, running through the estate. It was accessed by a flight of steps through the backyard of the off-licence. The backyard was full of bins, crates of empty bottles, and crushed up cardboard. It stank of cat piss, and Midge was careful to walk around the puddles in her thin pumps, never sure how deep they were.

Peggy's back door was open, and the warmth hit her as soon as she stepped in to the flat. Peggy was dragging some washing from a twin tub into the sink. Her arms were wet and scarlet to the elbow. She had once been a big, fleshy woman like Jean, but now she was slightly stooped and rangy. Tonight, she was wearing the tabard she used for cleaning fastened over her polyester old lady dress as Midge called it, but not to Peggy's face. Midge thunked the Littlewoods catalogue down on the little kitchen table as though it were a breeze block and prodded it with her finger.

'Grandma, this hoover thing will cost an arm and a leg through the catalogue. It's a rip-off. They'll have yer eyes out. Why don't you just get something from Rumbelows? Maybe a proper one that runs off electric?'

'Why don't you just mind your own business? It's my money,' snapped Peggy. 'Make yerself useful and put the kettle on, Miss Know-It-All.'

Peggy could be a bad-tempered bitch. Whenever Midge or Wendy was round at the flat, if they were hungry and asked what they could eat, she would stand with her hands on her hips and snap,

'You can chew on the bone of me arse! You kids don't know the meaning of the word *hungry*.'

Midge did as she was told. Peggy didn't use tea bags. She bought loose tea, which was kept in a dirty old tin with a Chinese pagoda picture on the front. It was measured out with a special spoon. *One for each person and one for the pot,* thought Midge, carefully tipping the tea into the brown pottery teapot, ignoring Peggy's instruction to warm it first. Peggy had a lot of weird old lady habits. The carpet sweeper, the loose tea, and the twin tub. The making of the beds with the striped flannelette sheets tucked in so tight you had to slide into bed and then lie there, unable to move, like being trapped in a sardine tin.

She also had a creepy holy water font by the front door, and everyone was liberally sprinkled when they came in or out. Protestant visitors got an extra dose, just in case. Peggy had a contact at church who supplied her with this water, in a plastic bottle with a blue lid shaped like Our Lady and sent, apparently, from Lourdes. Midge had drunk some of it once for a dare, but it didn't taste different to normal water, just a bit stale. When she asked Wendy about it, she shrugged and said,

'It's just a Catholic witchcraft made-up thing. Summat for old people to waste their money on.'

The flat was spotless and shabby. The main room was full of old-fashioned furniture; an uncomfortable lumpy dark blue settee with a plastic cover, a radiogram which took up an entire corner of the room, a big telly on legs, and a drum shaped object made of diamonds of thin leatherette sewn together. Peggy called it a pouffe. On the telly was an ancient, flaking red and white plaster statue of a little boy in a red and white robe, wearing a weird crown-like hat. He was, Peggy had informed her grandchildren, the Infant of Prague.

'If you keep one of these in the house, you'll never be without money, girls.' She would pat his head and nod slowly and deliberately as though she had inside knowledge direct from the Vatican.

'Well, that's a load of shite. Grandma hasn't got a pot to piss in. Look at all this ancient crap,' muttered Wendy to her sister, rolling her eyes theatrically.

A photograph of the Pope took centre stage on the wall. Peggy had bought it on a trip to Heaton Park in May when he visited England.

'Jesus Groupies,' Wendy had called them, shuddering.

Next to His Holiness was a picture of a lady with a blue face, another of a little boy crying, and an old black-and-white photo of a group of girls on the front at Blackpool. Jean was in the middle, head thrown back, laughing, and linking the arms of two other girls — one of whom was Carol, Peggy's older daughter, living in Canada. On the mantlepiece above the fire were photos of Midge and Wendy looking like miniature brides in their First Holy Communion dresses.

'Let's have a quick brew and then I'm off to get me hair done. If you come and meet me just about closing time, I'll be ready, and I'll buy you a chippy tea as a treat.'

Peggy felt guilty for snapping at the kid. She looked at Midge, who was tearing open a packet of Bourbon biscuits, and leant over to pat her forearm. She was so thin and plain compared to Wendy's red-gold glamour and curves. An odd kid. Too quiet. Into her books and animals, so unlike the rest of the family. Except maybe she had a slight similarity to Carol when she was that age. She watched her tipping the biscuits onto a plate and wondered how she would turn out, how adult life might shape her.

Peggy had her hair set every Friday afternoon at Bonne Maison. For years, she had worn her hair in a custard-yellow bleached Victory Roll. The same hairdo she had throughout the war, along with a slash of red lipstick, and her high heels. She still had the slim calves and ankles that had jitterbugged the night away with the American soldiers at every dancehall within a fifty-mile radius of the town. One night, she liked to recall, a young soldier had given her a lift home sitting on the top of an armoured car that was so loud she hadn't been able to hear for a week.

In recent years, she had ditched the Betty Grable look and had her hair cut short. During the week, she wore rollers, unless she had to leave the flat, when a good deal of back combing and hair spraying took place.

Later that afternoon, when Midge opened the door to Bonne Maison, the air was thick with the smell of hairspray, setting lotion, and fag smoke. She coughed and squinted through the haze, scanning the room. A bank of women sat under the beehive driers like a row of aliens, reading magazines and smoking while their hair gently fried. All looked identical; the same type of shoes, clothes, and faces. Peggy was in the middle, occupying prime position. She smiled as Midge came in and hovered in front of her.

'You look pale, kid. Probably about time you were starting your monthlies. Have you got belly ache?' She patted her own soft pillow of a stomach. 'What you need is a drop of Turkish brandy.'

Peggy examined Midge, a long worm of ash curling from her cigarette. She peered through the smoke, watching her grandchild closely. The row of aliens nodded in agreement and Midge could feel her face burning in mortification. She didn't want monthlies, or brandy, or anything to do with being a woman. She wanted to stay being a child forever. She looked away from them to a black-and-white picture on the wall of a woman wearing cat's eye glasses and elaborate hairstyle like a Walnut Whip.

'Are you courting yet?' asked Mrs Cavanagh, one of Peggy's best mates — a thin scarecrow with blue hair and pointy eye teeth.

Midge frowned and went slightly pink, shifting from foot to foot. The row of harpies shrieked with laughter. Midge smiled a fake chimpanzee's grin, her mouth stretched across her teeth in a rictus as she pleated her fingers together. She wished the old bitches would just shut up. Mrs Cavanagh whinnied at her own joke, licking her fleshy lips with a white-coated tongue as she enjoyed Midge's discomfort. Her lipstick was bleeding into the vertical lines on her upper lip. She reminded Midge of the grandmother in *Little Red Riding Hood*. A dreadful thought flashed across her brain. What if that old bag knew what Boston was doing and thought she wanted it? Enjoyed it? That she was his girlfriend, somehow? She felt sick to her stomach and turned away.

'Don't be mard. We're only having a laugh with you,' cried Peggy, indignant.

Midge flashed another forced grin to shut them up and moved away. She found a seat in the corner, under the coat pegs, picked up a magazine from the rack, and pretended to read a knitting pattern for a baby's cardigan. Reenie, the head hairdresser, swanned around in her overall and corrugated hair, brandishing a bag of rollers. The only young person in the shop other than Midge was the junior; a plump red-faced girl with a frizzy blonde bubble perm, snapping chewing gum with a bored expression as she swept up grey hair clippings vacantly, like a robot with a broom.

It was raining when they left. Peggy bought a plastic bonnet from the box of Rain Mates on the counter. There was some old people's music playing on the radio, and Peggy was humming tunelessly along as she fastened herself into her mac. She tied the rain hood over her pristine steel-grey curls and jerked her head at Midge.

'Now then, let's go to the chippy and I'll buy your tea. I'm ready for summat to eat.'

Midge sighed with relief. It was good to be out of that overheated shop and those nosy women. She could have Peggy to herself. She would revert to being Grandma. It was dark when they opened the door and stepped out into the wet street. Zipping up her parka, Midge pulled the snorkel hood over her face, linking Peggy's arm. When they returned to the flat, she'd tell her grandma what was going on. Grandma would be able to sort it without her mum finding out. Peggy might even concoct a tale explaining why she was leaving her job. Relief flooded through her. Safe in the depths of her hood, she allowed herself a small smile and nodded to herself.

The Friday chippy queue was long. It stretched out of the door, leaving everyone hunched against the rain. The smell was amazing. Midge strained to look through the fogged-up windows, stomach turning in anticipation. All she could see was a smear of stainless steel and someone in a white overall banging oil out of the fryer baskets. At last, the queue moved indoors to the warmth of the shop. Midge pushed her hood down, inhaling the hot vinegar. The counter was filled with towers of polystyrene trays, boxes of wooden forks, and enormous containers of salt and vinegar. Peggy ordered two portions of chips, a steak pudding for Midge, a fish for herself, and a carton of mushy peas.

'I can't believe a grandchild of mine isn't having fish on a Friday.' She shook her head at Midge, who smiled and watched as Peggy rooted in her purse. 'Your mother has raised a pair of bloody heathens.'

'I just don't like fish, Grandma, only when they're swimming in the sea. That's where they should be.'

'Well, I like mine battered and swimming in fat,' retorted Peggy, shoving the newspaper-wrapped parcels into her shopping bag. 'Come on, shape yourself before this lot gets cold.'

They marched back to the estate. The rain was coming down hard. Peggy was cursing, worried her hair was going to get spoiled. As soon as they got into the flat, Midge was tasked with brewing up while Peggy put the food in the oven to keep warm. She switched the gas fire on and dragged up the two armchairs. Peggy's fire had a fake log effect — a moulded, lumpy piece of dusty plastic that was supposed to look like coals, a noisy fan and a red lightbulb underneath to produce the illusion of flames.

Tea was poured and put onto a tray balanced on a stool in front of the fire. Peggy and Midge sat in their armchairs, the plated-up food on their knees. There was no sound other than the ticking of the fire and the rain on the kitchen window. Midge probed the soft fontanelle of her flabby suet pudding, making an exploratory slit in the crown with her knife. A scented plume of steam curled out. It was comforting sitting in the soft light filtering from Peggy's crooked standard lamp with its dusty fringed shade. Much more relaxing than at home where the telly or record player was always going, and Wendy or Jean were always shouting about something.

They finished the food and their brews, and Peggy had a fag. Then it was time for cards. Midge moved to sit on the floor opposite Peggy, who dragged over a little coffee table on flimsy gold-coloured legs. One side of her body was red hot from the fire.

'I don't like that woman, Mrs Cavanagh,' Midge ventured, trying to sound casual, watching Peggy closely.

'Oh, she's a daft cow. Pay her no mind.' Peggy was shuffling the deck mechanically, then licked her thumb to deal for a hand of Rummy. She was concentrating, not looking at Midge.

'I didn't like what she said about *courting*,' Midge persisted, spitting the word out as she watched Peggy dealing the cards.

'If she had half a brain cell in that thing she calls a head, it would be lonely. She's no right to talk about folk's personal lives. Not when she has a daughter who carries on with half the blokes in town and is pregnant with a married man's nipper, the dirty piece. She's had more fellers than Soft Mick, that one,' snapped Peggy, peeling a card from her hand and placing it on the table.

Midge watched Peggy's pursed lips as she examined her hand. Then she dropped her eyes and her heart sank.

Dirty piece. That's what she was, dirty. Gary would think so. Grandma Peggy would think so, and Christ only knew what her mum and Wendy would think. She wasn't going to be able to tell Grandma. Midge wasn't going to be able to tell anyone. She felt a hard lump rise in her chest and throat, and thought it might choke her.

They played cards until 8 pm. Midge struggled to concentrate, looking at her cards without seeing them. Losing repeatedly, until Peggy lost patience with her stupidity and suggested they stop. Midge nodded with relief, rubbing the space between her eyes.

'I'm just a bit tired, Grandma. D'you want the radio on?'

Peggy nodded and Midge fiddled with the radiogram for something to do.

'You can give me a hand with some stuff that's going to the charity shop if you like?'

Peggy had a small pile of clothes that Midge thought nobody in their right mind would buy, but she helped her grandma sort and fold them into two carrier bags to donate. She was glad of the distraction. When that was done, Peggy placed an old biscuit tin on the coffee table. It had a picture of a stag on the front, standing in front of a range of mountains with its head up, antlers surrounding it like a bony crown. It served as Peggy's jewellery box. Midge had loved playing with this when she was a little girl. She smiled as she remembered layering the cheap beads around her neck and arranging the rings in order of her favourite colours.

Peggy tipped the contents out onto the table, a tangled, glistening pile of treasure. She started to go through it, placing anything of value back in the tin and anything to go in a large, old, creased brown envelope. Midge watched, occasionally picking something up and examining it. Into the envelope went single clip-on earrings, their partners long-lost, plastic beads, and a couple of brooches with glass stones. Peggy stirred the mass of cheap glitter with a twiggy, arthritic forefinger.

'It's all rubbish, really. None of it's worth a blow on the rag man's trumpet.' She sighed, scratching her crispy curls with a forefinger.

She handed Midge a paper bag full of mint imperials. Midge popped a mint in her mouth and picked up a metal brooch in the shape of a black cat with green glass eyes, and turned it to the light, the eyes sparkling. 'I don't remember this, Grandma.'

Peggy smiled and took the brooch off Midge, running her wrinkled thumb across the surface of the cat. 'That's very old, love. A lad I once knew gave it to me during the war. He said it would bring me luck. I used to wear it a lot.'

Midge leant forward, examining it more closely as Peggy moved it through her fingers.

'What happened to him?'

'Well, he should have held on to it, because he went off and got himself killed.' Peggy shrugged. 'A lot of lads did. It was the war. *San Fairy Ann.*'

'Are you keeping it or throwing it?' Midge asked suddenly.

'Throwing it,' decided Peggy, nodding her head.

'Can I have it?'

'Of course you can, love,' smiled Peggy. 'Maybe it will bring you some luck.' She placed it carefully on Midge's outstretched palm.

Midge nodded slowly and pinned the dead boy's tin cat to her jumper with trembling hands. It was Saturday tomorrow.

Chapter 19
November 1982

It was Gary Butler who put an end to it. He had gone to Boston's to get some dog food for Butch, as he couldn't be bothered to go to Kwiksave. It was almost closing time and he had to run, panting as he turned the corner and crossed the street to the shop. It was time to cut down on the fags, he decided; his chest was burning.

When he got there, the sign was turned around to closed, but it was only 4.50 pm. The main lights were off, but the door was slightly open as if somebody had closed it in a hurry and it had bounced back open on itself. Gary eased his way in, pocketing a jazzy red cat collar and a small hard rubber ball from the revolving display by the fish tanks. The macaw looked at him, saying nothing. It inched along its roost, inclining its head, watching Gary carefully. He stuck a white-coated tongue out at the bird and gave it the vees. The bird stared back silently.

Gary was getting the creeps. He should have called out to Boston or Midge but now it seemed too late to say anything. He felt as if he had broken in and suddenly wanted to put the stuff back. The shop was too dark to still be open and it felt weird. Wiping his sweating hands on his thighs, he walked hesitantly towards the till.

The storeroom light was on. A thin, vertical ribbon of light was visible behind the counter and he could hear a low scuffling, breathing. He moved towards the noise silently, hoping his trainers wouldn't squeak on the filthy lino. The back of his neck felt cold. The quiet in the shop was unnatural, even the animals seemed to hold their breath. To the right of the counter, was a shelf full of rodent cages. Gary could see a white rat standing on its hind legs, forepaws holding onto the bars of its cage, whiskers vibrating. Its eyes glowed pink in the dimness.

Looking through the half-open door, he saw the back of someone. It was that weirdo Boston on the floor, grunting. Gary thought he was having a fit or a stroke but no, he was moving rhythmically on top of something, somebody much smaller. It looked like one of the mannequins in Scolbar's window, the ones dressed in school uniforms. But this one had a face. It was Midge Kenny, being held down across her chest. Boston's hand gripping her white face which was turned to the wall. Her feet were apart, the thin soles of her pumps covered in sawdust. He noticed two worn circles on each foot.

Gary watched for a couple of seconds to be certain that he knew what was happening. Holding his mouth, he couldn't get his head around it. He left quietly, hands trembling, taking a tin of dog food, a packet of Bob Martins, and a dried pig's ear for Butch.

The macaw called after him shrilly, 'Wait for me!' and let out a piercing shriek.

Once he was out on the street, he left the door open just as he had found it. Gary walked as quickly as he could back home, fighting the urge to run, and wondering if anyone had seen him go into the shop. His heart was galloping. He felt sick to the stomach and utterly terrified. The penny dropped and everything suddenly fitted into place. No wonder Midge had been so strange and silent all these months. He hugged the tin of dog food to his chest, running the final few yards to the flats.

Gary dropped the nicked pet shop stuff at home and walked the dark, wet streets with Butch. The image of what he had seen played through his head. He decided he couldn't ask Midge about it — Midge would be horrified and embarrassed if she knew he had seen what was going on. She would probably beg him not to tell anyone. He bit at the skin around his thumbnail. She might refuse to speak to him again, stop being his friend, and he didn't have many of them. But there was no way he could keep quiet about this. This was proper adult, serious stuff.

Boston was the sort of creep who would probably deny anything if he was confronted. Nobody believed kids like him and Midge. Most of the adults he knew were untrustworthy. But this was a situation that could only be fixed by involving a grown-up person. Gary walked on, head down, running through the list of possible adults he could speak to. Wendy was too unpredictable and didn't count as she was only *just* an adult in Gary's book. Mr

Crown was a possibility, but Gary didn't want to jeopardise Midge's paper round.

Then there were teachers, but that might mean involving a priest, or that arsehole sadist, Sister Philomena. And they may assume Gary was a lying pervert, and impose a marathon confession session or some such convoluted and shameful Catholic-related punishment. Father Scanlon was an option. He was alright for a priest, Gary conceded. The risk was he might have to do something involving the authorities that would embarrass Midge further. Gary paused to allow Butch to examine a lamppost and lick a rain filled polystyrene chip tray.

The police were discounted immediately. Gary had been cautioned for nicking more times than he cared to remember, and they just thought he was a lying toerag. There was the additional risk they might get the Social involved. His dad was out of the frame too; he was a drinker and wouldn't have the energy or inclination to do anything. He trudged on, brain fizzing as light rain fell in an orange veil through the streetlights.

Gary did and said nothing for a few days, frightened of telling anyone, struggling to find the words to express what he had seen. He even forgot about it for a while, pushing it out of his mind. Then he saw Midge at school, pale as always, but thinner if that was possible. She was quiet, but they chatted about the normal things and she seemed excited about going to the pictures next month to see *ET* when it came on at the Alhambra.

For all this surface normality in behaviour, Gary was pretty sure that whatever was going on between Boston and Midge, she didn't want any part in it. He watched the back of her head in geography, bent over her book, rabbit-coloured ponytail hanging down her narrow neck, fastened with a plastic bobble in the shape of a cat. He thought of Boston with his forearm across her chest, pressing her rigid, unwilling little body to the floor.

Revulsion and pity bubbled inside. That dirty old fat bastard hurting Midge. It was disgusting. Gary tried to concentrate on Father Scanlon and his moraine hummocks but couldn't get the image of Midge out of his head, crushed underneath Boston. Her chewed biro moved across the page of her exercise book, writing uncurling from her hand in a spidery slant. He watched the thin winter sunshine falling in a bar across the back of her bobbly jumper and decided. Gary was not a brave person by nature, but this wasn't going to go away unless he did something about it. It was the right thing to do.

After school one day, he waited for the crowds of smoking, screeching, fighting kids to disperse, and walked into town. He had decided he would make his way to Earnshaws, hoping to catch Jean when she knocked off. Unsure of what he was going to say, he was shitting himself. Gary feared Jean Kenny when she was in a good mood. Christ only knew what reaction his words were going to provoke. He nearly bottled it and went home, but then decided he couldn't keep quiet any longer. He couldn't let what was happening to Midge carry on.

With an hour and a half to kill, he wandered into town. Passing the bookies first, the door was open. Gary caught a glimpse of a row of cloth-capped heads looking in complete absorption at a telly on the wall. Then he popped into Woolies to do a bit of light shoplifting. The pick and mix were always a doddle. Filling the pockets of his jacket with sweets, he moved on to the small electricals. Gary picked up some batteries and pretended to browse the Ladybird clothing range before helping himself to more sweets and a packet of biros. The nosy cow by the records had started to stare at him, so he left and wandered up the main street towards WH Smith, mechanically unwrapping and shoving Blackjacks into his mouth.

It was quiet in Smith's, so he only managed to pinch a couple of comics, stuffing then down the front of his kecks, before heading off to sit in the bus station until it was Earnshaws knocking-off time — finding a seat in the corner away from the main entrance. Gary read *Commando* cover to cover and tucked *The Eagle* and *Shoot* inside his jumper for later. He worked his way through the rest of the sweets and suddenly it was time to go. His stomach lurched with anxiety and an overwhelming urge to just go home. It would be so much easier to just piss off back to the flats and pretend nothing had happened.

He wiped damp palms on his thighs and shoved his hands back in his pockets, jiggling his legs up and down in a nervous dance. No, he had to get it over with. He let out a long, ragged sigh. It was a bit like getting the cane or a bollocking off his dad; best get it done and dusted. Shoving the sweet wrappers in the bin, he left the bus station, heading away from the shops towards the familiar bulk of the mills to the east of the town centre.

Gary waited outside the factory gates until just gone five, watching the stream of men and women pouring out into the dark street. It was bitterly cold and a thin breeze was blowing rubbish and newspapers right past his legs. It had rained heavily when he was in the shops, and the gutter was chuckling and gurgling with filthy water. Rubbish was carried along like tiny boats, a dirty scum of lather gathering at the choking drain grids. People shouted goodbyes as they hurried home, and the crowd thinned quickly.

Jean was one of the last ones out. He recognised her instantly; her tall, bulky figure with its big tatty coat wrapped over her overall. Gary watched her meaty face in profile, lighting a cigarette, her head bent and hands cupped to shelter the flame. She hitched her handbag over her shoulder and marched up the street, away from the mill towards the estate. He had an intense urge to turn around and run away, but decided if he didn't get it sorted now, he never would. Rushing up to Jean, Gary pulled at her sleeve. She turned around in an instant, fag between her lips, eyes wide with surprise.

'Hiya, Gary. Bloody hell, you nearly frightened the life out of me! What's up?'

God, he was a weird-looking kid, she thought. *With his scarred face and nasal drone. What was it with Midge and her strange mates? She attracted many oddballs.*

'Jean, I need to tell you something,' he burst out, wrapping his arms around himself as if he was wearing a straitjacket. His voice was a high-pitched, nasal squeak. Eyes wide, he put a hand to his white, greasy hair.

'What's going on, Gary?' she demanded, suddenly frightened by his expression.

A cluster of fireworks went off somewhere close by, crackling and zipping, raining a shower of coloured fire in the darkness behind Jean's head. The sound was so loud she couldn't hear him at first and he found he couldn't speak anymore. His mouth had completely dried up. Gary stood motionless in a puddle turned to mercury by the light of a screaming rocket.

Jean stared at him, at his small, upturned face with its misshapen lip and nose, lit up by the fireworks. He looked like a little ugly goblin in an oversized Harrington jacket, his lips and tongue stained dark blue from the Blackjacks.

'It's Midge.'

Chapter 20
November 1982

Davey slipped into Ray's and Stella's bedroom, returning home after having finished work at the yarn warehouse. He felt a bit like a burglar; he rarely came in here. Davey didn't like to think of his mum in bed next to that arsehole. The air smelled of stale smoke, cheap perfume, and Ray's work clothes. The eiderdown was smoothed perfectly straight, its diamond patterns slightly raised, puckered in places. There was a fag burn on Ray's side of the bed, nearest the door; the edges of the fabric melted black and crispy. Above the bed was a large dent in the plaster where something had been thrown at the wall at some stage.

Davey looked at the wardrobe. It was an ugly, heavy, dark Victorian thing that Mum and Ray shared. It didn't close properly and there was a folded up brown envelope wedged near the handle to keep the door shut. He slipped it out with the tips of his fingers, hands trembling slightly, and the door swung open. It had a shelf with a couple of hats and shoeboxes on and beneath this, a single rail. The inside of the door held a full-length mirror, fixed in place by four rusty clips. He glanced at his reflection, looking back at himself in sepia, like a thin brown ghost in his work clothes.

He found what he was searching for; a man's navy-blue blazer with shiny elbows. Pushing some clothes to one side, the coat hanger hooks scraped noisily along the rail. Pulling the blazer out, he lay it on the bed and carefully looked at it. There was a metal bar on the left-hand side of the jacket with a row of dull, gold-coloured stars hanging from it. Davey didn't want to take the whole blazer with him. He bent the bar forwards and could see it was fixed to the jacket with a long pin, a bit like a large brooch. Pressing the pin, he unclasped the brooch and slid the pin out of the fabric of the blazer. His heart was beating so fast even though that shithead was at work and wouldn't know he was in here.

Picking the blazer up, Davey slid it back on the hanger. It was only then that he felt the weight in the right-hand pocket. He shook the jacket slightly and heard a soft metallic sound. Putting his hand in the pocket, he drew out a heavy handful of medals. These were circular and also hanging from ribbons, mainly silver metal but one gold coloured. He dumped them on the bed next to the stars. Davey realised he had nothing to hide them in to get them out of the house. He ran downstairs, feet thundering and got a clean tea towel out of the drawer in the kitchen, sprinted back up, wrapped the bar and the round medals up, and shoved them in his football holdall.

He rearranged the clothes in the wardrobe and closed the door before wedging the envelope back in an approximation of where it had been and smoothing out the bedcovers. Inhaling deeply, Davey closed his eyes and exhaled in a long-jagged sigh. A small internal voice asked him what he hoped to achieve by being told something he already knew was true, but he was too angry to think about that right now. He picked up the holdall and left to visit Chris and Jonty.

Taking the stairs at Mulberry Terrace three at a time, the bag lay slung over his shoulder. The door to the flat was already open and some haunting music was drifting out onto the landing. Jonty was whistling loudly, standing on a chair, changing a lightbulb. Chris was holding on to the chair, which was wobbling erratically.

'What is this playing?' Davey dumped the bag on the floor.

'This is Acker Bilk playing "Stranger on the Shore". It's a particular favourite of Cecil's.' Jonty's voice was muffled. Half his upper body seemed to be encased in a vast fringed lampshade.

Cecil, the brindle greyhound, was stretched out on a threadbare chaise lounge on his back. Head hanging off the foot end, he was fast asleep with his mouth half open and tongue lolling out of the side.

'He seems to like the clarinet, but Bacchus isn't fond. He's a lover of jazz, Stephan Grapelli and Django

Rhinehart in particular. He's more of a strings enthusiast, really. That's cats for you.'

Davey really had nothing to say in response to this and hovered in the doorway until Jonty had finished with the lightbulb. He emerged from the shade, brushing cobwebs out of his hair, and smiled at Davey.

'Well, I'll put the kettle on. Chris tells me you have some medals you'd like me to look at. I get them in from time to time. I'm always surprised how many people get rid of them.'

'Is that how people come to have them? People who they don't belong to, I mean? Can anyone just go and buy someone else's medals?' Chris gestured to Davey to come and sit down.

'Yes. People die, and perhaps the medals mean nothing to their relatives. The metal they are made from isn't especially valuable, it's what they represent that has value. They turn up in junk shops, antiques shops, people sell them through adverts in the newspapers. They are bought and sold for many reasons.'

Jonty strolled off to the kitchen and began making a lot of noise rooting through cupboards. He faffed about in the kitchen for a while, emerging with a giant silver teapot on a tray, three chipped mugs and a packet of ginger biscuits. Chris pulled a face as his father opened them.

'A much-maligned biscuit, the ginger nut,' announced Jonty, offering the packet round.

They drank their tea and listened to more Acker Bilk, and then it was time to look at the medals.

'Now then, Davey, what have you got for me? Shall we take a look?' Jonty rubbed his hands together, brushing a cascade of biscuit crumbs onto the floor and indicated the dining table with his head.

Davey nodded and jumped up and unzipped the holdall. Gently, he unwrapped the tea towel and carefully placed the medals on Jonty's dining table, straightening them out so they hung evenly in a line. They consisted of a row of dull, bronze coloured six-pointed stars. They all looked the same initially; all had a central boss with curly writing in the centre, but raised text around this. Each was suspended from a striped ribbon, and each of these had a different colour combination. Davey rummaged in the holdall and fished out some more, dumping them on the table in a jumble of silver, gold, and multi-coloured ribbon.

The animals came over to see what was going on. Cecil woke up, stretched and yawned, and wandered over to greet everyone, chattering his teeth in greeting and shoving his muzzle into Davey's hand to be stroked. Bacchus appeared, plinking his way across the piano keys in a discordant jumble of sound, making everyone jump. He leapt gracefully up onto the dining table to supervise proceedings.

Jonty raised his eyebrows quizzically. 'There's a fair bit of metalwork here. Someone must have had a busy war.'

He picked up the bar and held it up before placing it back down and putting his glasses on. Both Chris and Davey looked at him expectantly, watching him place his forefinger on each medal before carefully examining the next one. Jonty began plucking the larger circular medals out of the pile, smoothing down the ribbons and placing them in a row next to the bronze stars. In total, there were twelve medals.

He said nothing for a few minutes, paying special attention to the rim round one, tilting it to the light and frowning. Eventually, he raised his head, cleared his throat and looked at Davey closely. He knew there was no love lost between the lad and his mother's boyfriend. Even so, he might be embarrassed to hear what he was about to tell him.

'These *cannot* belong to the same person. I think it would be extremely difficult, if nigh on impossible to get this combination of medals as an ordinary soldier, unless you had the gift of time travel, and could be in the army, navy, and RAF at the same time.'

Davey nodded slowly; his hands deep in his pockets. Chris thought he saw a strange expression cross his face — relief, or maybe scorn. It was difficult to tell, his friend never gave much away.

'You see here, look at these,' Jonty indicated the stars. The boys moved closer; heads bent over the table.

'The ones on the bar?'

'Yes. It's actually called a brooch bar. Well, on here, they are in order from left to right as you're looking at them. Firstly the 1939-45 Star…'

'Sorry, Dad, what are the colours on the ribbons? What do they mean?' interrupted Chris. 'Why are they all different?'

Jonty nodded slowly, raising his head and closing his eyes for a moment to dredge up information. 'Well, I was just getting to that. They are the colours of the services. The dark blue for the Royal Navy, red for the British Army, and light blue for the RAF. The King is supposed to have designed the colours.' He looked up at the boys. 'Some represent the countries where the battles were fought. Or the region of a particular theatre of war, and so forth. I'll explain.'

Jonty prodded the next star with his forefinger, and Bacchus gently stretched out an inquisitive forepaw and slowly batted the star to one side, as if rejecting it. 'Thank you, Bacchus,' muttered Jonty gravely, 'most helpful. The 1945 Star is followed here by the Atlantic Star. So, you must have been on operational service in the Atlantic to be awarded this. Then, here is the Africa Star. The red, gold, pale and navy-blue colours on this ribbon represent the desert and the services, and to get this you would have had to serve in North Africa, Malta, or Egypt.'

He paused, noticing Davey rubbing his mouth and slowly shaking his head, expressionless. 'And this,' he pointed to the medal with the red, white, and green ribbon, 'is the Italy Star. So, this is for operational service in Sicily or Italy. And this one next to it.'

'That looks like the French flag,' interjected Davey.

Jonty nodded in agreement. 'Indeed. This is the France and Germany Star for service in those countries and others besides. Belgium and Holland too, I think.'

Davey let out a long, low whistle and looked up at Chris, who was slowly shaking his head.

Jonty's fingers moved to the next medal in the sequence. 'This here is the Burma Star, with its ribbon representing the sun and the Commonwealth forces.' Jonty tapped it softly.

The boys looked more and more incredulous as Jonty pointed to each of the stars in turn. Chris noticed that Davey's normally olive complexion was turning slightly pink.

'Oh, hello! Here's an Air Crew Europe Star. That was issued exclusively for RAF personnel. This is one of my favourites. The blue colours represent the sky, night flying, and enemy searchlights.' He smiled. 'I know of one man who has more than earned this one and that's Gregory Crown from the post office.'

Jonty moved on to scrutinise the heavy circular medals. Davey had already heard enough. He felt embarrassed yet jubilant. He folded his arms across his chest and waited for Jonty to continue.

'This is the War medal. Everyone got one of these, and this is the Defence medal. A person had to have three years' service for one of these.' He picked up another and smiled to himself, circling the cool metal with his forefinger and held it out to the boys. It was a beautiful, heavy bronze disc portraying a woman with wings in a long, flowing gown. 'This is a First World War medal. So, the soldier earning this would have been getting on a bit if he also fought in the Second World War too.' Jonty peered at its edge closely and murmured, 'This belongs to a Private Wilfred Gibbons, who was in the Durham Light Infantry.'

'Who? How do you know that?' Chris reached over to his father and picked up the medal, measuring the weight of it in his palm compared to the lightness of the gold stars.

Jonty pointed to the rim of the metal disc. 'Do you see there is a name engraved on the edge? Medals weren't engraved for individuals in the Second World War, but they were in the First World War.'

He picked up another circular, silver coloured. 'And this is an Australia Service medal from the Second World War. It's got the coat of arms of Australia; the emu and the kangaroo.'

Davey giggled. Chris was standing open-mouthed, silent for once. Jonty looked at Chris closely over the top of his glasses. He knew who this was about, guessing, when Davey took out the bundle from the holdall.

'Does he wear them all at once? He must look like a Christmas tree.' He puffed out his cheeks and made a low whistle.

'No. I only really see him wear the stars. Maybe a couple of the big round ones, too.'

'Well, theoretically, no more than five stars can be awarded to one person, as far as I'm aware. This wearing of medals that haven't been earned, it's not new, Davey. Plenty of people do it. Perhaps they're guilty that they didn't have a glittering war. Maybe they're ashamed that they shirked. Sometimes people who weren't suitable to be called up did it. It's about shame, but it's about wanting to belong, to be thought of as a good person.'

He paused and tapped the table, looking at Davey again. 'However, the thing that sets this apart is over-egging the pudding. If it was a couple of stars and the War medal, nobody would give it a second glance. The important thing to remember is there were hundreds of people who did incredibly heroic things during wartime and never got a medal or they did receive one but don't want to shout about it. The memories associated with it are too painful, both physical or psychological.'

Jonty absentmindedly stroked Bacchus under his chin. The purring ramped up a couple of decibels. He took his glasses off, rubbing the space between his eyes and placed his hands on the table like two white, wiry spiders.

'Why did you need to know this, Davey?'

Davey looked at the medals and then at Chris, who was slipping his fingers through the silk rags of Cecil's ears. The dog was leaning against Chris, eyes closed in ecstasy, grumbling in appreciation. Davey took a deep breath and leant his hands on the back of a chair, talking to the table.

'I know Ray's a liar and a bastard, but I just wanted to hear it from someone else, really. I'm certain he's never been to any of these places. I've seen people looking at him when he stands by the Cenotaph on Remembrance Sunday. People like Mr Crown, real war heroes.' He sighed. 'I'm not daft. I hear people talking, saying he's a Walter Mitty. I just wanted proof before I say something to him. It makes me sick, seeing him standing next to people who have really suffered and are still suffering. He's sacrificed nothing or done anything for anyone unless it's for himself.' Davey's eyes were black, furious. He was getting himself worked up now, just thinking about Ray.

'Be careful, Davey,' warned Jonty. He had known Ray for years and knew his sort. He knew he had no more been to the places marked on these medals than he had flown to the moon, but that was his business.

'Will it make a difference if he knows you know these aren't his?' he said softly.

Davey shrugged, pushing his hair back from his forehead. He closed his eyes momentarily. It might make a difference if his mum knew, but maybe she already did.

She wasn't stupid. Daft for staying with Ray, yes, but not unintelligent. He was confused. Did he want to confront Ray? Or did he want this to be the reason his mum could finally use to kick him out? Jonty put his hand on to Davey's arm and looked at him directly, his voice low and as serious as the boy had ever heard it.

'I wouldn't dream of telling you what to do. You are an adult, after all. But I would advise that you be very careful because his pride will be hurt. He may react badly to being exposed. You are a lot younger than him and you will probably leave home soon. Stella and Bobby may still have to live with him when you are up and gone.'

Davey looked at Jonty steadily, nodding slowly and inhaling deeply. 'Thank you, Jonty, but I just can't stop thinking about Gregory Crown, and Frank Singleton, who is always in the library reading room. Grandma told me he was a prisoner of the Japanese and ended up in a POW camp in Singapore. He had his tongue cut out and was starved almost to death.'

Davey paused, aware his voice was wobbling, attempting to slow it down. 'It makes me sick to think that my mum lives with a bloke who has the nerve to stand next to men like that when he's never done a good thing in his whole life.'

Jonty blinked and nodded. Bacchus pushed the Victory medal off the table with a fat ginger paw. It made a sharp ringing sound on the floor. Somewhere behind Chris's shoulder, the record player had turned itself off.

Chapter 21
November 1982

It was Sunday afternoon. The low cloud obscured the hills in a greeny soup, and the entire estate was rain-washed grey, slowly seeping into dusk. Bobby was at home, Wendy was out with some lad somewhere, so Bobby saw the rest of the dreary day stretching ahead of her; stuck in the house with Ray and her mum, everyone getting on each other's nerves. She might get her coat on and go up to Grandma Alice's at this rate. Bobby looked at the street through the nets; the steady downpour of rain, the occasional car whooshing past, throwing dirty water up over the pavement.

She didn't fancy staying here. Ray had come back from the pub early and was in a foul mood. He was on the piss, sitting in front of the telly, after having done his bit at the Remembrance Sunday parade — marching through town with the rest of the veterans to the Cenotaph in the marketplace. The cluster of old 'Tommies' from the First World War got smaller each year. The remainder were frail. Some were in wheelchairs, blankets tucked around their knees. This year was a special parade after the Falklands conflict.

Although nobody from Gritstone had served there, it was fresh in everyone's mind from the constant radio and telly coverage. There had been a good turnout of townsfolk for the brief service and wreath laying, even though the morning had been wet. A crowd of bared, bent heads stood still and silent as the mournful sobbing sound of the lone bugler playing the 'Last Post' drifted across the marketplace just before 11 am.

Ray loved the Remembrance Sunday ceremony in town, and he cut an impressive figure. Tall and smart in his slacks and blazer, he had a military bearing and was still in good nick for a man in his sixties. Enjoying the admiring glances when folk saw him marching through town from the Drill Hall with the other veterans, Ray ignored the sideways, sometimes amused, sometimes scornful glances from the other men around him when they clocked his chest full of medals.

Most of the veterans were too well mannered to say anything. They were here to remember lost friends and to give thanks for their own survival. This year, after the ceremony, as people were drifting away, he walked past the silent bloke from the library who had been in a POW camp in Singapore. Just as Ray drew level with him, the man hawked and spat on the ground, right in front of him, splattering Ray's shiny shoes. Ray glared, shocked, but the man remained impassive, eyes full of disgust.

There was a good half hour to fill before the pub opened, so Ray walked back to the Drill Hall. There would be the usual refreshments in the main hall and he could carry on playing the big man. It was a ten-minute walk back to the old Victorian building, and Ray strode quickly, reluctant to stop and talk to people. Not liking to admit it, the spitting bloke had really rattled him. Ray wasn't used to being disrespected.

He passed through the open, highly polished front door of the hall and into the small lobby — with its honour roll for the Boer War and both World Wars inscribed on marble plaques decorated with poppies and wreaths. Sitting under the Burma Star Association plaque and the Kohima Epitaph was a little old man with a collection tin for the British Legion. Ray ignored his smile and the offered tin, and marched inside.

Inside the hall, two trestle tables had been set up against the back wall and a small group of old soldiers were gathering, juggling paper plates and cups of tea. It was a large and high-ceilinged room, the regimental colours suspended from the roof in faded and sometimes tattered swags. Pale, watery sunbeams streamed through the windows onto the grey heads of the assembled men. Two Brownies wearing poppies were handing out limp toasted teacakes with a scraping of margarine.

Behind the trestle table were two women, busying themselves with plates, paper napkins, and teacups. One was an older woman, her scalp showing pink through its thin covering of white candyfloss hair. It was freezing in the hall and she was wearing a pinny over her coat. Next to her was a young blonde woman in a tight woollen dress and heeled boots, filling up the hot water urn with a metal jug. Ray liked the way the dress rode up to her arse when she stretched to fill the vessel with water. He smoothed his hair down and wandered over to work his magic. The girl was maybe twenty, with lovely pink skin and pale, slate-blue eyes. Her hair was held back from her face with a tortoiseshell clip.

'Tea, chuck?' She picked up the big metal teapot and filled a cup. Hands wobbling with the effort, she was slopping tea into the saucer.

Ray could see the old bat was talking to a couple of men and took the tea pot off her. 'Let me help you.' He carried on pouring. She smiled up at him, showing lovely white, even teeth. Smirking back, he could see she had clocked the medals.

'Thanks. It's so heavy when it's full. I've had a hell of a job setting up all this stuff with just Edie and the Brownies to help. I don't know how I got roped into this, to be honest.' She spoke in an undertone, rolling her eyes and jerking her head at the old lady who was clattering about with the crockery.

Ray puffed his chest out. 'Do you need help with anything else, love?'

'I don't suppose you could help me bring those chairs out? There're more people here than I expected.' She pointed to the open door of a storeroom and a stack of furniture crammed in beside boxes of sports equipment.

'Of course, my pleasure.' He followed her across the shiny polished floor, watching the swing of her hips in the tight dress. His shoes squeaked with each step.

'Thank you so much. I'd ask Edie, but she won't lift so much as a teaspoon before she starts skriking.' She shook her head and raised her eyebrows. 'She's a pain in the arse, to be honest,' she whispered to Ray.

He carried two stacks of chairs out for her to distribute. They were pretty heavy, but Ray made sure she saw he thought it was no more difficult than picking up a kitten. She quickly set them up around the perimeter of the hall and dashed back to fill up the teacups as more veterans drifted in. Accepting another cup of tea, he wandered back to her once the queue had died down.

'Are you courting, love?' he said casually, glancing at her left hand, which was bare.

Her face changed instantly into a tired, *here we go* expression. 'I'm not, no,' she said flatly, offering nothing more. She had noticed him staring at her tits when he spoke to her, his eyes moving greedily over her body.

'Would you fancy going out for a drink with me sometime?'

Her mouth set into a flat line, incredulous. Her voice was low, and she leant towards him, close enough to kiss him. Near enough for him to see the soft fair down on her upper lip. He thought all his Christmases had come at once.

'No, I wouldn't,' she said briskly. 'First, because you live with a woman whose kids are nearly the same age as me, and secondly because you're old enough to be me grandad. Piss off, you dirty old get.' She spat the last four words out so loudly, Edie turned to her with a scandalised expression and one of the old men chuckled.

Ray smacked the cup down so hard that the tea jumped out in a quick brown puddle. He marched out of the Drill Hall, nearly flattening one of the Brownies who was emptying ashtrays into a bucket. He had to get a drink inside him. Cheeky little slag. How dare she call him old? The bitch. Ray virtually ran up the street behind the Drill Hall, head bent against the drizzle, medals bouncing off his chest, heart pounding in rage. Two minutes and he would be in the pub.

It was a tradition of Ray's to go to the taproom in the Carders on Remembrance Sunday and soak up the admiring glances alongside the pints of Boddingtons. He walked in and shook the drizzle off his clothes, smoothing his hair down and fishing for his wallet. Ordering a pint and a bag of nuts, he was sure the lad behind the bar was looking at him funny. Ray felt on edge again, and didn't like it. *You need to get yourself together. You're getting paranoid.*

Standing by the bar, he watched the barman rip a bag of peanuts off the card hanging on the wall near the phone. The card was printed with a picture of a topless girl behind the packets. Barmaids always took the packets off from the outside first, so the breasts took ages to be revealed. The barman pulled off a bag from the middle, exposing a pink nipple. He tossed it across the shiny bar top and took the money off Ray, then as he turned away and went through into the lounge bar, he said something to the landlady, who looked at Ray and laughed.

Ray was sure he had said, 'A tit for a tit' but he couldn't be certain. His imagination was running riot. The pub was filling up with punters. Some had been at the Cenotaph, some were just drinkers, getting a few pints in. He stood by the bar for a bit. There was usually someone to talk to. But this year, he was on his own. Lighting a fag, he took a big swallow of his pint.

There was a group of younger lads standing between the jukebox and the fag machine. One of them whispered something to another and they all turned towards Ray and started laughing. He turned his back and felt an unpleasant and unfamiliar sensation of embarrassment.

Gregory Crown from the post office came in with a couple of other men, and the group of young lads parted respectfully to let them through. Gregory nodded at one of them, the shiny livid skin on his face stretching into a half-smile. One lad came up to the bar and ordered the older men drinks. Gregory tried to stop him, but was waved away.

'It's the least we can to for you, especially today. Three pints of Boddies please, Mandy.'

The landlady nodded, smiled and reached for the pint glasses. Ray lit another fag and kept his back to them all. He felt a sense of dissatisfaction, deciding to finish this pint, go home and start supping again there. This lot were a bunch of arseholes. Mandy pulled the hand pump towards her, the foaming bitter spuming into the tilted glass. Usually, she shared a bit of chat with Ray. He would make a flirtatious comment and stare at her shelf-like bosom in its low-cut top. Today, she kept her eyes on pulling the pints and ignored him, chatting to the young lad paying for the drinks.

Fuck this, he thought as he drained his pint, ground out his cigarette into the big glass ashtray near the drip tray, and left the pub. The group by the door parted to let him pass and he thought he saw the young lads smirking at him. Pushing the door open with the flat of his hand, he stepped out into the street and heard a shout of laughter as the door swung closed. Ray strode swiftly away, the medals tinkling against each other the faster he walked.

Bobby perked up as she saw Chris Clough come belting up the road from the town end of the estate, collar turned up and holding an umbrella which had turned inside out. Chris was always good for a laugh, and Bobby decided she might stay around for a bit longer before she retreated to her room. He crashed through the Armstrong's gate. Stella must have seen him coming up the path as the next moment he was in the room, shaking water over everyone like a lively terrier and trying to untangle the brolly.

Ray was watching a war film. The front room was hot and full of fag smoke, and as usual, when Ray greeted Chris, he got the merest twitch of the head and a grunt.

'Ah, *The Longest Day*. D'you like this film, Mr Short?' Chris shrugged out of his wet donkey jacket and pushed his quiff out of his eyes. He had to shout above the action on the telly.

Bobby indicated the settee with her head while Chris gave up with the umbrella and abandoned it under the window in a heap of crumpled metal and nylon.

'Aye, John Wayne, a proper war hero. I'll never forget that day, either.' Ray shook his head gravely and poked a yellow twig finger with its fag at the screen, snapping open the ring pull of another can of Tennants.

Bobby, out of Ray's line of sight near the window, rolled her eyes at Chris and mouthed, 'Bullshitter.'

Chris grinned at her, pulling his face straight when Ray looked back from the screen. Stella was hovering anxiously in the doorway, screwing up a tea towel like she was going to turn it inside out. She reminded Bobby of a man she had seen on the telly once, making poodles out of balloons.

'Would you like a brew, Chris?' she offered, voice high-pitched, hoping he would say no.

Chris was so unpredictable. He came out with all sorts of things; comments nobody else would dare to. It was like having a small wild animal in the house that could cause havoc at any second, or an unexploded bomb, ready to throw everything into confusion.

'No thank you, Stella. I'm fine.'

Chris settled himself down on the settee, one leg crossed at the ankle over the other, his foot dangling. He smiled at Ray with cheeky benevolence. Ray glared back. He had to be very careful about how he spoke to Chris. He could well go home and grass him up to his dad, and the cash in hand work might dry up.

'Well, what's interesting about John Wayne is he never actually went to war. So, he wasn't a hero at all. He never saw active service.' Chris's face was neutral, eyes on the telly. He started patting down his pockets, trying to find his cigs.

Stella stayed frozen at the door; the tea towel was now so tightly screwed up it had turned into a coil. Questioning the veracity of John Wayne's hero status in the Armstrong house was unheard of, sacrilegious. Her mouth was slightly open and eyes were already watering. She faked a humorous fluttering *'Ooh, get away with you'* gesture with her hand, and contorted her face into a mask of a smile. A pretend, high-pitched giggle escaped.

Bobby moved nearer the telly to get a better view of Ray's expression, but near enough to the door that she could bundle Stella out in a hurry. She was fascinated, but terrified at the same time. It was like watching someone poke a stick in the face of a furious bear.

'Don't talk shit!' Ray's face was furious, gob working. He was already burgundy with the drink, the blue veins on his nose a fine spidery net, like a miniature road map. Two little bubbles of spit had formed at the corners of his mouth. He'd had enough of people doubting him today.

'No, I'm afraid I'll have to disagree with you on that point.' Chris's voice was chirpy, young, confident. 'Sorry, Mr Short, but he was always an actor. He was never in the military, he just pretended. It's true. John Wayne never saw active service.'

Aye, you're right, thought Bobby, *he just pretended like you.*

Ray was at a pitch of drunkenness when he was at his most dangerous. Not pissed enough to be staggering, but drunk enough to be argumentative and violent. Bobby could see it was killing him to be civil to Chris. Chris eventually found the cigarettes in his donkey jacket pocket and offered the packet to Ray.

'Smoke, Mr Short?'

Ray shook his head and took another mouthful of Tennants, glaring at Chris.

'What are they?' Despite his simmering rage, he was curious about the paper packet of Gauloises.

'French cigarettes, Mr Short. You must have had these during the war when you were in Normandy? They taste disgusting, if I'm honest. But I've run out of Benson's and my dad smokes these sometimes. He lived in Paris for a while when he was a student.'

Ray said nothing and resumed his staring at the telly.

Davey came in then. He'd been out to Grandma Alice's and had a borrowed school chess set under his arm, wrapped in a plastic bag. He wasn't sure what was going on, but could see by the expression on Ray's face that he was about to kick off and Mum looked like she was about to cry or start shouting. Davey jerked his head at Chris and made a warning face, and Chris got up, rubbed his hands briskly, and picked up his coat.

'Goodbye, Mr Short, enjoy the film. I'm sorry if I spoiled it for you. It makes you look differently at someone when you know the full picture, doesn't it? James Stewart, Clark Gable, Paul Newman, David Niven — they all went to war, but definitely not John Wayne.' He saluted Ray smartly and turned to Stella and Bobby, making a small bow. 'Afternoon ladies, see you soon.' The lads left, and the front door slammed.

'He,' huffed Ray, 'is a cheeky little arsehole. And one of these days, he and that shithead of a son of yours are going to get a good hiding. I can see what they're doing, coming in here, shit-stirring and lying, and talking about things they know nowt about.' Draining the can, he dropped it to the floor, instantly cracking open another, the golden foam sighing out onto his hand. Bobby could see that he was trembling with rage. Something had happened today at the Remembrance service. He had been in a foul mood since he came back, and before last orders as well. She could never recall him coming back before last orders on a Sunday afternoon.

Bobby slipped out, followed by her mother, who walked into the kitchen, bending to light a fag from the gas jet on the hob. She stood upright, took a deep drag, and pointed at Bobby.

'Shut the door. That Chris is going to have to stop coming round here and winding up Ray.' She leant against the sink, scratching the instep of one foot against her shin. The grey fading afternoon light was behind her and the fag smoke rose in a blue haze above her head.

Bobby let out a short, mirthless bark. 'Good luck with that, Mum. He's only telling the truth and he's Davey's best mate. This is our house and we can have whoever we want round here. We were here before him.' She crossed her arms across her chest and stood up taller, pulling her head back.

Stella let out a long, exasperated sigh and dragged on her cigarette. 'How many times do I have to hear you say that? Why do you two make life so bloody difficult for me?'

'It's him that does that.' Bobby stabbed her finger towards the kitchen door. 'He makes life fucking impossible for all of us and you won't do anything about it.'

Chapter 22
December 1982

Slade was still belting out of the Carders' jukebox when the door to the taproom banged opened, onto the pitch-black ginnel, and Boston swayed out. A blast of music, laughter, light, and fag smoke followed him. He was really pissed and ready to make his way home. He stopped for a piss up against a keg, using one hand to steady himself against the wall, humming along to 'Merry Xmas Everybody'.

Christ, he was fucked. It hadn't hit him until he was outside in the cold air. There was a light covering of frost on the bins; the tops of the walls and the cobbles sparkled.

Jean and Lynne were waiting in a doorway halfway down the ginnel. He didn't even see them until he had zipped up his jeans under his beer belly and pushed the permed greasy mop away from his face. He was making his way down to Angel Street, bouncing off the walls and singing as he went.

'Hiya, Boston, yer fuckin' pervert. I'll give you a merry fuckin Xmas, yer dirty twat.' Jean's voice was a low, controlled growl.

She blocked his way, red tipped hands on her hips and shadowed face pushed forward, legs apart. Lynne stood beside her; they filled the ginnel. He couldn't see their faces at first. They had their backs to the streetlight at the bottom of the alleyway. Jean had him shoved down on the cobbles in a couple of seconds, her meaty forearm against his chest. He made a yelping sound as Lynne kicked his legs from under him and sat on them, looking scornfully at his shitty vinyl slip-ons.

'Yer can always tell a man by his shoes,' she spat, wobbling her head in disgust, pursing her mouth like a lip-sticked cat's bum. Jean had her face right up to Boston's confused gob. He stank of sweat, beer, fags, and crab sticks.

Bewildered, he groaned and whispered, 'What do you want?' in a strained and wheedling voice.

All he could see was her head; a large, back-combed frizz. A bleached halo in the gloom and an overpowering smell of Charlie perfume seeping from the opening in the neck of her overcoat.

'Don't you ever, ever, go near my daughter again. You're gonna be sorry you ever laid a finger on her, you fucking freak.'

The words came out quietly, slowly. Thick with rage through a rigid jaw, stiff with fury. Every word was punctuated with a finger stabbing in his chest. Lynne had a hand resting on Jean's shoulder, peering over at Boston's terrified face. Smashed as he was, Boston realised who she was then. A slow, wheezing sound huffed out of his throat. He looked fearful and stupid, like a cow Lynne had once seen in a documentary about abattoirs. Boston started to struggle and babble, but Jean punched him quickly in the face. He gasped and began whimpering quietly.

Jean massaged her fist, wriggling her fingers in the cold air. She unzipped his coat roughly and found what she was looking for; a small bunch of keys on a plastic fob with a sweaty blue gonk on the end of a chain. She put them in her pocket and took hold of his tie and slowly began to throttle him. It was taking too long. He was making choking, guttural sounds and wasn't giving her the satisfaction or result she wanted. Standing, she kicked him briefly in the head and he moaned. His eyes were puffy slits, mucus leaking from his slack lips.

Looking to the bottom of the ginnel at the junction with Angel Street, Jean smiled to herself, rubbing the space between her eyes with her thumb. Lynne stood over him, frozen, hunched like a skinny blackbird in a thin leopard print dress, fishnets, and high heels. Revolted by him rolling around, whimpering and sobbing, she wrapped her plastic mac around herself.

The booze was wearing off now, and she wished she hadn't agreed to help Jean batter this twat. It would have been easier just to ask a lad from the pub to kick the shit out of Boston, but Jean was having none of it. She wanted to look into his eyes when she shellacked him.

'Here, Lynne, help me shift him. I know how I'm going to sort the bastard,' she commanded, glaring up at Lynne, beckoning her with thick, swollen fingers.

Jean took one of Boston's limp feet. Lynne took the other, and they dragged him along the ginnel, his head rattling off the cobbles, moaning softly, hardly audible. A faint glow of orange from the streetlights lit a steep kerb where the old cobbles met the tarmacked road. Dumping her handbag up on top of a bin, Jean pushed her sleeves up as though she was going to do the washing up.

Lynne was panting now, her head aching after all that vodka. 'Hurry up, Jean, someone's going to come out any minute.' She pushed her hair out of her eyes, hands shaking with effort and anxiety.

Jean calmly and carefully straightened Boston out so his body lay across the pavement, at right angles to the houses — his legs sticking out into the road, across the steep drop of the stone kerb. His feet flopped inwards like a disjointed puppet, face flabby and limp

'Hold the bastard down, Lynne, this won't take long,' she hissed.

Jean quickly stood up, took a step back, hesitated for a moment if as if to measure her stride and jumped on Boston's shins in her stilettos with all of her eighteen stones. There was a small, dull splintering sound like the cracking of kindling, then a second of silence before an awful animal howl of pain filled the ginnel.

'Oh, God, fuck…' Lynne spewed up over Boston and started struggling to her feet, the thin soles of her shoes slipping on the frosty cobbles. A thread of vomit sparkled in the half-light. She wiped it away with the back of her hand and stumbled backwards, sobbing.

'Stay there, I haven't finished,' barked Jean, face stony with concentration.

'Jean,' Lynne started before the lounge door at the front of the pub opened briefly and they could hear the thin, high sound of a woman's laughter, drunken singing, and Wizzard playing 'I Wish it could be Christmas Every Day' before the door slammed shut again, muffling the sound. The street was deserted, just the sound of Boston's crying and gurgling.

Lynne stood, legs apart and hands on her hips, panting as Jean fumbled in her bag and pulled out a pair of rubber gloves; the ones she used at work to clean the toilets. Sovereign rings shining, face expressionless in the amber streetlight. She put the gloves on quickly and calmly, like a surgeon preparing to perform a routine procedure, humming all the while under her breath. She pulled something else from her handbag; something wrapped in a plastic bag, and opened it. The smell hit Lynne and she gagged, holding her thin white hand over her mouth.

'What the fuck is that?'

Jean ignored her, knelt down, skirt straining across her thighs. Carefully cradling the stinking bolus, she prised open Boston's jaws. It wasn't difficult. He was really wailing now; snot, blood, and spew dripping down his chin. His eyes were closed, swollen slits. She forced the wet ball of dogshit and nettles into his mouth, and then slapped him as hard as she could across his face. Lynne heard the sovereigns clack off his broken dentures.

'Right, let's go, Lynne,' sang Jean triumphantly, yanking off the gloves.

She struggled to her feet, dropped the gloves into the bin next to Boston, who was sobbing and choking next to them, his smashed-up legs still in the gutter with all the litter. Jean slung her bag over her shoulder, linked Lynne's arm through hers, and they strode off into the sparkling Christmas night, heading for the pet shop. Above them, blinking steadily over the houses, was Orion, swaggering across the clean winter sky with his belt gleaming, leading the way.

The streets were quiet. Curtains were closed and lights on. The sound of tellies going, one or two voices raised in anger or laughter, and the blurred coloured lights of Christmas trees glowed in windows fogged up with the heat of bodies. Lynne was struggling to keep up with Jean now. She kept stumbling in her stilettos and it was getting colder and slippier. Jean rooted in her bag and brought out two miniatures of Johnny Walker and her fags. Winking at Lynne, she nudged her with a sharp elbow.

'Let's take a minute.' Her voice was quiet, reassuring.

They sat down on the bench outside the hardware shop and Jean lit their fags. Lynne was trembling with cold and shock. Jean's hand was like a rock, the blue lighter flame steady. She passed Lynne a lit fag, took a deep drag on her own and emptied the whisky down her throat, feeling the spirit burn its warmth through her. Lynne sipped hers, eyes screwed up, shuddering. She wrapped her mac around her bones even tighter. Two minutes later, Jean slapped her thighs with purpose and stood up, dragging Lynne up with her, and they marched on. Past the tree in the marketplace with its Nativity stable, covered by a scratched Perspex window.

They stopped in the pet shop doorway and Jean glanced around to see if anyone was watching them — but the street was silent; everyone asleep, at the pub, or in front of the telly. Jean looked through the keys on the gonk fob and selected one, tried it, no joy. She tried another, felt the lock give and leant her shoulder against the sticking door. Her breath came in great long plumes, like a warhorse. Lynne was doubtful now. They'd broken a man's legs, half killed him, choked him with dog shit, and were about to break into his shop. She was freezing, nearly sober, and just wanted to go home.

'Do you not think this is going a bit far now, Jean?' She whined, rubbing her frozen hands together.

Jean turned, impassive, her slab of a face like an Easter Island statue. 'That fucker of a rapist is lucky to be alive. I'd like to kill him, but he's not worth doing time for. I haven't finished yet. Not by a long shot,' she spat.

Lynne looked at the floor, mute, lank hair covering her face. The door opened and the animal smell hit them both. The sweet smell of mouse shit, hay, sawdust, and pet food. Jean had a torch in her bag. It was cheap, with a weak beam, but it was good enough for her to do what she wanted. She daren't turn the lights on.

The shop was alive at night; the rodents awake and running on their wheels, climbing the bars of their cages, wrestling, playing, shagging, and fighting. Hundreds of tiny pink feet sounded like rain on a tin roof. Jean played the beam of the torch across the cages, and was met with pink eyes, brown eyes, and quivering whiskers. The rabbits and guinea pigs ducked into their nests, scuffling in panic.

Jacob the macaw had been asleep, head under his wing. Jean shone the light on him, and he turned, curious and wary, the colours of his feathers brilliant and jewel-like in the torchlight. She was struck by how out of place he looked in all this drabness.

'What have you got to say for yourself, you feathered fucker?' challenged Jean. Her voice echoing around the empty shop.

Jacob didn't answer, but cocked his head and made a small crooning sound.

'Okay, Lynne, let's start.'

Jean began methodically opening the cages of the mice, rats, rabbits, and guinea pigs. The mice began coming out almost immediately, climbing along the tops of the cages and shelves. The rats were slower and more cautious, but soon began exploring. The guinea pigs set up loud alarm calls and hid in their bedding, squealing in terror. Lynne picked up the rabbits gently, cradling their warm soft bodies in her arms and shooed them out into the street, then she started opening the bags of dog biscuits and fish food, tipping them on the floor, pulling the rubber bones and treats off a display carousel and throwing them around the shop.

Jean pulled bags of shavings and hay off the shelves and started piercing each one with her thumbnail, tipping the contents on the floor and the counter. Ripping open packets of Trill and sprinkling them into the open mouth of the cash till. She threw cuttlefish and sprays of millet into the fish tanks and made her way into the storeroom. Taking a broom, she ran the head across the shelves, dislodging tins of pet food and carefully stacked mouse cages. The noise was deafening. She jammed a plug in the sink, turned the taps on and started filling the sink with Bonios. It was creepy in here, a small skylight the only source of light and an overpowering smell of animal bedding and human semen.

'Come on, Jean, let's go, please. For fuck's sake,' begged Lynne, on the verge of tears.

Agitated now, they were making so much noise, somebody must have heard them.

'I'd love to torch the place, but I draw the line at burning animals.' Jean let out a long sigh.

She had one more job. She opened Jacob's cage door, the torch between her teeth. It had a heavy latch secured with a climber's carabiner hook to stop him from escaping. Jacob looked frightened now, moving slowly, mechanically, to the back of his cage, but Jean spoke to him quietly.

'You've been a prisoner in here a long time, haven't you? Since I was a kid, anyway. Come on then, now's your chance,' she whispered.

'Will he fly in the dark? Can he still fly? He's been in there years. Will his wings work?' gabbled Lynne.

'Dunno Lynne, I'm not fuckin' David Attenborough. Let's see,' snapped Jean.

'Hurry up, Jean. Coppers will be here soon.'

'Shut it, Lynne. Give him space. Let him see the door.'

They stood back, away from the doorway of the cage, feet crunching on the spilled food, cat litter, and sawdust. Jacob moved forward, perched on the threshold, tilting his head this way and that, considering. His grey scaly feet carefully, slowly, gripped the bars as he leant into the darkness at the edge of his known world.

'Come on, go. Get out, go,' urged Jean. She shoved her hand in the cage, trying to shoo Jacob out. But he retreated to the back of the cage, fearful, squawking loudly.

'Fuck off! Fuck off!' He screeched and nodded his head up and down furiously, darting at Jean with his beak open, enraged and terrified.

'He'll have you, Jean! Watch his beak. Look at them claws!' shrieked Lynne.

'Oh, shut it, Lynne. You're scaring him as much as me. Stop being a mardarse.'

Jean had an idea. She flicked the shop lights on and Jacob stopped screaming instantly, like his sound had been turned off. He blinked once, slowly, and then flew out towards the open doorway of the shop. A gorgeous, shocking, jewel-flash of jungle as he disappeared into the darkness.

'Do you think he will live in the cold? Don't they come from somewhere hot, like Africa or South America? Won't he die?' Lynne was almost weeping with fear.

Jean shrugged, her voice flat and careless. 'If I was him, I'd rather die of cold than rot in that nonce's cage.'

Jean left the shop door wide open and used a big tin of Chappie as a door stop. A cautious stream of rodents began a steady exodus out into the quiet street. Above them, perched on the warm window ledge of the commercial laundry, a macaw tilted his head and observed the starry night sky for the first time in fifty years.

Jean opened her handbag and rooted around for her fags. 'Let's go home, Lynne. I could murder a brew.'

Chapter 23
Christmas Day 1982

Stella plugged the tree lights on as soon as she got up, to look at them in the dark without the big overhead light on. She would have liked a real tree; she loved the smell and it always reminded her of being a kid in Flint Cottage. Alice would drag in a newly felled fir tree, stick it in a bucket, and wedge it upright with wet mossy rocks. It would sit in front of the low window, the delicious piney fragrance filling the cottage. The tree would be sparsely decorated. No tinsel, just a handful of passed down, ancient glass ornaments and a star made from a few twigs and twisted silver wire. Stella used to complain that it looked bare, but Alice would shake her head.

'Let the tree speak for itself. You don't need anything extra. Nothing can make a tree look more beautiful than it already is.'

Not Stella's tree. The one they had now was artificial; made of white plastic and literally smothered in tinsel and baubles. It was actually difficult to see any of the branches, just a solid triangle of gaudy decorations covered in a net of fairy lights. Under the tree were a handful of presents. When the kids were little, there had been a pillowcase full of gifts for both of them. Ray had never bought them anything, but said they were spoilt. Stella would rack up a fortune on the catalogue, buying them toys and clothes and then paying all year to clear the debt.

Now they were older, it was just a few things. This year she bought Bobby some new tights, make-up, and the record she wanted. She had got Davey a book, some socks, and a jumper that looked as though it was already going to be too small for him. For Ray, always the same: a bottle of whisky, some socks, and a box of the sugary crystallised jellies made to look like segments of oranges and lemons. She looked to see if there was anything for her. There was, two things, a small, badly wrapped heavy object which she could tell was a bottle of perfume and would be from Davey, and something soft and squashy from Bobby.

Opening the curtains, it was still dark outside, but she could make out a little lad on a brand-new bike, wobbling down the street, watched by a hungover looking woman in slippers with a coat over her nightie. She smiled, remembering Davey and Bobby when they were that age, up before it was light, excited for Christmas.

Stella put the kettle on and had a fag. When the kids were nippers, they would have been up hours ago, whingeing and mithering to open their presents. She used to take them to midnight Mass, and they were allowed to have one small present before they went to bed. Ray put a stop to that, saying it was papist shite. Now the kids went out to the pub or parties on Christmas Eve and slept in on Christmas Day. Last night had been loud on the estate; a police car and an ambulance shrieking past the main road into the town at about midnight.

There was a sound at the back door and Stella opened it quickly. Tiger slid through, bringing a blast of cold air, miaowing peevishly. Stella opened a tin of cat food and tipped it into a saucer, stroking his cold glossy coat as he ate noisily, tail fluffed up like a bog brush. Every year, with unfailing optimism, Stella would think, *this is going to be the year it's all nice*. A Christmas Day where there's no aggro, no shouting. It would be a Christmas like in the films. She had a quiet fantasy that she re-ran in her head each Christmas morning.

They would spend Christmas Day in a beautiful house with ceilings so high the Christmas tree would be nearly twelve feet tall and covered in fabulous decorations. At the base of the tree was a mountain of beautifully wrapped presents and they would sit around in gorgeous clothes, opening their presents in front of a raging log fire, carols or Bing Crosby on the record player in the background. Ray would hand her a stunningly wrapped present. She would tear off the thick gold paper and there would be a slim hinged leather jewellery box. Opening it, she would look down onto a diamond necklace nestling on a bed of white padded satin. She would sigh and coo and Ray would say,

'I'm glad you like it, darling.'

She would bend her head, holding the black cloud of hair out of the way of her white neck, and he would fasten it. She would look up at him, eyes wet with tears, the pear-shaped diamond resting like a star on her cashmere bosom.

'Thank you, Ray. It's gorgeous. I love it.'

Ray would smile at her indulgently, and everything would be perfect. They would all drink sherry, eat their turkey dinner, play games, watch the telly, and go to bed without a cross word or a black eye. It was the fantasy Hollywood white Christmas of her teenage dreams.

The sound of movement from upstairs brought her out of the daydream and she brewed up and shoved some bread in the toaster. The turkey had been in the oven early, just the veg to do when they got back from Alice's. Stella had cleaned the house in the days leading up to Christmas day, and put up decorations and paper chains with Sellotape and drawing pins. On the day itself, she liked to get the fire going early, banking up the coal. By the time everyone was up and downstairs eating their breakfast, the room was warm and cosy.

Before the festivities could start properly, they would visit Alice. She wouldn't come to Stella's, not while Ray was in the house, and he didn't want her there either. Alice saw right through him; she knew it and he knew it. It was just easier for Stella and the kids to go to Flint Cottage for a couple of hours. He needed to be in the pub when it opened and didn't like hanging about. Ray always dropped them off. Stella didn't drive. Ray had discouraged her every time it was mentioned.

'Why would you want to learn to drive? If you need to go anywhere, I'll take you.'

It was bitterly cold when they got in Ray's car and followed the white-coated frosty road out of town. They saw little traffic, just the odd taxi. Within ten minutes, they were getting out of the car again and up the short, cobbled path to Flint Cottage.

Alice was waiting at the open door, calling out, 'Merry Christmas' to them as Ray sped away down the hill. She was in her second smartest jumper as a concession to Christmas; bottle green wool with darned elbows and a frayed neck. She wore man's cords, which were bald at the knee and stuffed into thick odd socks.

She had the range going full blast and the cottage was beautifully warm when they stepped in from the thin wind coming off the moors. Ganymede and Perseus were asleep, stretched out on the hearthrug in a tangled mass of fur. A rich, clean, resinous smell from the tree filled the air and Bobby and Davey both looked at each other, silently wishing they could spend the day here. They hated Christmas at home; the terrible pent-up tension waiting for Ray to get to that pitch of drunkenness that he bickered with Stella and it would all start. He would be okay until teatime-ish, then when he started on the whisky, it was all downhill from there.

Next year, thought Davey, *we'll both come here. We're not kids anymore. We're only staying around for Mum.*

Alice hugged them all and Davey ducked to avoid the swags of holly hanging from the roof beams. The austere little tree with its few decorations filled the window. Stella looked about while the kids chattered with Alice. She didn't come up here often and it had changed little since the Christmases of her childhood. Still the same pictures on the walls, the collections of rocks, skulls, and fossils that the kids loved so much, and that gave her the creeps. She ran her fingers over a jam jar full of feathers, staring out of the tiny window to the frosty fell beyond.

Under the tree were three presents. The kids and Stella handed theirs to Alice first. Peppermint creams from Stella, a book on ferns from Bobby and a new kindling axe, and some rolling tobacco from Davey. There were treats for the cats and a large poinsettia from the indoor market with crimson leaves. Davey handed over the small cannonball of a pudding that Alice would have later, steamed with tinned custard poured on top. Alice smiled, remarking on each gift, however modest, stroking the leaves of the plant and kissing her grandchildren.

Alice handed her presents over, all wrapped in ancient wrapping paper that was reused year after year. Stella got a knitted scarf in blue and pink stripes, hand knitted and very rough looking. Alice was a practical woman who could turn her hand to most things, but her knitting was decidedly on the rustic side. Stella wouldn't wear it; it wasn't fashionable enough.

She nodded and smiled and said, 'It's lovely,' in an unconvincing voice, but her reaction meant it would end up around Bobby's neck.

Bobby was delighted with her geography book full of illustrated world maps and a purse. Unzipping it with a smile, she noticed 10 pence in the bottom. Alice winked.

'Don't worry, love, I didn't forget to put the lucky silver in it.' Bobby smiled and nodded, hugging her quickly.

'I knew you wouldn't. Thanks, Grandma.'

Davey got new football socks and was then handed a long slim package that rattled. He glanced at Alice, intrigued. She made a little shrugging gesture and tilted her head. When he peeled back the Sellotape, he saw a beautiful chess set in a wooden box with a sliding lid and a folding board. He gasped in surprise and pleasure. Slowly, he drew out a knight from the box, its polished, curved head glowing in the dim light.

Alice nodded. 'Rosewood. It's a lovely colour, isn't it?'

He beamed with delight, smoothing his fingers over the chess piece. 'Thank you, Grandma, that's ace. I'm sick of borrowing them from other people. I love it.'

'I thought you'd like it, love. Now, let's have a brew, eh?'

They sat down with tea and mince pies as they listened to carols on the radio. Alice watched the grandkids.

Bobby, so like her mother in colouring, but with a leaner shape and more prominent nose, maybe inherited from her father. Her mouth curved upwards too, she had none of Stella's moody petulance. Alice noticed how tall Davey had become. He folded himself almost in half to sit in the small armchair he used to curl up in just a few years ago. His bony wrists stuck out from his jumper, which she had got him last Christmas.

The kids were young adults; they'd be eighteen soon. Next year might be a different Christmas altogether. Alice glanced at Stella, who was standing now; busy combing her hair and applying lipstick in front of the old mirror above the shelf of fossils. *She can't settle for a minute,* thought Alice. *She can't wait to get away. Nowt changes.*

At the dot of 10.30 am, Ray was outside in the car. The atmosphere in the cottage changed abruptly. Everyone could see Stella getting worked up as the twins took their time getting their coats on, saying goodbye to Grandma and stroking the cats. Alice stood at the door to see them off. She would go back in and start preparing her own Christmas dinner. Watching the car disappearing down the hill away from the greenness and into the grey pocket of the town, Alice was grateful that she didn't have to spend Christmas day with Ray Short.

Stella was a good plain cook and Davey always helped her with chopping and peeling veg. Ray did nothing, just made a start on the beer. He usually snapped the ring pull off his first can before 11 am, and as soon as the pub opened, he would be gone for his pre-Christmas dinner drink. He made an exception in his wardrobe choices for Christmas day, wearing trousers instead of his boiler suit, a shirt and tie, and was cleanly shaven. Ray wore a pair of oxblood brogues, highly polished, and his hair would be brushed and swept back.

As soon as the pub opened, he would pull on his overcoat and be off down the road to the Spinners, the Carders or occasionally Giddons or the Cartwright. The last two pubs were a further walk, but both had pretty barmaids who hadn't heard quite as much of his bullshit and were amenable to his tall tales. By the time the pubs had closed for the afternoon, his dinner would be ready and he would have put away a few pints and needed some food before he started again.

In preparation for dinner, the small table was dragged out in front of the window and the leaf pulled out so all four of them could sit together. They rarely sat at the table, most meals were eaten on their knees, in front to the telly. A paper tablecloth that didn't quite fit was laid down crossways with a single bedsheet underneath it. Bobby laid out four skinny crackers, mismatched cutlery, and some glasses. She added salt and pepper pots nicked from the café. A centrepiece of plastic holly stuck in a jam jar completed the festive ensemble.

Returning home, Ray's face was purple from booze and the cold as he settled in front of the telly. The kitchen was fogged-up; pans boiling, the turkey sitting on the table under its blanket of foil waiting to be ferried through to the front room. Condensation streamed down the windows and walls. Davey was stirring a pan of gravy whilst Stella flapped around. Bobby flicked through the *TV Times*. She was going round to see Wendy after dinner, determined to get out of the house before the drink started talking and *The Two Ronnies* came on. Davey was also out tonight, going to Jonty and Chris's flat for food and to take his new chess set round for a game. They'd both had more than enough Christmases at Ribbon Street.

The phone rang, and Bobby jumped up to answer it, shutting herself into the cold hallway. It was Chris, ringing up to wish everyone happy Christmas and to see what time Davey was coming round. She chatted to him for a few minutes, resting her forehead against the cool wall, picking at a loose a blister of woodchip. Chris drivelled on; there would be turkey barm cakes for tea, and most of the Mulberry Terrace neighbours were invited. She could come as well if she liked. Bobby finished the call and went back into the smoky furnace of the front room. Tiger ran out. Even he'd had enough of the heat and the smoke.

Everyone sat down at the tiny table for Christmas dinner. Ray always insisted on carving the turkey, making a big deal about being the man of the house. He made a right pig's ear of it; hacking off great collops of meat. Bobby and Davey exchanged small smiles across the table as he clumsily loaded everyone's plates. Crackers were pulled, lame jokes read out, and the paper hats went on. Ray's was crammed well down on his head. He looked like a king on a playing card, hollow cheeked and expressionless. There was little conversation, heads down and eating steadily.

Instead of Christmas pudding, Stella brought her speciality trifle in and Bobby watched greedily as she plunged the spoon into the pristine cream top, waiting for the slurping suction sound of the jelly and cream coming out. By teatime, dinner eaten, half a tin of Quality Street and a box of Family Circle biscuits nailed, Stella was sitting in her armchair opposite Ray on the other side of the fireplace. Bobby and Davey sprawled on the settee, comatose with food.

Everyone's eyes were streaming with the fag smoke and Bobby got up to crack a window open. Stella had put a record on. Ray was pissed. His Christmas stash of cans had diminished throughout the day and he was now on the whisky. Bobby had drunk a couple of cans of lager but was always on alert, treading on eggshells and waiting for Ray to kick off. And Davey wasn't drinking until he got round to Chris's. Stella was slurring slightly, getting to the stage where she would start answering Ray back when he began sniping. The red paper hat from out of the cracker was making its way down her forehead and was now sitting just above her eyes.

She turned to the kids. 'What time are you two off out?'

'Soon. Waiting while me dinner's gone down,' offered Bobby, patting her belly. 'Jean has got Peggy there and some other people, so I'll wait a bit.'

'What about you, love?' Stella turned to Davey, who was reading a book, feet curled under him on the settee.

'Yeah, I'll go over to Chris's soon. They're having neighbours over tonight for a buffet and drinks.'

Stella nodded and hiccupped loudly, clapping her hand over her mouth and giggling.

Ray made a long sneering sound and put on a pretend posh voice. 'Buffet and drinks. Who the fuck do you think you are? Knocking about with that shit-stirring little queer. I'm glad you're not my kid, all that poncing around with books and chess and drinks and buffets. I wouldn't stand for it. A-levels and university, and all that shite.' He looked over to Stella to see her reaction, and then back to Davey again who was pale and expressionless.

'You should be out of school and earning money. Not sitting on your arse and reading fucking poetry. When I was your age, I was fighting for my country.' His face was purply red with drink and rage, pushed towards Davey in provocation. 'You do a few hours a week at the yarn warehouse and you piss around the rest of the time.'

Stella instantly started shouting in Davey's defence, but Ray cut her off with a raised hand. She shut up as quickly as a budgie with a tea towel thrown over its cage, crouched in her chair, pleating the fabric of her skirt with nervous hands.

Davey sat quivering slightly, like a woodland creature — a tall leggy deer, large eyes and lean head, watchful and on high alert. 'It's okay, Mum.' Inhaling deeply, he turned to Ray, leaning forward on the settee and said quietly, 'No, you weren't fighting for anyone, you lying twat. And I'm glad I'm not your kid. I couldn't think of owt worse.'

Ray forced a quick, triumphant smile, picked up the chess set from the arm of the settee, and shoved it neatly onto the fire. The board changed colour instantly, the coloured paper of the checked coating peeling in an instant, blistering and popping. The blackening chess pieces made the flames leap. Stella made a furious yelping sound and went to grab the pieces, but Bobby dragged her back by her arm.

'Don't be bloody stupid, Mum, you'll burn yourself. It's red hot!'

'You stupid bastard!' she screamed into Ray's face, going at him with hands up, nails out. She looked like a small monster; red faced, hair wild, teeth bared, enraged.

Ray, almost casually, languidly, slapped her hard across the face and picked up a handful of her hair, holding her at arm's length and flinging her backwards onto the hearth. She missed the fireplace and crumpled between the coal bucket and the settee. He stamped on her quickly and stepped back, ready to kick her soft belly.

'Hey.' The voice was soft, conversational.

Bobby was trying to pick up Stella and fend off Ray, but at that moment they all turned to Davey in complete surprise, and he said it again,

'Hey, Ray.' And he punched Ray once, hard, in the middle of his face.

Nobody knew what to do. Instantly, the normal order of things had been turned on its head. Bobby always thought something in the air automatically changed when Ray came into the room. It always felt fuller, as though there wasn't enough room for everyone. But there was space now. An enormous space as though a dangerous animal had suddenly been captured and contained in a cage, its teeth pulled out and its claws broken.

Davey was suddenly the grown-up in charge. Taller, younger than Ray and it appeared, much stronger. He pointed a completely steady finger at Ray who was crouched on the floor, looking absurdly, Bobby thought, like a runner about to stand up in the blocks — knuckles resting on their backs on the floor, blood and snot streaming from his nose down his slack corned beef face with its small, hard, piggy eyes.

'Now, fuck off and get out!' bellowed Davey. He moved towards Ray again.

Stella was crouched, holding her face, blood and coal dust covering her white top. Bobby arm was around her shoulders, watching Ray warily. He bared his teeth, picked up his keys and coat off the back of his chair, wiped his hand across his face, and left. It was as simple as that. The passage of time while a child grew and a single short sentence. Bobby had dreamt of this moment for years. Now it was here, it felt weird, exhilarating, frightening. Elvis was softly reminding everyone from the stereo speakers that it was going to be 'Lonely this Christmas'. Suddenly the room was silent, just the crackle of the record player and then the click and snap as the needle lifted and drew off the vinyl. Then Stella started a quiet wailing.

Bobby dragged her mum up and pushed her gently into her armchair, scattering the empty cans with her feet. Davey sat down heavily in Ray's chair. It occurred to Bobby that she had never seen anyone else sit in that chair before. It had moulded itself to his bulk over the years. The chess pieces were incinerated now, the board a curled piece of paper like a grey leaf, a faint chequered pattern still visible.

She looked about her at the mess, retrieved Davey's crumpled gold paper hat from under the upended Christmas tree, feet crunching on the pulverised baubles ground into the carpet, and placed it tentatively on his head with hands shaking from the shock. Davey looked completely calm, whey-faced, chin up, his crown slightly askew. Bobby was the first to speak, exhaling in a long, wobbling breath.

'Fucking hell. I'll put the kettle on. I think we could all do with a brew.'

Chapter 24
New Year's Day 1983

Ribbon Street was silent as a fine drizzle fell. Midnight was long passed and most people who had gone to the pub and then on to parties, had seen in the new year, then drifted home and to bed. When Ray got to the house, he was careful not to go through the gate. It creaked and scraped on the concrete, and he didn't want anyone to hear anything until it was too late.

He glanced up and down the street, but it was deserted except for a cat trotting down the opposite pavement, white socks flashing in the streetlights. He pulled his hood over his head and slid down the narrow drive at the side of the house where the old car was dumped, squeezing between that and the overgrown privet hedge. The wet leaves saturated his jacket and trousers. He didn't need a torch; there was enough of a glow from the streetlight two doors down. He looked at his watch, tilting the face towards the light. It was almost 3 am.

The house was in complete darkness. Curtains closed, no sound of talking or music. He tiptoed to the front door and crouched down low, opening the letterbox slightly with his fingertips and put his face to the slot.

The hallway was pitch black and he waited until his eyes had adjusted to the lack of light. The front room door was open and he could make out the shape of the Christmas tree. In the hallway, Stella's handbag was hanging from the banister. Its mouth open, her big housewife's purse sticking out of the top like a tongue, mocking him. Looking at a personal object belonging to a woman he could no longer control made his head spin.

He was suddenly filled with an overwhelming rage. A fury that was so hard to contain, he almost gave up on his plan and opted to smash the door down and gallop up the stairs to smash that bitch's head in, as well as her bastard kids. He took a deep, quivering breath and wiped his clammy hands on the thighs of his boiler suit. No, this would be far better in the long run. They wouldn't be expecting this and it was just what they deserved after everything they had put him through.

All those years he had provided for that ungrateful cow and those spoilt bastard kids that weren't even his. He'd been too soft on them all. That was the problem. He was a nice guy who had been pushed to the limit by arseholes. Taking a ragged breath, he was careful to make as little sound as possible. Slipping back to the side of the house, Ray carefully lifted out from under the hedge the items he had hidden two nights ago; a petrol can and a bin bag with an old folded up blanket tucked inside. Quietly, he carried the stuff round to the front door, aware of the sound of his own breathing and nothing else.

Somewhere close, a dog barked and a door slammed. There was a buzzing in Ray's head. Taking a Stanley knife out of his jacket pocket, he methodically and quickly slashed the blanket into rough squares, each about the size of a newspaper. He laid them on top of one another as if he was going to make a stack of felt sandwiches. Picking up the petrol can, he slowly unscrewed the metal cap, wincing at the squeaking sound it made. Ray tipped it and the smell streamed out first, then the fluid. Pouring it slowly over the piles of blanket, soaking them before he recapped the can. Precise and careful, his hands were perfectly steady.

One by one, Ray folded the squares of saturated blanket into smaller squares and fed them through the letter box. They made a fat, soft sound as they landed on the floor in the hall, one on top of the other. Excess petrol ran in greasy streams down the door. The smell was overwhelming. Suppressing the urge to cough, Ray turned his face away from the fumes.

He dried his hands on a piece of dry blanket and pulled his coat sleeve over it, taking a ball of rag from his pocket. This was anointed with black engine oil and the moment Ray flicked his lighter, it set alight. Quickly, before it burned his hands, he opened the flap of the letter box and stuffed it through the slot. He released the flap with a click. It felt like only a second before the blankets caught and there was a soft whumph.

The glass above the door was suddenly filled with orange and blue flame as the blankets and the doormat caught fire. Ray turned and slid down the side of the house, smiling, satisfied, calm. He hurried down the street towards the main road, his head down and hands deep into his pockets. The wagon was parked behind the Carders. Nobody had seen him. Nobody knew what had happened. In a few minutes, he would be well away. By the time he turned the corner on to the main road, the flames in the Armstrong house were licking slowly along the hallway to the stairs like a stealthy little orange army.

Gary heard his dad come in and start crashing around in the next room, making a brew and something to eat before we went to bed. He looked at the clock next to the bed; it was nearly 2.30 am. Christ only knew what time his dad had started drinking, and he must have had a lock-in somewhere, or been in someone's house.

Butch farted and jumped off the bed. Gary groaned. Feeding him the leftovers from tea had been a bad idea. If he didn't get up and let Butch out, the dog would shit all over the house, and the last thing his dad would want when he got up with a raging hangover would be to tread in a dog turd or a puddle of luminous yellow spew. Flicking his lamp on, he looked at the little dog, peering up at him anxiously. Butch let out a tiny whine and trembled. An ominous gurgling coming from his belly.

'Fuckin' hell, alright.' Gary pulled on his tracksuit bottoms and a jumper over his underpants and vest and grabbed his coat, shoved his feet into his trainers and opened the door. The lights were on in the kitchen and the front room. He turned the gas off under the chip pan and went into the front room.

His dad was fast asleep in his clothes on the settee. Gary looked at his sleeping face, sallow and stubbly, mouth hanging ajar. It was a drinker's face, and Gary sometimes wondered if he would have looked like that if his mum had been here to sort it all out. He didn't have time to philosophise any longer. Butch was scratching at the door of the flat in desperation. They stepped out into the walkway and Gary picked up the dog. It would be quicker to leg it down the stairs and onto the patch of grass in the courtyard.

The lift was always knackered. Gary didn't even try it, galloping down the stinking stairwell. They passed the spray canned cartoons of cocks and balls and names listing who was a lying twat and who was a slag, *Thatcher out* and *City*. They crashed through the double doors at the bottom and Gary dropped Butch on the tired litter strewn grass. The little dog instantly squatted and the remains of a week-old Christmas leftovers tea were ejected noisily in a stinking stream. Gary held his arm over his nose, gagging at the stench.

Once Butch had finished, Gary was tempted to go straight back up to the flat, but experience had taught him this might not be the end of it, so he may as well wander for a few minutes to make sure the dog's stomach was empty. He fastened the lead and they walked towards the older part of the estate. Butch had perked up. Gary didn't see a soul. It was a mild night and a steady drizzle fell.

Shoving his hands further into his pockets, he enjoyed the quiet. He turned into Paterson Street and watched as the headlights of a wagon lit up the front of the Carders and drove away, accelerating towards the main road.

'Just round the block and we'll go back, Butchy. Not a good start to the New Year for you.'

They turned into Ribbon Street, and Gary was aware of a burning smell. It wasn't the usual winter smell of coal fire smoke; this was more metallic and plasticky. The drizzly air was smoky too, and the acrid smell was getting stronger as he made his way further up the street. Gary suddenly could hear and see that the entire front of the Armstrong's house was alight. His first thought was that someone would think he had done something wrong. His second was that if there was anyone in there, they would almost certainly be dead by now.

There was nobody out in the street. *Probably all pissed*, he thought. Gary ran up the nearest path and started hammering on the front door, then ran back into the street, shouting and screaming in the middle of the road like a lunatic. *Please let someone would take notice*, he thought, panicking. This was the sort of street where someone screaming in the street in the middle of the night was a common occurrence. However, lights started coming on in windows.

Someone opened a window and shouted, 'Shut the fuck up!'

'Fire! Fucking fire!' Gary screamed and belted off to the phone box on the corner of the main road, running like a greased whippet, praying that it was still working and not just functioning as a toilet. The dog galloped behind, panting, enjoying himself. Gary yanked open the heavy door, nearly squashing Butch. The receiver was in place on the cradle, and when he picked it up, he sighed in relief, hearing a dialling tone. He stuck his trembling finger in the number nine hole of the rotary dial and tried to control his breathing. He looked down. The directory was on the floor, sitting in a puddle and had swollen to twice its size like a big grey paper sponge.

'Fire brigade, please.' He tried to control his breathing, but he could hear the tremble in his voice, the high-pitched piggy whine.

By the time he came out, the street was full of people. There was a lot of shouting and screaming, then an upstairs window was smashed at number eight. Gary could see curtains on fire downstairs, and the toxic, plasticky smell of smoke was overwhelming. In the distance, he could hear a siren. He was trembling now with the shock and picked up Butch, hugging him to his chest, fighting the urge to sob. A fat woman wandered over, fag lit, smelling of drink in a quilted dressing gown and a hairnet. She smiled at Gary as if they were in a queue at the chippy and she said conversationally,

'They're nowt but trouble, the Armstrongs. If that Ray Short isn't shouting and carrying on, it's Stella screaming. And now they're burning their fucking house down. Fucking savages.' She shook her head, took a deep drag on her fag, and folded her arms across her chest, thoroughly enjoying the drama.

Two men from up the street were trying to get a ladder around to the back of the house, but the old car was alight now and they couldn't make their way past. The crowd stepped backwards; the heat had intensified, and the fire was spreading upstairs.

Bobby woke first. She had slept deeply; they all had since Ray had gone. She heard a slight shifting sound downstairs. Maybe a tapping sound. Then she could smell smoke and stepped out onto the landing, which was as bright as day and overwhelmingly terrifyingly hot. All she could see was the hallway below consumed in a fireball and a curling flame, twisting like something alive and coming up the stairs quickly.

The wallpaper was peeling from the walls as she watched. The nylon stair carpet was melting black, giving off the most horrendous acrid smell. The paintwork on the banister was blistering like cheese under a grill. In front of her, Tiger was standing transfixed on the top step, miaowing in a high, keening wail — a sound she had never heard before. His fur standing up all along his back, and eyes like black, terrified saucers.

She scooped him up and he clung to her, claws digging into her shoulders. It was agony, but she knew if she let him go, he might run under a bed and they would never see him again. The next few seconds were a blur, Bobby screamed like a banshee and suddenly Stella and Davey were on the landing, bewildered at the noise, befuddled with sleep, Davey with his hair on end in his pyjama bottoms, face masklike. He could smell petrol, and, in an instant, knew exactly what had happened; Ray.

Stella was shrieking, incoherent. Bobby pushed past her, ran into the bathroom and wrapped a viciously protesting Tiger in a towel, her forearms and shoulders lacerated from his claws. Tucking him under her arm, she turned on the bath taps with one hand, put the plug in, threw three towels into the bath and, while they were soaking, ran out onto the landing, her whole body shaking.

Bobby had no time to think. There was no way out downstairs. They would either have to jump out of the back windows or burn to death. It was as simple as that. She felt quite calm now. The noise was tremendous; she had never realised fire made such a sound. Davey was breaking his bedroom window with a chair and shouting at Stella to fucking hurry up. They would all get out through here; it was the only escape route. He was shaking her and telling her she was going to have to jump out and a broken leg was better than burning to death, wasn't it?

She was shocked at how calm and cold his voice was as he talked to Stella, as though she was a small child, trying to pull her into the bedroom by her flailing arm. Bobby passed Tiger to him, swaddled like a furious baby in a yellow towel. Stella was motionless. Paralysed with terror in the doorway, unable to think about anything other than *Ray has done this. Ray is trying to kill us.* Bobby gently led her mother through into the bedroom, pushing her towards to window. Davey, one arm around the cat, pulled her towards the window, his feet lacerated by the broken pane, not feeling anything but utter fury.

Bobby sprinted back to the bathroom and lifted out the three soaking towels from the bath, surprised at their weight, dragging them into Davey's bedroom, steaming. Once they were all inside, Davey shut the door on the landing with his foot. The metal handle was too hot to touch. It was getting hard to see and breathe now.

Bobby looked at her mother, still standing mute, in complete shock. The flames were so intense the thin bedroom door was glowing orange and the room was dark with smoke. Bobby passed the towels to Davey and Stella. They were all coughing uncontrollably, even the cat.

'Hold them over your nose,' she bellowed.

The landing outside was fully ablaze now and Bobby could feel the heat under her bare feet and knees. She was startled at the speed at which the fire had galloped up the stairs. Suddenly, there was a rushing, smashing noise from downstairs, shouting voices and a siren above the roaring of the fire. A ladder appeared at the window. Bobby closed her eyes as the fire engulfed Davey's door and she realised her nightie was alight.

Chapter 25
July 1983

Midge woke, and for a second, didn't realise where she was. Then she looked out of the small oval window and saw a fluffy cotton wool bed of cloud stretching as far as she could see, drifting underneath the aircraft, tinged gold in places by the sun. Above this, the sky was the deepest, most intense blue she had ever seen. She reached out and touched the glass. It was icy cold and vibrated under her fingers. Clenching her fists in excitement, she inhaled deeply. It was actually happening. Midge was in an aircraft, flying for the first time in her life all the way to Canada.

She glanced over at her mum. Jean was asleep, head back, mouth open. Midge studied the open pores on her nose, and the waxy pale colour of her skin. For a few seconds, she wondered how Jean would cope in another country, then dismissed the thought. This was a new start in a new place. Everything would be okay. She stretched in her seat and folded her hands in her lap. The plane was quiet. All she could hear were muted conversations, and the ever-present low hum of the engines. The meals in the little foil trays, the smiling air hostesses, even the weird cramped toilets with the funny little doors were a fabulous novelty. Midge closed her eyes again, willing the hours to pass. There was still a long way to go before landing.

A small knot of excitement in the pit of her stomach rotated slowly as she reflected on the past few months. The year had not started well for the Kennys. Jean had lost her job in the cold, short, and skint post-Christmas dark days of February. Cheap imports and the deepening recession hit the town hard. Mills closed every day. The small, family-run businesses were the first to shut and then the bigger factories started to cut back. Earnshaws had put many people on restricted hours, and then they let people go.

Jean's older sister, Carol, came over to visit from Canada at Easter. Smaller and leaner than Jean, with a strange accent and kind, practical manner, she could not have been more different from her younger sister. She and her husband Duncan were teachers in Vancouver. They went fishing, sailed, hiked, and travelled.

Midge couldn't believe Carol was actually related to her mother. She couldn't imagine Jean hiking anywhere, except a very short distance to the pub. Carol's personality was so cheerful and positive, she seemed to infect everyone with her energy. The last time Carol had been in Gritstone, Midge had been a baby. She had no recollection at all of meeting her auntie, who was always spoken of as being eccentric, a rebel, the black sheep of the family.

The days leading up to Carol's visit had been busy. Jean had actually cleaned the house, a rare event involving much bleach and irritability. The tiny box room, which was full of junk, had been cleared out and a clapped-out single bed borrowed from Lynne's brother was hastily installed.

'I don't know why I'm bothering, to be honest,' remarked Jean to the girls, while she scrubbed the bathroom. 'Our Carol would be just as happy in a friggin' tent in the garden. She was always going off doing daft things when we were kids. Hitchhiking around Spain. Living with hippies in Israel. Looking after goats.'

'I think that's a kibbutz, Mum,' interjected Midge, scrubbing mould out of the grouting around the sink with an old toothbrush.

'A Kib what? Isn't that a Turkish barmcake?'

'No, Mum,' explained Midge patiently, suppressing a giggle. 'That's a kebab. A kibbutz is a collective farm, a community.'

'I don't know where you pick all these words up from. Too much reading, that's what it is. Pass me that bog brush, kid.'

Carol finally arrived on a brilliantly beautiful spring day. Midge had gone with her mum to the bus station to meet the coach from Manchester. There were only a few passengers, and Midge spotted Carol at once. It had to be her descending the steps. A small, lean woman with spiky brown hair, crazily patterned jumper, freckles and an enormous backpack. She was half the size of Jean, and the dead spit of Midge. The thin, angular face broke into a grin when she saw her sister and the niece she had last seen as a baby.

'Our Jean, you look just the same. But look at you Amanda, you're almost as tall as me now.'

The accent was a weird hybrid of Gritstone and American to Midge's ears. Carol hugged her, Midge squirming with embarrassment at being called by her Sunday name.

'Come on then, Carol, let's get you back home. Nowt has changed here,' sang Jean, linking arms with her sister and marching them all towards the estate. 'We'll drop your bag off at ours and get to Mum's. She'll have the kettle on. She's dying to see you.'

All the apprehension at meeting her older sister after so many years melted away. Jean suddenly realised how much she had missed her company. It was as if she had seen Carol yesterday as they passed all the familiar landmarks, Carol laughing at the Carders and the Spinners, unchanged since she left.

The days passed in a blur. Midge's Easter holidays were spent hanging on Carol's every word, persistently quizzing her about her travels and dragging her all over the town and up into the hills. The stories of Canada fascinated Midge; icy blue-green lakes, mountains, forests and endless prairies, bears, moose, caribou, porcupines, and wolves. She questioned Carol constantly, her atlas open on her knees, tracing the cities and lakes with her forefinger. Even Jean was captivated.

Carol had always been a free spirit. She had left home young and never stopped travelling until she met Duncan, when they were training to become teachers. And even then, they were always off doing something: hiking, sailing, camping, fishing expeditions. It was Carol who suggested they move to Canada. Wendy was out one evening and Midge had finally fallen asleep after a marathon question-and-answer session about Canadian wildlife. Jean and Carol were sitting quietly in front of the telly, turned down to a low murmur.

'Would you consider moving out to live in Canada, Jeanie? You and the kids? I know Mum won't come. I've asked her, but you and the girls might?' She tilted her head at her sister. 'Don't take this the wrong way, but life isn't easy for you here, is it? I didn't realise until I saw it for myself. The factories closing, the unemployment. Just all the depressing crap on the news about the economy.'

Carol paused, looking to see Jean's reaction. Her face was impossible to read. She sat opposite her sister, hands in her lap, quiet for once, face stonelike, impassive.

'Jean, Gritstone doesn't change, but it seems a real struggle now, with the job situation for you, I mean. Canada isn't perfect, there're problems there too, but so many more opportunities.'

Carol looked over at Midge, curled in the chair, wrapped in Jean's big coat, her atlas slowly sliding off her knees. 'For the nipper, especially.' Carol leant over and closed the book, placing it softly on the floor.

Jean shrugged, taken aback. Her first instinct was to say no. Peggy wasn't getting any younger, and Wendy was still living at home. But for how much longer? Who knew?

Carol opened her palms towards her younger sister and made a small shrug. 'Think about it. All of those things are absolutely solvable. Maybe talk to Mum and the girls. See what they think. I'm not forcing you. It's your decision, but the offer is there, and I think you would love it.'

She paused and yawned, stretching her hands to the fire, leaning back in her chair, eyes fixed on Jean. 'You might not like the outdoor lifestyle, but you don't have to adopt it. Vancouver is a busy place compared to Gritstone. I bet Midge would love it. She's got such an inquisitive nature, hasn't she?'

'Aye. She's like you. Just like you were at that age. It's more obvious now as she's getting older. Books, animals, nature, geography, all that stuff.' Jean wafted her hand as if the gesture encompassed the whole of the natural world. She smiled at the sleeping child.

Carol thought she detected a bit of sadness and pride in Jean's voice. She got up and stretched. 'Well, I'm off up to bed, Jeanie. Think about it, I'm serious. There's a chance of leaving one country that's old and tired to join one that's just getting going. We would help you get started, you know. You wouldn't have to sort it out on your own.'

She made it sound straightforward and simple. They could live with her and Duncan. They had plenty of room. Jean would soon find work. The economy wasn't as tough as it was in Britain. Midge could start school in the autumn without a gap if they left in the summer. They could try, see if they liked it. It would be a shame to waste the opportunity, reasoned Carol.

Jean looked around the room. At the crappy furniture and tired wallpaper. The broken stuff that never got fixed. The things that never changed. She hadn't really thought about it before. Carol had swept in and made her see everything with fresh eyes. She should have been resentful, but she wasn't. Carol wasn't judgemental, she was practical, positive, and generous. Jean sat up for a long time after Carol had gone to bed. She thought about her children and Peggy. But she thought about Boston as well and pushed these other thoughts to the back of her brain. Thoughts that would serve no positive use if they came to the fore.

She stood up eventually, stiff from sitting down for so long, and pushed the fireguard over the dying coals. Quietly, she tucked the coat around Midge, who stirred slightly with a soft mumble. She flicked through the atlas quickly to the page Midge had marked with Carol's postcard. She looked at the outline of Canada. It was enormous. She traced her finger to the right, from the east coast of Canada to the west coast of the UK.

I suppose it's not that far away, she thought idly, then closed the book quickly and placed it back on the floor near Midge's chair. Out in the hallway, she looked in the mirror. The light from the landing shone down on her broken, badly permed hair, the greasy open-pored grey smoker's skin. Years of hard graft, booze, and fags showed in her face and she knew it. Dispassionately, she lifted her chin and smiled into the glass. Maybe there was some time to turn things around.

Carol returned to Canada after three weeks, and Midge went back to school, deflated and sad. Everything seemed a little more colourless and boring, even more than it had been before Easter. The atlas went back on the shelf and Midge started on *The Call of the Wild,* her present from Carol, when she left to go home.

A week later, Jean sat down with Midge and asked her if she would like to live in Canada, with Auntie Carol and Uncle Duncan. She knew the answer before she asked the question. They were sitting on the settee and Jean got up and turned *Coronation Street* off, so Midge knew something of momentous importance must be about to happen. The only time the telly was off in this house was if the meter hadn't been fed.

'We won't do if you don't want to. I reckon — and your auntie Carol thinks as well — that it's a great opportunity for us. What d'yer reckon?'

Midge was speechless at first and then overcome with excitement, talking and asking questions one after another, the words tumbling out, almost incoherent. And then she stopped and asked,

'Wendy and Grandma, and Baz and Jasper. What about them?'

'Well, I've spoken to Wendy and your grandma, and they are happy here. They really don't want to move, but they think it' a good idea for us two. They will look after the animals. They offered, they didn't need asking. We can come back for holidays, or they could come to us.' Jean breathed deeply and twisted her sovereigns around as Midge pleated her school skirt with a nervous hand. 'It's not that we wouldn't see them again, it's just not for them. Your grandma especially thinks it would be good for you. She'll be sad to see you go, but she wants the best for you, love.'

For Midge, the overwhelming excitement was tempered by the loss of Wendy, Grandma Peggy, and the animals. There was too much to think about. It all swirled around in her head, impossible to make sense of. Jean had never considered living anywhere but Gritstone. Her life was here, her friends and family. It might be shit, but it was home. It was familiar. *Better the devil you know*, Jean told herself. But, after initially dismissing the idea as a fairytale, she considered a different life with more possibilities.

Peggy encouraged her to go, and after everything that had happened with Midge and Boston, for Jean, it felt right to have a new start somewhere else, if not for her, then for Midge. They sat together in Peggy's flat, playing dominoes on a tray in front of the fire. Midge was cautious about discussing the move, frightened that her grandma would get upset. Peggy swirled and shuffled the dominoes with her knotty fingers.

'I'm just rattling the bones, kid. Are you looking forward to going to live with our Carol?'

Midge looked wary, not meeting her grandma's gaze, watching as Peggy stacked up the pieces and divided them. She shrugged and whispered, 'Yes, I think so.'

'Good. Double six, me to go. I knew girls in the war, not much older than you, upped and went to America with young lads they'd known for five minutes. GI brides, they were called. Remember, you're not going alone. You'll be with your mum and auntie and it will be a big adventure. Next time I see you, you might have your own feller to show off.'

Midge blushed and picked up a domino, placing it next to Peggy's.

Wendy couldn't think of anything worse when Jean asked if she would like to move with them. 'Nah, not for me, thanks. I'll be fine here with Grandma.'

She shuddered at the thought of going anywhere further than a holiday in Spain.

Once Midge was reassured Peggy, Wendy, and the animals were happy, she felt sick with anticipation. She had never wanted something so much in her brief life. Her biggest fear was that Jean would change her mind. There was a succession of drunken leaving parties at the house and in the Carders. Stella and Lynne were inconsolable, and Midge prayed they wouldn't put her mum off, leaving with their dramatic, grief-stricken histrionics. *They're carrying on as if we're going to live on Mars,* she thought irritably.

But a few weeks later, two cheap suitcases were ready to be packed, lying open on the floor of Jean's bedroom, like two open hungry mouths waiting to be filled and the airline tickets were bought. Midge didn't know where the money had come from to buy them and didn't care. She suspected Carol had sent it to Jean to make it harder for her to say no to the move.

The second week in July, Midge met Gary to say goodbye on the waste ground near the railway shed. Neither of them had been there since their visit before the start of the autumn term last year. He hadn't really mentioned the move. It sat like an unspoken awkwardness between them. Midge felt embarrassed at the exciting opportunity ahead of her, but for Gary, nothing much was changing. He was stuck here in Gritstone with his dad and Butch.

They sat on the car seats, looking out over the railway tracks. Midge noticed Gary's legs were longer. They stretched out much further into the dust than last September.

'Are you looking forward to it? Canada? It's a long way.' Gary didn't look at her when he spoke. He stared into the distance, shredding the seeds from a long stem of grass and flicking them onto the ground.

'Yes and no. It will be a lot different. I'm not sure what the school will be like, and if Mum will get a job. She won't want to be reliant on Auntie Carol. She'll want to be paying her way and all that.' She was playing it down, not wanting to sound too excited, keeping her voice carefully neutral.

'Well, if you don't like it. You can always come back,' he reasoned, flinging the naked stalk away and massaging Butch's ears.

Midge smiled sadly. She knew right now, for certain, that if she got on that plane, there would be no coming back. That she would never see him or Gritstone again. She had an uncanny, strange feeling that their friendship was about to change anyway, even if she wasn't leaving. Gary hadn't altered. He was as honest and open as she had been secretive and guarded. Boston had changed her, changed everything, and somehow fractured her bond with Gary forever. *It's just as well I'm going away.*

They got up to walk to the river. The bushes were full of cow parsley, meadowsweet, and foxgloves. Purple and white flower heads littered the ground in front of them. Neither Midge or Gary had any coppers to put on the railway line. It seemed a childish thing to do now. They followed the worn path through the silver birches, dodging dried up dog turds and a used, knotted condom.

'I'll send you postcards, anyway,' she offered in a small voice that sounded like an apology.

He screwed up his plain pale face and finally looked at her, and his small grunting voice said quietly, 'It will be good for you to get away from…after everything…'

His voice faded away and suddenly with a great rush of shock and sadness, with a leaden, stabbing weight in her stomach that made her legs quiver, Midge realised he knew about Boston. He knew what had happened to her. He knew everything.

With a painful, tight, invisible pressure in her chest, she reached out and hugged him fiercely, feeling his wet hot tears on her neck. Then he pushed past her, wiping his face, and walked away quickly, dragging Butch by the lead, back towards town.

The aeroplane started its slow descent. The seatbelt signs came on, and Jean stirred and stretched. Around the cabin, hundreds of clicks and taps signalled passengers fastening themselves in for landing. Midge blinked dry, weary eyes that felt gritty and sore. Her ears popped. She looked out of the window for what felt like the hundredth time but saw only darkness and her own blurry reflection looking back at her in the glass. She sat back in her seat and took a deep, ragged breath, waiting for landing. Stretching her neck to peer again through the window, and could see lights below, getting closer. She closed her eyes, overwhelmed.

Suddenly, the plane bumped down abruptly, Jean clutched Midge's arm, whispering, 'Fuck!' as it eventually roared to a stop, engines screaming.

Midge exhaled unevenly, almost vomiting with excitement. A ripple of murmuring activity travelled around the cabin whilst a bored, disembodied voice announced something in the same funny accent as Auntie Carol, speaking rapidly, telling them what time it was and welcoming them to Vancouver.

Midge turned to Jean, her face a pale oval in the dimmed cabin lights. She grabbed her hands tightly and shook them excitedly. 'We're here, Mum. We're in Canada.'

Chapter 26
November 1983

Wendy stretched out sideways on the bed, propping her feet up on the chair and observed Bobby. She looked so different and she'd only been here at university in Newcastle for a few weeks. In the brief time since they had last seen each other, Bobby had cropped her hair short. It formed a curly black halo around her narrow olive face. She was wearing her student's uniform of jeans, frayed black jumper, and Doc Martens. The tartan-lined donkey jacket that Wendy hated was hanging on the back of the door.

She glanced at all the familiar possessions that used to be in Bobby's room back in Gritstone: the small portable record player, the books, and posters. She felt a momentary spear of sadness that the nights sat on Bobby's bed in Ribbon Street drinking tea and smoking were gone. The evenings of tarting themselves up for a night out in front of the wardrobe mirror were over, too. They had both moved on.

'You look like a proper student now, with all yer miserable dark clothes. Are you still using a hedgehog to brush your hair?'

Bobby snorted and kicked her shoes off. She loved her warm little room in the hall of residence. A narrow single bed positioned against the wall. A modern desk of smooth, pale wood and a chair which didn't wobble. A wardrobe and chest of drawers, and her own sink in an alcove. The carpet was made of hairy orange and brown checked tiles, but a massive improvement on the mind-bending nylon swirls of her room at home.

She had her posters, books, and a new spider plant. Bobby felt completely safe and at home here. She missed Gritstone in a way, but more the people than the place. She worried about Stella and had never been apart from Davey for so long. Sometimes, she felt as though a limb was missing when she woke up and realised they didn't live in the same house anymore.

'How's your Davey?'

'He loves London. He won't be back when he graduates. Made lots of mates and sees Chris all the time. He's got a job in a bar on a night. He was itching to leave even before the fire and all that shit.'

Wendy nodded and shrugged. 'Aye, I know. I get it. How many people live here then, in this building? *Hall of Residence*. It sounds dead posh.'

Bobby smiled. 'It's not really. Just like a big house, I suppose. There're four floors, and forty rooms on each floor. All mixed, lads and girls from all over. Posh people and people like us, ordinary people.'

Wendy swept her arm in an arc, wafting her fag, taking in the small space. 'It's like a nicer version of your room at home, Bob. Look at all your student-y stuff. New pens and notepads, books and all that. It's great, although weird to see everything of yours here.'

Bobby grinned. 'Yeah, but there's no peeling damp woodchip, and I can keep the heating on as long as I like. Luxury, mate.'

When Bobby had got off the train with her cheap suitcase and heard some of the unfamiliar accents around her, she had thought she might be wiser getting the next train back home. Central Station in Newcastle seemed vast compared to the tiny, two-platform railway station at Gritstone. For a few seconds, she was overwhelmed by a wave of homesickness and anxiety. She had wished and longed for this moment so long, and now it was here she wondered if she had made a big mistake. *You're good enough to be here. Your grandma Alice told you that. Give it a few weeks. Give it til Christmas and if it's no good, you can always jack it in and go home.*

But Bobby soon fitted in and had already made a couple of friends. Her flat northern vowels and cheap clothes didn't matter. There were plenty of others like her here, and she slowly felt confident that she would find her own way. She had broken up with Gritstone. This was home now.

Bobby joined Wendy on the bed at the head end, leaning on a pillow. They were both drinking brews, smoking, and working their way through a packet of custard creams. An ashtray lay between them on a cushion. She shuffled her bum up to Wendy and took the lighter out of her hand, lit her cigarette, and inhaled deeply and contentedly.

She had already taken Wendy on a tour of the halls, the refectory, the library, and the tiny bar. Proudly, she had shown her the line of phones in individual booths, the common room with the giant telly, and the poolroom. She really missed Wendy. Missed her just being there, the nights in front of the telly, familiar as sisters, no conversation necessary. Bobby missed her relentless pursuit of pleasure, her live-for-the-moment attitude, energy, and abrasive wit. Bobby had worried Wendy wouldn't want to visit her. But she seemed perfectly at ease with the change, curious and enthusiastic about Bobby's new life, with no intention of wishing to change her own.

'It's another bloody world, Bob. I don't know how you cope with all this.' She fluffed out her hair and made a lemon-sucking face. 'Too many students here. There're some right weirdos.'

Bobby burst out laughing. 'It's a bloody hall of residence. Of course there's going to be students here, you dick.' She elbowed Wendy in the ribs. 'And there's people here from all over. It's bound to be different to home.'

Wendy pulled a face, shuddering. 'It's not for me, this communal living lark. Like a kind of nice prison.'

Bobby smiled and shrugged. 'It's peaceful, you know. Even though there're loads of people. There's no kicking off. Well, not much, just students after a night out on the piss. Not Ray-type kicking off, anyway. Everyone just lets everyone else get on with it.'

She frowned, realising suddenly that she hadn't had a single broken night's sleep since she had moved here. No waking in the small hours like she used to before the fire. No hearing voices downstairs, worrying about what Ray was going to do, or if Stella was okay.

'Have you heard owt about him? Shithead, I mean?'

Bobby shook her head slowly, instinctively rubbing the raised burn scars on her hands. They still itched as they slowly healed but were much improved. She took a drag and exhaled slowly, head up to the ceiling.

'No. He's still in Strangeways. Not coming out anytime soon, the bad bastard.'

They sat in silence for a few seconds, Bobby loudly slurping her tea and smoking. The faint sound of music drifted up the corridor outside, followed by a stream of laughter.

'You don't think Stella will have him back when he's out, do you?' Wendy frowned and narrowed her eyes against the cigarette smoke.

Bobby put her head on one side, considering. She had wondered this off and on since the fire and the trial, and she realised it didn't really matter. She had given up trying to save her mum. It was time to move on now, to save herself. Davey had done it. He'd broken free, and wasn't going home anytime soon.

'No, I honestly don't. I think the thing that finally made her wake up was that woman from Stockport turning up; the woman he's married to with the grown-up kids.' Bobby shook her head, still amazed at Ray managing to keep a family hidden for all those years.

Ray's wife had seen an article in the *Manchester Evening News* about the fire and saw his photo, recognising him instantly. He hadn't changed that much since he had walked out on her and the kids. She tracked him down to Gritstone, knocked on a few doors, and then turned up at Alice's cottage, asking to talk to Stella.

By this time, Ray was in prison for arson and attempted murder. Stella got the full story from Mrs Short. All the lies about the war, Ray's stints in the nick, his children, the beatings. Stella didn't believe it at first. Until the woman opened a cavernous handbag and fished out photographs of the kids; little versions of Ray. Then yellowed newspaper articles recording violence and theft. Stella had sat and listened to this woman; teacup chattering in its saucer, knee nervously trembling, a digestive biscuit disintegrating into the carpet. She knew it was all true, but she felt no relief at hearing it.

Wendy shook her head slowly; she knew Ray had come unstuck. Gritstone had followed the fire and the aftermath with relish. It was like an episode of *Coronation Street* gone mad. She reached for another biscuit and dunked it in her almost cold tea.

'What do you think your mum will do now? Do you think she will stay with your grandma in the cottage? I mean, she's been there for nearly a year, hasn't she?' She slotted the full biscuit in her mouth like someone posting a letter.

'I don't know.' Bobby shrugged. 'What with Davey living in London now, I'm not sure. She doesn't like the countryside. She gets bored easily. Tiger is in his element, though, with all the mice up there.'

As much as Bobby loved it here, she worried about her mum. The fire had fucked her up and she wasn't going to adjust to life without Ray quickly, regardless of what he had done. Wendy raised her eyebrows and grinned. Bobby knew that smile, and it meant Wendy had some gossip.

'Go on. What d'you know?' Bobby put her face in her hands, not sure she wanted to know.

'Well, I've seen your mum in the Spinners and the Carders with Jonty Clough a couple of times, all dolled up!' Wendy threw back her head, shrieking with laughter, spraying crumbs everywhere, her amber eyes crinkled up.

'Get away!'

'Yes. I have! She could do worse. He's a nice bloke, and you know, although he's a scruffy get, I think he's a proper *gentleman*,' reasoned Wendy, stuffing another biscuit in her mouth.

Bobby shook her head. Stella would never change, but at least that psycho Ray was locked up. That was the main thing. She got up to fill the kettle.

'So, what else is happening in town?' she asked over her shoulder, ramming the kettle on its side to get it under the tap. 'Have you heard from your mum and Midge? You must miss them?' She shook her head and turned to Wendy, shouting over the noise of the tap, 'Canada is a bloody long way from here. I can't believe they're gone.'

Wendy put her head on one side and looked at her nails, her voice deliberately casual. 'Yeah, sometimes. It's a lot quieter with them gone. Lynne misses them the most. I think they're having a great time with Auntie Carol.' She brought both knees up under her chin and hugged them. 'I really didn't think they would like it, but they love living there. When Mum said she was thinking of going to make a new start, I kind of didn't believe her. But bugger me, she was true to her word. They went and did it!' She slapped the bed, slopping tea over her legs.

'What's it like living with Peggy in the flat? Is it still okay?' Bobby couldn't see that lasting, and searched Wendy's face for the familiar eye roll.

'It's alright. But as soon as I can, I'll get a place of my own. I'm lucky to still be in work.' She drained the cup with a final swig and handed it to Bobby with a small burp, 'Jasper and Baz love it, though. Both as fat as pigs. Grandma never stops feeding them.' Blowing her cheeks out, she closed her eyes. 'She does my head in with the religious crap sometimes. And she gets nowty if I leave my clothes on the floor or smoke in the bath. Last week she asked if I was going to go to Mass.' Wendy made a scandalised face and ground out her fag, shaking her head slowly.

Bobby snorted with laughter. 'Any other goss?'

Wendy considered, head on one side, while Bobby rinsed out the empty mugs and brewed up again. She opened her bedroom window to retrieve a pint of milk balanced outside on the windowsill.

'Not really.' Wendy shook her head.

'That freak, Boston, from the pet shop. Whatever happened to him?' asked Bobby. 'That was weird, him found fucked up like that in the street last Christmas Eve... I mean, he must have really pissed someone off to break his legs over a kerbstone. That's brutal.' She made a spewing face and mashed the tea bag against the side of Wendy's mug.

Wendy smiled blandly. 'He fucked off out of town and hasn't been seen since he left hospital. He was in there months and when the coppers interviewed him, he said he had no idea who had done it. Mum thought he owed somebody money, maybe.' She smiled and reached out for the fresh mug of tea, not meeting Bobby's eyes.

She knows more about that than she's letting on, Bobby thought, chucking the spent tea bags in her wastepaper bin and sitting down on her desk chair.

They sat drinking in silence for a while, listening to the sounds of the building on a Friday night. Feet running past the door, muffled sounds of music, voices, and laughter. The sound of students getting ready for the weekend. Bobby got up to draw the curtains, reflecting suddenly how much had changed in the last few months. Wendy flicked through a tattered copy of *Smash Hits,* wondering if she should bleach her hair.

'Anyway, any new blokes on the scene? Did you ever hear from that dickhead, Matt?'

Bobby shuddered. 'No, I have not, thank Christ. I'm well shot of him. No blokes. I'm happy as I am for the minute, thanks.'

Wendy threw the magazine on the floor and stretched, poking Bobby with her foot as she walked past. 'Well, are we going to this student's union or what? You might have given up on men, but I haven't.'

Wendy fished in her bag for her lipstick. Bobby shook her head.

'Come on then, Wendy, they won't know what's hit them.'

Chapter 27
November 1983

It was getting dark, a late November afternoon, already turning to a blue-pink dusk. Alice switched the lamp on, a small pool of light illuminating the ancient grey stone flags, worn to a soft sheen by centuries of feet. The cats didn't move from their bed as she attended to the range, loading it with fuel and shutting the cast iron door. Alice could see their soft furry bellies slowly rise and fall.

She pulled her thick jacket on and added a scarf and woolly hat. It was going to freeze tonight and there would be some good stars to see. She shoved her feet into men's work boots and stepped out into the sharp, icy cold air. It stung her nose as she inhaled. Alice slammed the door and a flock of crows wheeled away from the roof like a charred cloud of black confetti, cawing loudly.

Jupiter was already waiting by the gate that led into the small yard. He whickered to her, his breath pluming white in the cold air. She lifted the latch, and the gate swung open. He trotted stiffly out of the paddock, across the yard and straight into the barn. He was an old pony now, his face frosted with grey hair.

Alice followed him into his stable and he turned for his evening treat, rustling through the thick straw covering the floor. She held out half an apple and he took it quickly and gently from her palm, his lips and muzzle velvety soft. She ran her hand down his silky neck. His winter coat had come in, thick and woolly. The pony turned to pull hay from the rack on the wall, grumbling contentedly. Alice lifted the zinc lid on the food bin and scooped out a measure of his feed, tipping it into his bucket. She placed it in the corner, and he waited patiently until she had moved away before he started eating.

'Well, I'd better go, or I'll be late and he'll be waiting for me,' murmured Alice softly.

The pony's ears moved back and forth like furry radar, head down, listening, munching steadily. Alice moved over to the hens, squabbling as they put themselves to bed for the night on their roost. She checked their food and water and left the barn, fastening the door on the fragrant warmth of animal breath.

It was a beautiful, clear, chilly afternoon. A thin crescent moon hung low on the horizon and the sunset had streaked the western sky with pink and apricot skeins of cloud. Alice went through the small paddock onto the fell, and the sheep moved to greet her. Once they realised she hadn't brought food, they wandered away, cropping the coarse tufted grass as they went. She patted their greasy, fleeced heads as she passed through them.

Alice climbed steadily up to the stone circle where she could get a panoramic view. Her legs swished through the low-growing wimberry bushes and heather. Town tumbled below her, a jumble of grey buildings in a grey-green hollow. The mill chimneys were outlined like a mismatched jigsaw above the lampposts. House lights were slowly blinking on. Away to the north west, the green Cheshire plain stretched out. The telescope at Jodrell Bank was still visible as a bump and the glow of lights from Manchester, a haze beyond.

She turned around and looked south, to the distant blue shadows of the Welsh mountains on her right. An owl called as it made its way out for an evening's hunting, flying low and silent towards the fields below. She turned around again, pulling up her collar against the thin chilly wind and watched as a small arrow of white geese honked their way across the sky, travelling eastwards towards the bulk of the higher Pennines. They were in a hurry to get to shelter by nightfall.

Alice reached the stone circle, the wind sounding lonely and hollow as it passed through the rocks. She sat on one of the fallen stones and waited, a small knot of anxiety settling in her stomach. She rubbed a patch of lichen absentmindedly, her fingertips catching on the rough lacework. It was almost dark now. Maybe he wouldn't come. Maybe something had happened.

The lights in town were getting brighter as dusk deepened, daylight just a pale, drained sapphire ribbon on the horizon. She watched the occasional car lights winking as they passed along the main road out of town. Somewhere on a distant farm, a dog barked.

Familiar constellations and planets appeared as the dark deepened to indigo overhead. Beautiful Venus blinked just above the horizon in the southern sky. She was getting cold. It was almost completely dark so she stood up stiffly to go home, dispirited. Suddenly, there was a flapping sound of wings and a raucous screech behind her. Alice whirled around and he was there, swiftly landing on her surprised, outstretched arm like an outsized, comical, multicoloured bird of prey.

'Jacob! Here you are, at last. I thought you wouldn't come.' The relief sounded as a tremble in her voice.

Alice rummaged in her coat for the other apple half and held it out. Jacob picked it up with one claw and devoured it greedily. She smoothed her hand along his jewelled back, and he shivered with delight.

'Home,' he croaked.

Alice smiled and turned around; the macaw balanced firmly on her arm. She left the stone circle and strolled down the narrow sheep track back to the cottage, just as the last of the light faded from the sky.

Acknowledgments

The town in this book, Gritstone, is a fictional mill town, loosely based on my hometown of Macclesfield. Whilst some of the characters and stories are inspired by real people and events, this is a work of fiction.

Thank you for reading When the Small Creatures Wake. I have got many people to thank for helping and supporting me whilst I wrote this book. Firstly, heartfelt thanks to Helen Aitchison, author, editor, and the founder of publishing house Write on the Tyne. Helen supported and mentored me throughout this process, offering encouragement, practical advice, and never-ending positivity and energy. She has been with me all the way and never doubted me. Thank you, Helen.

Andrew Jukes from The Medal Centre in Hexham, who gave generously of his time to talk to me and share his knowledge about military decorations. Brian Tilley, journalist and resident of Northumberland, a fellow Maxonian who was kind enough to advise me on the Barnaby mill holiday. Elaine Gardner, author and poet who is always so kind, positive and encouraging.

The ladies of the Park Village Book Club, especially Nicola, who picked Helen's novel The Dinner Club as her reading choice and inspired me to contact Helen to begin my writing journey. Thank you to Neil and my family and friends, both home and abroad. I won't name you for fear of forgetting someone, but you know who you are. Thank you for everything.